## A KISS ON THE HAND

Vincent, looking into her eyes, felt a warm glow suffuse his being. "Well, you're nothing like I ever expected an American lady to be," he said.

Constance smiled. "Am I not? But you know you must not judge all American ladies by me, Lord Yates. Even back in Boston, I am accounted something of an eccentric."

"I don't think you're eccentric at all," said Vincent. "I think you're *wonderful.*"

There was a brief silence, during which Constance looked at him and he looked at her. Finally she gave an uncertain laugh. "That is a great compliment, Lord Yates," she said.

"It's the truth," said Vincent. Emboldened by a certain something in Constance's eyes, he reached out, took her hand between his, and kissed it. . . .

## Books by Joy Reed

*An Inconvenient Engagement*

*Twelfth Night*

*The Seduction of Lady Carroll*

*Midsummer Moon*

*Lord Wyland Takes a Wife*

*The Duke and Miss Denny*

*A Home for the Holidays*

*Lord Caldwell and the Cat*

*Miss Chambers Takes Charge*

*Catherine's Wish*

*Emily's Wish*

*Anne's Wish*

*The Baron and the Bluestocking*

*Lord Desmond's Destiny*

*Lord Yates and the Yankee*

Published by Zebra Books

# LORD YATES AND THE YANKEE

*Joy Reed*

## ZEBRA BOOKS
Kensington Publishing Corp.
http://www.kensingtonbooks.com

# One

Vincent, Lord Yates, stood looking moodily out the window at the mausoleum where his remains were destined to lie.

He wondered if his ancestor, the first earl, lying there now with the second, third, and fourth earls and their countesses, had purposely chosen to locate his final resting place where it must forcibly strike the view of his descendant on arising each morning. "Probably so," Vincent muttered to himself. "Probably struck him as a jolly notion, by Gad. Sort of a variation on the old death's-head-at-the-feast business: 'Eat, drink, and be merry, for tomorrow ye must die.' What ho! It's a damned depressing business, being an earl."

Vincent pronounced these words with great bitterness. It was a bitterness that would have startled his friends and relations if any had been at hand to hear him. Bitterness was the last emotion anyone would associate with Vincent Yates. In the general way, there was no man in London with more unquenchable high spirits or a more irrepressible sense of humor. His exploits at Eton and Oxford were still legend, and only the previous fall he had won a wager by riding a course over rough ground in a lady's side-saddle. But on that February morning, looking out toward the first earl's mausoleum, Vincent felt a distinct sense of gloom.

The mausoleum itself was not to blame. Assuming that a man must die and be buried somewhere, he could hardly hope to have a more splendid resting place, Vincent told himself. The Yates family mausoleum was no mere chapel, but a magnificent domed rotunda large enough to house a whole regiment of deceased earls. Yet for all its size and splendor, it had nonetheless the grisly associations that any funerary monument must bear.

Normally, Vincent's cheerful and insouciant temper rendered him indifferent to such associations. It had never before occurred to him to question his ancestor's motives in placing the family mausoleum in direct view of the rooms traditionally occupied by the current Lord Yates. But Vincent had awakened that morning in a low mood, and the sight of the mausoleum looming in the distance had served to awaken in him some uncomfortable reflections concerning his own mortality.

Such reflections might have been thought premature, for Vincent had no immediate prospect of being gathered to his ancestors. He was only thirty-five and in excellent health, as he assured himself. There was no reason why he should not live to achieve his full biblical three score and ten years, as his father and father's father had done before him. But try as Vincent might to comfort himself with this thought, he could not avoid the realization that his present age, thirty-five, was exactly half of three score and ten. That meant that in all probability, his life was half over. It seemed somehow a significant fact.

With an impatient gesture, Vincent turned from the window to regard the cheval glass that stood beside it. What he saw there was hardly less disquieting than his previous object of contemplation. When had the lines about his eyes and mouth become so prominent? And the scattering of gray hairs at his temples had surely never been so noticeable before. He was still good-looking, of course, blue-eyed, fair-haired, with handsome, regular features, but his first youth was past him now, and he was beginning to look it.

"I'm getting old," Vincent said aloud. The words struck him as smacking of self-pity, and he summoned up a smile. "But there, you're not on your deathbed yet," he told his reflection. "A lot of years left yet to kick up your heels, what?"

Try as he might to speak cheerfully, however, Vincent could not help being depressed by the futility of it all. Assuming he had another thirty-five years to live, what had he to look forward to? Existence, frankly, was beginning to pall on him. It was futile to tell himself that he had everything a man could desire. In a dim way, Vincent could see this was part of the problem. He had wealth; he had leisure; he had an enviable position in society and the means to indulge any reasonable whim along with some that were not so reasonable. In theory, this ought to have made him a happy man. But looking back on the last few years of his life, Vincent realized that it had been a long time since he had felt anything like real happiness. He certainly sought it energetically enough, plunging himself into the manifold gaieties of London in the spring and Brighton in the summer with hunting and shooting parties during the fall and winter months and the occasional house party to fill in the gaps. But had all this whirlwind activity really made him happy? Examining his heart with sober introspection, Vincent decided it had not. Even his celebrated pranks and escapades were no longer outpourings of high spirits as they had been in his youth, but rather a desperate attempt to infuse interest into an existence that was growing increasingly monotonous.

*But that's nonsense,* Vincent told himself robustly. *If life's becoming monotonous, then all I've got to do is make a few changes. Nothing stopping me from doing anything I like, by Jove. I could travel, perhaps—make a trip to the Continent and see Rome and Paris and Vienna. Or I could take up politics, or music, or amuse myself with painting bad portraits of my friends and family. Or I could become a dab at farming*

*like Mr. Coke and see how many extra bushels an acre I could
get out of my land.*

Somehow none of these ideas struck Vincent as very
appealing, however. It was hardly necessary for him to
dabble in the management of his land, which already
turned a handsome profit under the management of a
capable bailiff. There was already a surfeit of politicians
and musicians and landscape painters in the world,
Vincent reckoned, and as for travel, what difference
did it make whether he passed his days here or in
Rome, Paris, or Vienna? The problem did not lie in his
surroundings, but rather in himself. He was *bored* with
himself—bored both with his way of life and way of
thinking. Vincent recognized this truth with a sense of
dismay. Still, he immediately sought to make light of it
in his own characteristic way.

*I'm just blue-deviled, that's all,* Vincent assured himself.
*It's being mewed up here at Larkham that's the trouble. Any-
body'd be blue-deviled with nobody but Mama to talk to and
nothing much to do. If I were in London, now, I'd be out having as good a time as anybody.*

Yet he knew in his heart the matter wasn't as simple
as that. It had been boredom that had driven him out
of London and up to Larkholm in the first place. Now,
in mid-February, the *ton* were flocking back to town for
the beginning of the Season, but somehow the round
of balls, assemblies, drums, routs, and ridottos that he
normally looked forward to had lost its appeal. It was
rather like his first term at university, when he had
gone out carousing every night with a band of like-
minded companions. After a time, the misery of
waking up after a night of heavy drinking began to
outweigh the pleasures the indulgence provided, and
in the end he had cut out drinking altogether apart
from an occasional glass of wine at dinner.

Likewise, upon first entering society, he had gone
through a stage when heavy gaming was the heart and
soul of his existence. To risk several thousands of

pounds on the turn of a card or the roll of the dice had seemed the most exciting thing in the world. But one day he had awakened to the realization that standing around a green baize table, breathlessly watching the progress of a couple of bits of ivory or scrutinizing the patterns on a handful of pasteboard cards was a silly way for a grown man to spend his time. The fact that his whole future might be jeopardized by it made it even sillier. Richer men than he had been reduced to penury overnight through gaming, as Vincent well knew. And so he had simply laid down his cards and dice that day and had never taken them up again, except to take part in an occasional friendly game of whist where the company was the attraction rather than the stakes.

But in this case it was not merely one pastime that had palled, it was the whole of existence. Previous to now Vincent had never been much of a deep thinker, preferring action to thought and laughter to philosophizing, but he found himself this morning in a mood to contemplate life's deeper mysteries. Here he was, a wealthy earl endowed with every worldly advantage, and what good had it really done him? More to the point, what good had he done with himself, given the potentialities of his position? Could he say that he had accomplished anything really memorable or worthwhile during his thirty-five years on earth?

"No," said Vincent, answering his own question. All he had done was earn the distinction of being the man to ride over a rough course in a lady's sidesaddle; the man who had once taken a coach and four backward down Pall Mall; the man who had once hung a chamber pot on the Martyr's Memorial at Oxford. He had been proud enough of these accomplishments at the time, but they struck him now as a paltry legacy for a man who had been born to the dignities of the earldom of Yates.

This reflection led Vincent to reflections still deeper and darker. Would anyone miss him if he were

to suddenly depart this life? Oh, his mother would
mourn him, of course, and his older sister Beatrice,
but their sorrow over his death would hardly be in-
consolable. He knew very well he had always been a
disappointment to them. They had often expressed
disapproval of his mode of life, telling him that a man
in his position had no business frittering away his existence with drinking, gaming, and silly pranks. As
for his so-called friends, he knew better than to look
for deep or sincere grief from them. They might
shake their heads and look solemn when they heard
the news of his passing, but it would not stop them
from eating their dinners with as good an appetite as
ever, or discussing the latest Pet of the Fancy with
their customary interest.

*Well, what would you expect?* Vincent told himself. *It's
the way of all flesh, as the religious fellows say—here today,
and gone tomorrow.* He supposed this idea might be
faced with fortitude by persons of a firm Christian
faith, but when he examined his own faith he found it
rather shaky. He believed, or rather hoped, in heaven
and an afterlife, but he could not help feeling that such
a trifling fellow as he was presumptuous to aspire to it.

Vincent was still musing over this idea when he went
down to breakfast a half hour later. As usual, his mother
had preceded him into the breakfast parlor. She was
seated at the table, consuming tea, toast, and kidneys,
and poring over a ledger of household accounts. The
Dowager Lady Yates now resided at the dower house
rather than at Larkholm itself, but when Vincent was in
residence she made a practice of coming over to take her
meals with him—to keep him company, as she told him.
Vincent, however, suspected that economy might be her
real motive. The dowager had an enthusiasm verging on
mania for paring her living expenses to an absolute min-
imum. There was no need for such economy, for she had
been left a handsome jointure by the eleventh earl,
Vincent's father, but her penny-pinching apparently

served as a hobby for her, a kind of pastime to fill her days and occupy her thoughts. Vincent supposed it was as legitimate a hobby in its way as knitting mufflers or keeping lap dogs, although not quite so genteel. He had now and then been embarrassed by his mother's tendency to wear dresses that any self-respecting beggar would be ashamed to be seen in, but having never been one to interfere in other people's amusements, he generally dismissed the dowager's tendencies as harmless eccentricity. Still, he could not resist the urge to poke a little fun at her now and then.

"Good morning, Mama," he said now, as he seated himself at the table. "Looking over the accounts, eh? I hope the butcher hasn't made the mistake of charging you an extra sixpence again."

The dowager gave him a perfunctory smile. "He won't do that again in a hurry," she said. "The fact is, I've stopped eating butcher's meat altogether, Vincent. Too dear by half, and I've come to believe a body's better off without all this flesh food. Why, my rheumatism hasn't bothered me at all since I stopped eating meat." With which statement, she helped herself to another kidney.

Vincent could hardly conceal a grin, in spite of his somber mood. "I see you've got no prejudice against eating meat at other people's tables," he said, eyeing the dowager's plate. "Last I heard, kidneys were flesh food."

"Well, of course they are," said the dowager, in an "anybody knows that" tone of voice. "But there's no harm in a well-broiled kidney now and then. A vegetable diet is all very well, but it doesn't do to carry anything to extremes. Moderation in all things: that's what I always say." With which words, she speared another bite of kidney, put it in her mouth, and went on poring over the account book.

Deciding there was no point in baiting her further, Vincent took a couple of kidneys for himself along with a cup of coffee and a hot roll. He had little appetite, for his thoughts had reverted once again to the subject of life and mortality. It was such an absorbing subject that he did not realize he had lapsed into silence until the dowager's voice broke in on his thoughts. "I must say, you're very quiet this morning, Vincent."

"Am I?" said Vincent, with a would-be smile. "Well, there's not much point in talking when you're busy with your accounts."

"I'm busy with my accounts most mornings, but that don't stop you from babbling like a brook just the same." The dowager looked narrowly at her son. "I noticed when you came down that you looked a bit peaked. Not feeling quite the thing, are you?"

"I *feel* well enough," said Vincent. "Mean to say, if something's amiss, it don't seem to be my health." He hesitated, torn by the urge to confide in someone and a desire to conceal feelings that might be laughed at. In the end the former urge won out, and he went on with another would-be smile. "The fact is, I'm feeling a trifle blue this morning, Mama. Everything seems stale, flat, and unprofitable, as what's-his-name says in the play."

The dowager gave him a searching look. "Oh, yes?" she said. "'Stale, flat, and unprofitable,' eh?"

"Aye, it does. I don't seem to have any taste for anything."

The dowager nodded. "I wondered what brought you to Larkholm this time of year," she said. "Normally I wouldn't look to see your face till summer."

"I s'pose not," said Vincent. "But London just didn't seem as interesting as it usually does." Summoning up another smile, he added, "It's left me at something of a loss, what?"

Again the dowager nodded. "It would, of course," she said. "You've never done much but fool around in society and go to parties from the time you left Oxford. It stands to reason that kind of life would pall on a body eventually, assuming he or she wasn't a complete fool."

Vincent was beginning to regret his urge to confide.

"I thank you for the compliment, Mama, if compliment it be," he said. "But I don't think—"

"It wasn't a compliment," said the dowager.

Vincent shut his mouth firmly on what he had been about to say. After a moment he went on, through clenched teeth. "Never mind," he said. "I'll confess I was hoping for something more, Mama—some advice, maybe, or at least an encouraging word. But I ought to have known better than expect such a thing from you."

The dowager regarded him with a not unkindly eye. "To be sure, you might have known better than that," she agreed. "I've never been one to sugarcoat my words, as you very well know. But believe it or not, I'm not at all unsympathetic to your feelings, Vincent. Otherwise I'd have simply advised you to take a dose of rhubarb and wait until the mood passes."

"Much obliged," said Vincent with a short laugh.

The dowager gave him an indulgent smile. "Mind you, the rhubarb probably wouldn't hurt you," she said. "But if you're to the place where you're—how d'you put it?—'don't have any taste for anything,' then I doubt it will help much, either."

"It sounds pretty foolish, I suppose," said Vincent, flushing. "But I don't know how to put it any better. It's not that I'm afraid of death, or anything like that. I trust I'll go out like a man when my time comes, but I just don't see the point of it all." Bitterly, he added, "And if you tell me that this world's only a temporary business and we'll know all the answers in the next one, I tell you plainly I'm not convinced. How the deuce can you know that's true? How can anyone?"

The dowager gave him another indulgent smile. "Heaven knows *I* don't know," she said. "I've met folks who claimed to know all about this life and the next, but I'm a skeptic by nature, and I've never much believed they had more of an idea than the rest of us. To spend eternity sitting around playing harps and sitting on a cloud don't sound much of a heaven to me. I sometimes wonder if the Jews don't have the right idea. They don't believe in our notions of heaven and hell, from what I understand. Instead, they consider that a man lives on through his descendants after he dies."

Vincent gave her a long look. "The Jews may very well be right, for all I know," he said. "But if you'll forgive me for saying so, Mama, this sounds remarkably like a prelude to your usual speech, the one where you advise me to get married and produce an heir to carry on the family name."

The dowager looked guileless. "Does it?" she said. "Ah, well, I don't mean to preach. You know your duty in that direction as well as I do—or should know it, at least." She spoke acidly, but when Vincent failed to respond, her voice softened once again, becoming low and persuasive. "The fact is, we're none of us getting any younger, Vincent. I can see why you didn't want to tie yourself down with a wife and family when you were just out of university, but it's high time you was thinking of it now. Beatrice hasn't produced anything but girls, so there's no one to inherit the title and property after you're gone except that oaf of a cousin of yours. And I tell you plainly I'd rather see the title die out than have it go to him."

Still Vincent said nothing. The dowager went on, her voice growing even more persuasive. "You say you've been feeling low lately and bored with everything. To my mind, that's a sign that you're ready to turn over a new leaf. There've been times I've despaired of your ever developing any sense, but what you've told me today gives me hope that you might yet come about."

"What, because I'm bored with society?" said Vincent.

"Exactly," said the dowager triumphantly. "Good lord, I was bored with society before I was seventeen. What's the point of trying to outdress and outspend your neighbors and throw parties for people, most of whom detest you as cordially as you detest them?"

Vincent shook his head. "Don't you think you're

exaggerating a bit?" he suggested. "I know there's a bit of backbiting that goes on among the *ton*, but I never thought it was as bad as that."

"I might be exaggerating a little," allowed the dowager. "There's society folk that are decent enough, I'll admit that. And I still enjoy going up to Town for a week or two in the Season. But I've never tried to make it a way of life like you have. This business of doing the social round year in and year out—why, it's bound to bore any sensible person sooner or later. It's taken you a while longer to get bored with it than most, but the fact you're finally feeling it gives me hope you've got more sense than I gave you credit for."

"Much obliged," said Vincent dryly. "But I'm not sure I care for your diagnosis, Mama. According to you, the reason I'm feeling blue-deviled is because I'm developing sense?"

"That's what I'm hoping," said the dowager with a brisk nod.

"Then if you'll forgive me, I'd just as soon *not* develop it. Besides, even if you're right, I don't see how running out and getting married is likely to make me feel any less blue-deviled."

The dowager did not respond to this statement directly. Instead she said in a nostalgic voice, "There was that Hancock chit you was so crazy about. I thought for certain the two of you were going to make a match of it."

Vincent shook his head. "Desdemona married Sidney Carlyle last June," he said. "Besides, you told me at the time you'd as soon I didn't marry a Hancock. You said there was bad blood in the family."

"So there is, but it would have been a decent match all the same," said the dowager. "Still, if she's married now, it obviously won't do."

"Obviously," agreed Vincent.

"So you'll have to find someone else." The dowager pursed her lips and looked meditative. "Cordelia Ellis has a couple of daughters who are supposed to be nice-looking gels."

Without undue haste or temper, Vincent got to his feet. "That's it," he said. "If you're going to start making matches for me, Mama, I'm going back to London. I can stand being blue-deviled, but I won't be nagged into marrying."

The dowager, looking martyred, said that she had no intention of nagging him. "You must do just as you think best, of course, Vincent," she said. "I didn't mean to drive you from your home."

She sounded so penitent that Vincent's irritation abated. "That's all right, Mama," he said. "I think I'd be better off in London anyway. Town ain't precisely gay right now, but it's better than it is here. What with it raining every day, and the first earl putting his damned mausoleum where a fellow has to look at it first thing every morning, and the fact that I can't even eat my breakfast without staring at his ugly phiz—why, it's enough to make anybody blue-deviled." He looked with distaste at the portrait of the first earl that glared down at him from over the breakfast room fireplace. "I wouldn't be surprised if that wasn't half my problem."

The dowager said absently that the first earl's portrait was commonly held to be a poor likeness. "But there's no doubt the country in this Season *is* rather slow. Town would probably be better, as you say." With a thoughtful voice, she added, "Besides, if you are in Town, it will give you a chance to look over the latest crop of girls making their bows at St. James's."

Without a word, Vincent turned and left the room.

# Two

Having made up his mind to return to London, Vincent lost no time in shaking the dust of Larkholm from his feet. By the time twenty-four hours had passed, he was back again in his house in Mayfair and wondering why he had been in such a hurry to return to it.

Nothing was changed. The outlook was just as dreary as it had been at Larkholm. To be sure, he didn't have to look at the first earl's mausoleum every morning, but life as a whole held no more joy than before.

There had been fully a dozen envelopes lying beside his breakfast plate that morning. All of them contained invitations of one sort or other. Yet somehow, not one of them appealed to him. Neither did it seem worthwhile to take a look-in at his club, examine the latest cattle on the block at Tattersall's, or put in a session at Jackson's boxing salon. He felt restless, yet overcome with inertia.

"This won't do," Vincent said aloud. Making an effort, he pushed the invitations aside along with his scarcely touched plate of breakfast and rose to his feet. "I'll go for a walk in the park," he decided. "Some fresh air will blow the cobwebs from my brain. Might give me an appetite, too. Seems like I haven't felt really hungry in weeks."

It was too early in the year for the park to be very busy, even if it had not been so early in the day. The walks and drives that were jammed with Fashionables

during the height of the Season were virtually empty
now. This suited Vincent, who was feeling distinctly an-
tisocial. He strode along the path with his hands thrust
in his pockets and his shoulders hunched against the
February cold. There was a stiff breeze blowing, which
nipped at his ears and nose, making him wish he had
bundled those features in a muffler. Still, the walk was
not wholly unpleasant. It felt good to stretch his legs
and breathe the cold, crisp air. By the time he was ready
to return home, he was feeling less oppressed in spirit,
if somewhat chilled in body. This latter circumstance
made him decide to take a hackney coach home rather
than walk all the way. He was looking about for an available cabman when a barouche passing in the street
slowed and came to a stop in the street opposite where
he was standing.

"My Lord Yates?"

Vincent looked to see who was hailing him. The
barouche contained a single lady passenger, clad in a
sumptuous chinchilla-lined cloak with matching muff. A
little blue velvet toque sat jauntily atop her blond head.
Her expression was a trifle uncertain, but it gave way to
a radiant smile when Vincent's eyes met hers. "It *is* you,"
she said. "I thought it must be, my lord, though I certainly didn't look to see you abroad as early as this. And
on foot, too." Her eyes made a quick survey of Vincent's
figure, then dropped as though overcome by a sudden
shyness.

Vincent felt a little shy himself. There had been passages between him and Desdemona Hancock, now
Lady Carlyle, that made a meeting between them now
a somewhat awkward business.

Still, he was glad to see her. As he took the kid-gloved
hand she gave him and bowed over it, it struck him as a
curious coincidence that he should run across her today.
His mother had spoken of her just the other morning,
saying she had expected him to propose to Mona. Vincent wondered now why he had not. Certainly Mona was

a lovely woman and a charming one as well. They had had some good times together. It made him a little sad to think that those good times were now irretrievably over. He gazed at her with mingled sensations of regret and admiration.

Mona was regarding him with much the same expression. "It's been an age since I've seen you, my lord," she said. "Have you time to talk, or are you on your way someplace?" She gestured toward the seat opposite her in the barouche. "I would be happy to take you wherever you are going. Indeed, my lord, my carriage and coachman are quite at your service."

Vincent assured her he was in no hurry to go anywhere and happily seated himself in the barouche. Again Mona scrutinized him. "You're looking well," she said.

"And so are you," said Vincent, sketching a bow. "Very well indeed, Mona. Even prettier than when I last saw you, 'pon my soul. And that must have been—why, I suppose it must have been at the wedding."

"Yes," said Mona. She looked down briefly, then looked up again with a forced smile. "I suppose it must have been at the wedding."

Vincent was aware of a constraint in her manner. He thought it better not to seem to notice it, however, and rattled on as though unconscious of her looks. "Gad, but that'll be a year ago this June. Time flies, don't it? Have you been on the Continent all this time? I know Sid said you were going there for your wedding trip."

"Yes, but Sir Sidney and I returned from the Continent several months ago," said Mona. She had regained her composure by now and spoke quite matter-of-factly. "We have been staying at Sir Sidney's home in Surrey since returning and only arrived back in Town yesterday."

"Then I'm lucky to have seen you so soon," said Vincent. "And looking very well, as I said before. Married life seems to suit you, 'pon my word."

Mona gave him a quick look, seemed about to say

something, and then thought better of it. "You are very kind to say so," she said.

Vincent made a light reply to this, but inwardly he was wondering. He was not so obtuse as he appeared, and he had caught the expression on Mona's face when she had spoken of her husband—an expression of discontent, it seemed to him. Taken together with what she had said and *not* said, it seemed to indicate matters were not as well between her and Sir Sidney as might be hoped.

Vincent had heard the rumors surrounding Mona's marriage, of course. There were people who said she had taken Sid for his money, and others who opined she would have married any man who enabled her to put the apellation "Lady" before her name, but the prevailing opinion was that she had chosen Sir Sidney, a close friend of Vincent's, as the best available substitute for Vincent himself.

Vincent was in no position to know how much truth was in these rumors. He did know that at one time Mona had expected, or at least hoped, that he would ask her to marry him. When it came to the point, however, he had been obliged to disappoint her hopes. It wasn't that he didn't care for her. He had cared for her sincerely, and there were times when he fancied he might even be in love with her, but it hadn't been enough to carry him over the barrier of his reluctance.

Looking at Mona now, sitting across from him in her opulent furs and velvets, Vincent wondered why he had been so reluctant. Had it been cowardice, or fickleness, or simply a desire to remain unencumbered by a wife and family? Vincent couldn't have said. He did know that Mona had no serious reason to complain about his behavior. True, he had stolen a few kisses from her, but kisses were nothing in this day and age, as he assured himself. Mona must have known better than to take his dalliance seriously. He had no reason to feel guilty about disappointing the hopes that she had evidently cherished. And yet as Vincent sat in the barouche, watching the look of discontent flicker across Mona's face, he did feel guilty. Had she chosen to marry Sid only because of him? Balked of love, had she chosen a marriage of convenience to his best friend as the next best alternative?

Somehow Vincent couldn't believe it. He simply wasn't conceited enough to imagine that any woman could be crazy enough about him to let it ruin her life. Particularly a woman like Mona, who was admirably practical and levelheaded beneath her frivolous exterior. He had wondered a little at her choosing Sir Sidney as a husband, but he had never seriously questioned her decision. Looking back, he supposed he must have felt a little guilty about his treatment of her after all, since his chief emotion on hearing she was engaged to Sid had been one of relief. He had been glad to think she was settled so credibly and that he was off the hook so far as offering for her himself was concerned.

But was it possible he had been premature in thinking he was off the hook? He could hardly be expected to marry Mona now, of course, but if she was unhappy, then her unhappiness must be in some measure his fault. Vincent scrutinized her face, noting more and more the discontented droop of her mouth and the restless, unhappy look in her eyes. He wanted to say something to her that would address the questions uppermost in his mind, but a moment's reflection showed him that he had much better let well enough alone. Therefore, he chattered on lightly about parties and balls and the Prince Regent's latest folly, not seeming to notice that Mona was hardly responding to his talk. When they reached his house in Mayfair, he rose and prepared to quit the barouche.

"Thanks for the lift," he told her. He was about to add some conventional polite remark about its being a pleasure to see her again when Mona seized his hand between hers.

"My lord, *must* you go?" she asked.

There was appeal in her voice, and something more than appeal in the smile with which she regarded him. She went on, pressing his hand tighter between her own as she spoke. "I have so enjoyed talking with you again. Can't you cancel your other engagements so we can spend a little more time getting reacquainted?"

Looking into her lovely, imploring face, Vincent knew a strong urge to say yes. There was no reason he might not say yes, for his other engagements were hardly pressing. He had planned nothing more important that day than a visit to his tailor and perhaps a look-in at his club.

Yet something compelled him to refuse Mona's invitation in spite of his desire to accept it. Perhaps it was the very strength of his desire that gave him pause. Mona was the wife of Sir Sidney now, and even if there was no harm in their spending time together (which of course there was not), they ought to refrain from behavior that might give rise to gossip. A five minutes' ride was one thing, but to extend the ride without a maid or other third party to bear them company was another and more dubious action. So Vincent shook his head with unfeigned regret. "I'm afraid I can't stay, Mona," he said. "Dash it, I'd like to, but I'm all booked up."

"Truly?" said Mona. She looked at him keenly. "Or is it that you simply don't wish to spend time with me?"

"No, indeed!" Vincent assured her. "Why, there's nothing I'd rather do if I had my way about it. I'd like to spend the whole day with you, by Jove."

As soon as the words were out of his mouth, he realized that this was hardly an appropriate statement to address to a friend's wife. But it appeared that he had not offended Mona, for she smiled and pressed his hand again.

"That's all right, then," she said. "I will accept your excuses this time, my lord. But if you really are glad to see me, then I shall expect you to call on me now you know

I am back in town. And I shall also expect you to give me as much of your company in the evenings as you can conveniently spare." She reached up and kissed him lightly on the cheek. "I'm giving a party in a few weeks' time—just an intimate gathering for a few of my closest friends. Please oblige me by saying you will come, my lord."

"Oh, aye, I'll come," said Vincent. He could hardly have refused, with Mona's kiss still tingling on his cheek. After he had bade her adieu, however, and watched her drive off in the barouche, he found himself prey to a sudden unease.

Ought he to have accepted Mona's invitation? He could see nothing wrong about doing so on the face of it. There could be no possible objection to attending a party at a friend's house at the behest of that friend's wife. Vincent supposed it was Mona's description of the party as "intimate" that had made him feel uneasy. He told himself he must have a lewd mind, to let that word arouse such illicit possibilities in his mind. Or perhaps it was the kiss that had preceded it that had done the mischief. There was nothing wrong in Mona's kissing him as she had, for she might have kissed a brother the same way with perfect propriety, but the fact was that the touch of her lips had affected him in a way that was hardly brotherly.

The thought increased Vincent's unease. He had no wish to be disloyal to Sid, who after all was one of his closest friends. Likewise, he did not wish to hold Mona in disrespect. But he could not rid himself of the notion that there had been something provocative in her manner. He was not a conceited man, but he had enough experience to know when a woman was deliberately trying to entice him. What was even more disquieting, he could not deny that something in him had responded to Mona's enticement.

Vincent was not a fool, whatever his mother might say. He knew it was no uncommon thing for married women to have their cicisbeos, just as many a married man kept a mistress. Still, he would never have supposed Mona would participate in this practice. For his own part, he had never dallied with married women, feeling there were enough pretty, willing women in London without trespassing on someone else's property. But this was a different situation, as Vincent told himself. This was Mona, the woman whom he probably would have married if he had been a marrying man. If she was unhappy and it was in some measure his fault, was it not his duty to do something about it?

It seemed a logical argument, yet Vincent felt convinced there was a flaw in it somewhere. For one thing, it had not been his experience that duty ran so smoothly in yoke with inclination. For another, there was Sid. Of course it might be that Mona wanted him only as a platonic friend, but that wasn't the impression Vincent had gotten. He was too honest to shut his eyes to the possibilities. Seeing her today had reignited the spark of attraction that had lain dormant in him since they had parted ways. Mona had made it clear by her own behavior that she still felt something for him, too. And that meant both of them were, in a sense, already betraying Sid, even if they never let their attraction go any further. Vincent could not like this idea. Like most of his contemporaries, he tended to laugh at conventional morality, but he did have a personal code of honor that he had always prided himself on keeping.

*But Mona's unhappy,* he reasoned to himself. *She didn't actually say so, but it's obvious from the way she talked. I'll bet a monkey Sid's been neglecting her. He always was a careless sort of fellow. Probably he's been spending all his evenings at White's and Watier's and leaving her to her own devices.*

Following this line of reasoning, Vincent told himself that Sid had nobody to blame but himself if his wife took up with another fellow. Still, his chief justification for pursuing his acquaintance with Mona was a selfish one. Meeting her that day had temporarily dispelled the melancholy that had been plaguing him for the past few weeks. It had given him something new and interesting to think about, and the more he thought about it, the more convinced he became that he really had loved Mona all along. It had only taken this chance meeting to show him his own heart. There could be no doubt that the idea of seeing Mona again held a real excitement. It might be a guilty excitement, but after so many weeks of boredom and malaise, Vincent thought guilty excitement was better than no excitement at all.

Having resolved the matter in this fashion, Vincent entered his house, handed his hat and overcoat to his butler, and inquired if there were any callers while he was out. "Yes, my Lady Beatrice has called, my lord," said the butler. "I have put her in the small parlor."

"She's here now?" inquired Vincent, a little surprised. He and his sister were on friendly terms, but it was rare that she called on him. Lady Beatrice Evers was a blue-stocking renowned for her literary salons and a person of note among London's intelligentsia. She was wont to turn up her nose at her brother's more pedestrian companions and pastimes, while Vincent, for his part, tended to apostrophize her companions and pastimes as intolerably dull and stuffy. As such, they seldom saw each other except on those rare occasions when their circles overlapped, such occasions being about as common as a total eclipse of the sun.

It was thus a surprise for Vincent to hear that his sister was calling on him today. He knew it could not be merely a formal call to welcome him back to town, for she might have accomplished the same object by simply leaving a card. For her to call meant she wanted to talk to him about something. Vincent knew from experience that this was not a favorable circumstance. She had frequently rated him in the past for indulging in undignified spectacles like the sidesaddle race. He searched his memory to see what he had done to earn his sister's displeasure this time, but his conscience was reasonably clear apart from his intentions regarding Mona, and he was reasonably sure Beatrice could have no inkling of those as yet. Still, as he entered the parlor he looked warily to see if she was about to favor him with another blast of sisterly disapproval.

On this occasion, however, Lady Beatrice seemed to have other fish to fry. Her handsome countenance wore an amiable smile as she rose to her feet and put out a hand for her brother's salute. She inquired after his health with solicitude and said she was glad to hear he was feeling well. Vincent studied her curiously as he seated himself opposite her on the parlor sofa. "To what do I owe this honor, Trix?" he inquired. "Surely you didn't come just to ask after my health."

"As a matter of fact I did," said Lady Beatrice. She went on, her voice betraying a tinge of embarrassment. "I had a letter from Mama yesterday, you see. And in it, she mentioned that you were feeling . . . not quite the thing. And she asked me to wait on you and see if there was anything I could do for you."

Vincent scowled. More than ever did he regret making the dowager the recipient of his confidences. "Mama makes too much of it," he said shortly. "I was just feeling a trifle blue-deviled last week, that's all."

"Is it?" asked Beatrice. She looked searchingly into his face. "You do look a trifle pulled-down, Vincent. Heaven knows it's no wonder, considering the pace you've been going."

"Nonsense," said Vincent. "I'm in perfect health. Never felt better in my life, by Jove. You can tell Mama so if she asks." With asperity, he added, "And you can also tell her that if she's worried I'm going to put a period to my existence, then she needn't."

"I don't think that's it," said Beatrice. "She just thought you were low and wanted something to divert you."

"And she thought *you* were going to do that?" inquired Vincent, in a voice not so much rude as incredulous.

Lady Beatrice smiled, revealing a sudden and unlikely

resemblance to her brother. "You may well ask," she said. "I've been wondering myself why Mama wanted me to come. I suppose she just wanted me to show a little filial support, as it were." In a more serious tone, she added, "I hope you know that I *do* support you, Vincent. Even if I do not precisely approve of your mode of life, I wish you nothing but well."

In spite of his irritation, Vincent was touched by this avowal. "That's very good of you, Trix," he said. "Much obliged, I'm sure."

"Not at all," said Lady Beatrice. In a lighter voice, she added, "I am your sister, after all. Of course I don't want you falling into a Slough of Despond."

"No chance of that," said Vincent. "I might have been a bit mired last week, but that was only because I was at Larkholm."

Lady Beatrice agreed that Larkholm in February was a dreary place. "How Mama bears it year in and year out, I do not know," she said. "I am sure I would perish if I had to live there year around."

"Here, here," said Vincent fervently. "It's good to be back in London. Although things are still a bit slow, being as it's only February."

Lady Beatrice shook her head with a patronizing smile. "Perhaps things are slow in *your* circle," she said. "In mine, I assure you there is excitement enough."

Vincent opined that her circle got excited every time somebody strung two sentences together. Lady Beatrice gave him another, even more patronizing smile. "Not at all," she said. "In this case we have sufficient cause for excitement, for Samuel Locke has come to town."

"That's not exciting as far as I'm concerned," said Vincent. "Never heard of the fellow."

Lady Beatrice made a noise both exasperated and amused. "Vincent! Is it possible that you haven't heard of Samuel Locke?"

"Just told you I haven't, Trix," said Vincent impatiently.

"Like I said before, I never heard of the fellow. Who is he? What's he done?"

"Why, he is an author—an American author. He wrote *Moccasin Tales* and *The Scout's Story* and several other books as well."

Vincent shrugged. "That's nothing to me," he said. "You know I'm not much of a reader, Trix. I've no use for literary fellows—or for colonials, either."

Lady Beatrice smiled. "Well, just between you and me, I haven't any use for them either in the normal way," she said. "But Samuel Locke is an exception to the rule. He really is a tremendously talented writer and such an original character, too. Everyone in my circle is quite charmed by him."

"Well, you're welcome to him," said Vincent with a yawn. "He don't sound any great shakes to *me*."

Lady Beatrice, with just the suggestion of tartness in her voice, said she hadn't supposed Vincent would be interested in Mr. Locke. "If I had thought you would be, I would have invited you to meet him at my house this evening. I'm holding a small reception in honor of him and his daughter, who is visiting England along with him. But of course I knew you would not be interested. What would *you* have to say to Samuel Locke? You haven't a thought in your head for anything besides gaming and sports and playing childish pranks."

If Lady Beatrice had leveled this charge against him a month ago, Vincent would have laughed and agreed that she was right. Today, however, it touched him on the raw. Beatrice obviously thought him a trifling fellow incapable of deep thought and meaningful conversation. Although he would never have claimed to be an intellectual, he had *some* thoughts that went beyond gaming and sports and childish pranks, Vincent told himself. Heretofore he had not minded if people dismissed him as a fool without a serious thought in his head, but now he found he resented it. He also resented Beatrice's implication that he would have nothing to say to Samuel Locke. He was an English peer and a man of the world, and he prided himself on being equal to any situation. It was ridiculous to suppose a mere backwoods colonial could put him at a loss, no matter how many books the fellow had written.

So Vincent leveled a look at his sister and said, "On the contrary, Trix. I'll wager I'd find plenty to say to Mr. Locke if you invited me to your party."

Lady Beatrice drew her fine brows together. "Are you saying you want to come to my party?" she asked. "To a *literary* party?"

The incredulity in her voice goaded Vincent into recklessness. "Why not?" he said. "Never been to a literary party before. It'll be something new for me. A change from gaming and sports and childish pranks," he added maliciously.

Lady Beatrice did not seem to feel the sting of this, being still occupied in a dubious survey of her brother's face. "Of course you are welcome to come to my party if you like, Vincent," she said. "But I truly don't think you will find it the least bit entertaining."

"Maybe not," said Vincent. "But I'd as soon be the judge of that myself. What time should I come? Will there be dinner and dancing, or do we just talk all evening?"

Lady Beatrice, looking as though she were regretting her permission, told him that it would be merely a conversational evening with light refreshments. "You may come anytime after nine o'clock," she said.

"I'll be there at nine o'clock sharp," said Vincent cheerfully. "Got to lend you my brotherly support, don't you know."

Lady Beatrice made no reply to this, but merely said she ought to be going, as she had preparations to make for the party that evening. Vincent, grinning to himself, wished her a good afternoon, and saw her off the premises with a strong sense of satisfaction.

# Three

Although Vincent had enjoyed getting the better of his sister, it was not long before he realized that his victory was a hollow one.

Why should he wish to attend a literary party? Particularly a party given in honor of a colonial who wrote books about Red Indians and probably ate with his knife? Vincent could only suppose he had suffered a brain-storm. He had been piqued because Beatrice had dismissed his intellectual pretensions, and he had forced her to issue the invitation as a form of revenge. But in truth, what intellectual pretensions did he have? He had fooled away most of his time at Eton and Oxford, and nowadays he rarely opened a book unless it was a racing journal or French novel. Beatrice had always been the brainy one of the family. What could he possibly hope to achieve by challenging her position now?

*Don't know what I was about,* Vincent told himself gloomily. It seemed unlikely that he would have a good time at Beatrice's party with no dancing, no dinner, and nothing but talk to while away the evening. Of course he could talk well enough after a fashion, but the kind of talk that served at *ton* parties and White's probably wouldn't answer in Beatrice's circle at all. Vincent realized he didn't really know what Beatrice and her friends talked about. Books, undoubtedly: seeing that this was a literary party, it stood to reason they would discuss books. And since Samuel Locke was the guest of honor, it likewise stood to reason it would be his books that were discussed. And he, Vincent Yates, had never read a single one of Samuel Locke's books. In fact, he knew nothing about them apart from the two titles Beatrice had mentioned.

Vincent ran his fingers through his hair. He was just beginning to realize he had let himself in for a ghastly ordeal. He almost had a mind to send Beatrice his regrets, citing some just-remembered engagement as an excuse. Beatrice would not hold it against him if he cried off. Probably she would be relieved, for he could see she had not liked above half the idea of his attending her party. She probably thought he would do something to embarrass her. *Like the time Johnny Crossman and I dressed up that old orange coster and introduced her to half the* ton *as a Russian grandduchess,* Vincent recalled with a grin.

Yet beneath his amusement was a feeling of hurt. Beatrice ought to know he would never do anything to embarrass her in front of her friends. She ought also to know that he was quite capable of behaving with propriety when he chose. Somehow, the idea that even his own sister dismissed him as a scapegrace prankster brought back his depression.

This depression continued to plague him as the afternoon passed. A visit to White's Club did nothing to alleviate it, and when he stopped by the tailor's to order a new topcoat, he could not even interest himself in the decision of whether it should be made of Bath cloth or superfine. Searching desperately for something to shake him out of his despondency, he summoned up the image of Mona as she had sat across from him in the barouche that morning. There was still a pleasure in that memory, he was happy to find. If only Mona had been going to Beatrice's that evening! Then it would have been an occasion to look forward to, not to dread. But after all, even if the party turned out to be deadly dull it was only for the one evening, and he would be seeing Mona again soon. She had spoken of her own party as being only a

week or two away. And there was nothing to stop him
from seeing her before then, if he liked. She had urged
him to call on her. The thought of seeing Mona soon—
possibly even as early as tomorrow—restored Vincent to
a better humor. There was, after all, something to look
forward to in life.

With this fact established, Vincent was able to face
the evening in a more philosophical frame of mind. He
would talk about books with the best of them and look
as though he liked it, a strategy that would inciden-
tally show Beatrice he was not the trifling fellow she
thought him. It occurred to him, however, that he
could probably make a better job of this business if he
were to some extent prepared. So instead of going
straight home from his tailor's, he stopped by a bookseller's and bought a copy of *Moccasin Tales.* Of course
he could not hope to read the whole book before
evening, but he might at least read a chapter or two
and gain a general idea of what the story was about.
*And if it's too dull to be endured, at least I can tell Mr. Locke
I own it,* Vincent told himself comfortingly. *That ought
to satisfy him, even if he is a literary genius. I daresay even literary geniuses care more about their royalties than they do
about compliments and criticisms.*

As it happened, however, Vincent found *Moccasin
Tales* not in the least dull. Thumbing through it at the
bookseller's, he had received an off-putting impression
of outlandish Red Indian names and unfamiliar North
American locations, but once he started reading he
quickly became so absorbed in the story that these details ceased to matter. When his butler came into the
library to announce that dinner was served, Vincent
brought the book down to the dining parlor with him
and read while he ate. After dinner, he adjourned to
the library to read some more. So intrigued was he by
the tale that was unfolding that he came close to forgetting the whole reason he was reading it. It was a
quarter to nine when he remembered Beatrice's party,

laid the book aside, and made a hasty scramble to get into evening clothes. As he was waiting for the coachman to bring around his carriage, he surveyed *Moccasin Tales* with satisfaction. He had made a healthy dent in the first volume and he felt there was no reason he couldn't participate in a discussion about its characters and incidents, even if he wasn't sure how it was all going to come out.

*Best of all, I can tell Mr. Locke I liked it and be telling the truth,* Vincent told himself as he went out to his carriage. *A jolly good book, by Jove. Haven't read anything in years I enjoyed so much.*

Arriving at Beatrice's town house, he was ushered into the saloon with its crimson velvet hangings and gilt-framed oil paintings. A goodly company were already gathered there. Glancing around, Vincent would at first have taken them for any gathering of London society folk, but a closer inspection revealed certain differences. The men were, in general, less meticulously tailored than their less intellectual counterparts; the women were less *décolleté*, and a number of guests of both sexes appeared to have thrown on their garments with a complete disregard for either fashion or the exigencies of their own figures. A stout dame in a hoopskirt was holding forth in the corner on the subject of Greek antiquities, while a gentleman in a wig and laced coat who appeared to have stepped out of a Hogarth engraving was earnestly discussing Elizabethan verse with a party of other guests.

Beatrice herself was the center of a lively group near the door. She caught sight of Vincent as he entered and came hurrying over to greet him. Her "Good evening" was perfectly cordial, but Vincent noticed she looked him up and down with a hint of anxiety. It was evident she was still expecting him to disrupt her party in some manner. "There you are, Vincent," she said. "I had nearly given you up."

Vincent said gravely that he had been reading and lost track of time. Beatrice gave him an incredulous smile.

"It's perfectly true," he told her. "You needn't think you're the only literary one in the family, Trix. I thought I'd take a dip in one of that fellow Locke's books. It turned out to be a jolly good tale, so good that I came near to losing track of time entirely."

"Well, I'm sure Mr. Locke ought to be gratified by your approbation," said Beatrice. Her brow had smoothed a little, but she was still looking faintly apprehensive. Vincent reached out to pat her arm.

"Don't worry, old girl," he said. "I promise I'll be a pattern-card of propriety tonight. You needn't fear I'll kick up a dust."

"I'd be very glad to know that is so," said Beatrice. "To speak truth, I don't know how much more dust I can stand this evening. We've already had one near-incident. Mrs. Osbourne disagreed with Miss Pinkley about whether Lord Elgin was justified in removing the Elgin marbles from Greece, and they nearly came to blows about it. Oh, dear, they're at it again." She looked with distress toward the corner, where the stout dame in the hoopskirt was now addressing a younger woman with close-cropped hair and spectacles.

"Surely even you cannot believe it to be right to deprive a country of its own cultural treasures? I think it an outrage, an affront of which England ought to be justly ashamed."

The younger woman smiled a superior smile. "Such rhetoric is all very well, Aurelia," she said. "But if the marbles were to be preserved at all, it was vital that they be removed from Greece. In this case, the end may be said to justify the means. The preservation of antiquities of such value justifies any measures, including removal from their native country."

The stout dame, appearing on the verge of apoplexy, began an impassioned rebuttal to this speech. Beatrice touched Vincent's arm. "Excuse me for a moment, Vincent," she said. "I must go see what I can do to avert a battle."

"Anything I can do to help?" inquired Vincent. "I'd be glad to throw myself into the breach, what?"

Beatrice started to make a hasty refusal of this offer, then stopped in midsentence. "Well, and why not?" she said. "If you could only distract Miss Pinkley for a few minutes, it would probably answer." Casting a sardonic smile at Vincent, she added, "I expect you can distract her very nicely if you try. There's no doubt that you can be very charming when you make the effort, Vincent."

With a sense of gratification, Vincent promised to do what he could in the cause of peace. He trailed interestedly after his sister to the corner where the two ladies' conversation was rapidly devolving into an exchange of personal insults. "My dear, ma'am, you have not met my brother, I think," said Lady Beatrice, breaking in on the exchange to address the elder lady with a winsome smile. "And neither has Hester, have you, Hester? Aurelia, Hester, this is my brother Vincent, Lord Yates. Vincent, this is Mrs. Richard Osbourne, authoress of *Life with the Greeks*. And this is Miss Hester Turnbull. You may have heard of her also, for she published a book of verse last Season—*Songs of Solitude*."

Vincent had never heard of *Songs of Solitude*, or of *Life with the Greeks* either, but he bowed politely and said he was honored to meet both ladies. "So you're a poet, eh?" he continued, addressing Miss Turnbull. "Never met a poet before. Except for Byron, of course, but I never had much to do with him. Bit of a loose screw, don't you know, even before he went jauntering off to the Continent."

Miss Turnbull, smiling her superior smile once more, said Lord Byron's verse was poetry only in the loosest sense. "It's been my observation that what is generally popular is almost always inferior," she told Vincent, and went on to explain why this was so, and why her own verses were far superior to Byron's. So eloquent was she on this subject that all Vincent had to do was make an occasional comment on the order of "Indeed?" and "You

don't say," and "Very shocking, 'pon my soul." This he
did patiently for the best part of an hour, and was re-
warded by having the poetess declare him a gentleman
of discerning taste. "Not many people hold such enlightened views on the subject of verse," she told him. "As
a general rule, the standard of popular taste is woefully
low. I do my best to raise it, of course, but it's a thankless
task."

"I'm sure it must be," said Vincent. Another gentleman came up just then to ask Miss Turnbull if she had
attended the reading of Mr. Gibson's new blank-verse
play last week. This caused Miss Turnbull to launch
into a denunciation of Mr. Gibson's blank verse-writing
abilities. Seeing that she was occupied, Vincent made
good his escape and went to the parlor to get some
well-earned refreshment.

After helping himself to a glass of punch and a few
sandwiches, he wandered back into the saloon and
stood looking around him. His sister had been so intent on averting hostilities between Miss Turnbull and
Mrs. Osbourne that she had had no time to introduce
him to any of the other guests. Vincent wondered if
Samuel Locke, the guest of honor, was among them.
Since dipping into *Moccasin Tales*, he found he was
quite eager to meet its author. Scrutinizing each of the
gentlemen in turn, he decided at last that Mr. Locke
must be the tall, dark-haired gentleman, dressed in a
somewhat outdated topcoat and knee breeches, whom
he saw chatting with Beatrice near the fireplace. He
strolled over to see if he could get an introduction.

Beatrice greeted him with affection. "Vincent! There
you are. I was meaning to go and rescue you soon if you
did not manage to break free from Miss Turnbull. I
cannot thank you enough for the heroic way you took
charge of her. It was wonderful of you to be so self-sac-
rificing, but I am afraid you have been having a rather
dull time of it. She can be rather long-winded when
once she gets started."

Vincent returned a polite, noncommittal answer to this and looked expectantly at the dark-haired gentleman. Beatrice took the hint. "By the by, Vincent, I have been wanting to introduce you to Mr. Locke, our guest of honor this evening," she said. "Mr. Locke, this is my brother Vincent, Lord Yates. Vincent, this is Mr. Samuel Locke."

Mr. Locke bowed and smiled. "I'm very pleased to meet you, Lord Yates," he said. He had a full, rich voice faintly colored with the accents of New England, and his face, without being precisely handsome, was full of character and good humor. Vincent found himself liking him at once.

"Indeed, I'm very pleased to meet *you*, sir," said Vincent sincerely. "Not much of a reader in the usual way, but I've just started reading your *Moccasin Tales* and like it very much."

Mr. Locke smiled and inclined his head. "Do you? I'm sure I'm much obliged to you for the compliment, Lord Yates. It happens part of my reason for coming to England was to arrange for a new edition of that book with my English publisher. But of course it's partly a pleasure trip, too. I've always had a hankering to see old England, and when this chance came along, I thought it a fine opportunity to combine business with pleasure."

"Are you staying in England long?" asked Vincent.

"Perhaps as much as a month or two. It depends partly on how long it takes to settle my business, and partly on my own inclinations—yes, and those of my daughter. You must know my daughter Constance has accompanied me here to England."

Vincent said politely that he had not yet had the pleasure of meeting Mr. Locke's daughter. Mr. Locke looked mildly surprised. "Haven't you? Constance is somewhere hereabout, I'm sure." He peered vaguely around the room. "Is she—? No, I don't see her. Perhaps she's stepped into the next room. Ah, well, as I was saying, Constance is here with me, and I don't know what I would do without her. She's an invaluable helper—makes all the arrangements, you know, and sees to it I'm kept up to the mark."

Vincent said politely that he was sure Miss Locke was a great help to her father. Mr. Locke agreed that she was and went on. "After we're done with our business in London, we're thinking of making a jaunt to the Continent and seeing some of the sights there." He smiled at Lady Beatrice. "I must say, however, that we've met with such a kind reception in London that I'm half tempted just to stay right here."

Beatrice said graciously that that would be London's gain and the Continent's loss. She then excused herself, leaving Vincent and Mr. Locke to talk between themselves. Vincent was wanting to say more about *Moccasin Tales*, but Mr. Locke very adroitly turned praise of his works aside in favor of more general conversation. He seemed particularly interested in discussing the differences he had found between England and America. Since Vincent was both an earl and a landowner, Mr. Locke had a number of questions about leases and holdings and hereditary license that Vincent did his best to answer, although he was rather embarrassed to find how ignorant he was concerning the laws of his own country. Overall, Mr. Locke seemed much better informed on the subject than he was. When Vincent said as much, however, Mr. Locke waved the compliment away with one of his self-deprecatory smiles.

"Not at all, sir; not at all. If I've learned anything during my stay in England, it's only because you and your fellow countrymen have been gracious enough to answer my questions."

He might have gone on to question Vincent further had he not been interrupted just then by a sharp-featured dame in a turban who requested (or rather demanded) his opinion on a matter she and some of the others were discussing. Mr. Locke good-naturedly acceded to her demands. "It's been a pleasure talking to you, sir, a very great pleasure," he told Vincent, shaking the latter's hand. "I hope I'll have the pleasure of talking to you again while I'm in London."

Vincent expressed the same hope. It was a hope which he found himself sincerely cherishing. He had been most favorably impressed by Mr. Locke's manners and personality.

*Trix was right, by Jove,* he told himself. *For a colonial, he's a very decent fellow. I wouldn't mind talking to him some more, but it looks as though that harpy in a turban has collared him for the rest of the evening. What's the time? Nearly midnight, by Jove. I could push off now if I like and consider I'd done my duty.*

Still, Vincent did not immediately push off. He continued to stand looking about the saloon. It was still early by his standards, and the party had proved quite enjoyable once he had shaken loose from Miss Turnbull. He cast his eye about, wondering if he ought to take the chance of introducing himself to some other congenial-looking individual. Beatrice had gone off somewhere, and the only other people who might have performed introductions for him were Miss Turnbull, whom he was reluctant to approach again, and Mr. Locke, who was occupied. Finally he decided to take the risk and make his own introductions. This was unconventional, but as Beatrice's brother, he reasoned that he was almost in the position of a host and might bend the rules without offense.

There was a young lady standing by herself not far off. Vincent gave her a tentative smile. The young lady regarded him coolly, then gave him the faintest of nods in return. Vincent, running an experienced eye over her, decided she was not in the least pretty. She had a mass of curly dark hair twisted into an untidy knot atop her head and a figure that was thin almost to the point of skinniness. Her face was somewhat enlivened by a pair of fine dark eyes, but her other features were rather plain, and so was her attire. She was wearing a simple round dress of white muslin, modest as to neckline and worn without any ornament apart from a gold cross on a chain. Yet in spite of these deficiencies, something in her appearance was pleasing and even striking. Vincent was struck by it, at any rate, and he decided to approach the young lady, even though her expression was more discouraging than encouraging. "'Evening," he said, strolling over to where she stood.

"Good evening," said the young lady. She turned her head as she spoke, and Vincent observed that there was a red, white, and blue cockade tucked among her dark curls.

"Decent party, what?" he ventured, studying her profile with its firm little chin and aquiline nose. "Are you having a good time?"

"Not particularly," said the young lady.

Vincent was taken aback by her frankness. It did not really surprise him, however, for none of the people he had met that evening were precisely conventional. It stood to reason that this girl, too, was an eccentric of one sort or another. Surveying the cockade in her hair, he thought he could guess which sort. "Are you a revolutionary?" he asked.

The young lady gave him a frosty stare. "I *beg* your pardon?" she said.

"A revolutionary," repeated Vincent, gesturing toward the cockade. "Thought you might be a revolutionary. You're wearing the what-d'ye-call-it—the *tricoleur* in your hair, don't you know."

The young lady eyed him disdainfully. "I'm American, not French," she said. "Perhaps you are unaware that our flag uses the same colors as the French one."

"Does it?" said Vincent. "Well, that's quite a coincidence, what? Still, I suppose if it comes to that, they're the same colors as the jolly old Union Jack!"

He smiled, but the young lady acted as though she had not heard him. "And I am *not* a revolutionary," she said. "Although I do confess to having a certain amount of sympathy with the French republicans. It is a pity their claims have been subjugated once more to the tyranny of the so-called aristocracy."

Vincent, as an aristocrat, might have been expected to resent this speech, but his brain had been working while the young lady was speaking, and enlightenment had come to him in a flash. "You say you're American?" he said. "Then you must be Constance Locke. I was talking to your father a bit ago."

"I am *Miss* Locke," said the young lady, laying a heavy emphasis on the "Miss." She surveyed Vincent with disfavor. "May I ask who you are, sir? It seems you have the advantage of me. I don't believe we have been introduced."

"No, we haven't," agreed Vincent cheerfully. "Trix ought to have introduced us, but she's busy somewhere else at the moment, so I thought I'd introduce myself. I'm Yates, her brother."

"Lady Beatrice's brother!" repeated Constance. Her color had risen, and she looked Vincent up and down with growing perturbation. "Then you must be—I beg your pardon, but would it not be *Lord* Yates?"

"Aye, that's right," said Vincent. "Vincent, Lord Yates, at your service." He accompanied the words with a smile and a bow.

Constance started to curtsy in return, stopped, then put out her hand instead. "It is a pleasure to meet you, sir," she said. There was no pleasure in her voice, however, but rather an edge of hostility.

Vincent, as he shook her hand, was puzzled. He could think of no reason why this Yankee girl should regard him with hostility, unless it were because he had violated convention by introducing himself. He had often heard that New Englanders were very straitlaced. Hoping to soothe her outrage at his faux pas, he went on, flashing her his most winning smile. "As I said, I was talking to your father just a bit ago," he told her. "If you like, we can go over and have him introduce us properly. 'Deed, and

I didn't mean to presume, but I enjoyed talking to your father very much, don't you know, and I thought I wouldn't mind meeting his daughter, what?"

"Indeed," said Constance. Her voice was contemptuous. She looked down her delicate aquiline nose at Vincent as though at some particularly offensive piece of rubbish. Vincent found he was beginning to be irritated. He was trying as hard as he could to be agreeable, but Miss Locke was clearly having none of it.

*By Jove, you'd think I was a leper or something,* Vincent told himself indignantly. *What a cross-grained girl! Her manners make Miss Turnbull's look downright charming.*

Still, he did not allow himself to be driven away by Constance's manners. Instead, he redoubled his efforts to be agreeable. "May I get you something from the refreshment room?" he asked her. "A glass of punch, or a few sandwiches?"

"I thank you, no," said Constance, lifting her chin still higher. "If I want something to eat or drink, sir, I am quite capable of going to the refreshment room myself."

"Well, of course you are," said Vincent. "Nobody doubts that, ma'am. Only thought I might save you the trouble if you did want something."

"I thank you, no," repeated Constance. Even she seemed to feel this was rather rude, however, for after a moment she added, "But it's very kind of you to offer."

Vincent regarded her with increased exasperation. "What makes you so deuced reluctant to let me get you a glass of punch?" he said. "I'm not a complete Yahoo, I hope."

"No, you are a nobleman, which is a far worse thing," said Constance.

This rejoinder was so unexpected that Vincent blinked. "Oh, yes?" he said.

"Yes, indeed," asserted Constance with warmth. "I think the whole system of rank and title in this country is an abomination. Why should one class of men be granted special privileges over their fellow men only because of their birth?"

Vincent shrugged. "Why was I born with light hair and you with dark?" he said. "Why was you born a lady and me a man? It's just the way of the world. I didn't *ask* to be an earl, y'know."

"No, but you are one," shot back Constance. "And being an earl is not an immutable physical thing like hair color or sex. It's a role you've voluntarily taken on, and I don't suppose for a minute that you'd renounce it now you've got it."

"Well, of course not," said Vincent "Nobody'd be such a noddy."

Constance smiled contemptuously. "So you say," she said. "But it makes me sick to see the way people in this country bow down to lords and ladies, only because you have titles to your name and are from what you are pleased to call good families. For my part, I honor a man far more who wins the respect of others through his own efforts, rather than one who is content with respect that is merely inherited."

Vincent thought this over. "That *sounds* all right," he said. "But it seems to me you're getting respect and authority mixed up. What I mean is, I might have a certain amount of authority because I was born an earl, but nobody's bound to respect me. As a matter of fact, I don't think anybody does," he added ruefully.

Constance brushed this aside as mere frivolity. "In any case, you don't deny you have a hereditary authority," she said. "As a nobleman, you can do whatever you please, even to the point of making laws which the common people are forced to obey."

"Here, now, I know *that's* not right," said Vincent, pleased to be able to refute one of her arguments. "*I* don't make the laws; Parliament does."

"But you are a Member of Parliament, are you not? As a nobleman, you are automatically entitled to a seat in the House of Lords. That means you and your fellow nobles can basically agree to do whatever you please with the law."

"That just shows you've never been in the House of Lords," said Vincent. "If you had been, you'd know there was precious little agreement going on . . . a lot of wrangling is more like it. Besides, the Lords are only the one House of Parliament. There's the Commons, too, and they're elected by popular vote."

"In my country, *all* our officials are elected by popular vote," said Constance. "I think it a much superior system."

She looked at Vincent as though expecting him to dispute this statement. But he only responded agreeably, "Ah, well, I expect it's all a matter of what you're brought up to."

Constance's lips thinned. "I suppose people who have never tasted freedom might conceivably embrace a form of government that oppresses them," she said coldly. "The people of my country feel differently about such things. We don't endure oppression from anyone. I think we demonstrated that adequately during the recent conflict between our two countries!"

"Aye, poor old Pakenham," agreed Vincent. "Got beat hollow at all points, didn't he? Still, it's a question whether he might not have done better if he'd had the full force of the British Army and Navy behind him. You know we were engaged in fighting a war with Boney on the Continent while that little skirmish in the States was going on."

Constance frowned. "Even if the whole of the British Army and Navy had been involved, the outcome would have been no different," she said coldly. "Americans will never bow to English tyranny—*never.*"

"Well, we won't likely know now," said Vincent. "The war's over and done with, what? Unless you intend we should fight the whole thing over again by proxy."

A reluctant smile curved Constance's lips. "No," she said. "You have a point there, sir. I am glad enough our countries ~~are at peace~~ once more." She paused for a moment, and when she went on there was a note of apology in her voice. "Perhaps I should not have expressed myself so strongly concerning you and your country. I know I should not, for I am a guest in your sister's house, and it's a poor return for her hospitality to spend the evening abusing her brother. And indeed, since coming to England I have seen much that I admire—even some things I think my own country would do well to emulate. But I do feel strongly that the English system of aristocracy is a blight on an otherwise progressive nation."

"Aye, I can tell that's how you feel," said Vincent politely.

Constance burst out laughing. She had a charming laugh, low and musical. "You are impossible to quarrel with, Lord Yates," she said. "No matter how hard I poke at you, you refuse to get angry. You simply poke back in such a well-bred, offhanded way that all my arguments end up sounding quite foolish."

"Oh, now, I wouldn't say that," said Vincent. "You've got a point, y'know, about some of the things you were saying. About the aristocracy and all . . . I've often thought myself that it's a queer system, giving so much to one fellow just because he happened to be born the eldest son in a particular family. Fine thing if you're that fellow, of course, but hard lines for everyone else, what?"

Constance shook her head. "You are very good to take my part, sir," she said. "But I know very well I should not have spoken as I did. The fact is that one of the young ladies here tonight rubbed me the wrong way. She told me in the most condescending way that I must find London very different after living in a primitive place like America with no culture or society or educational amenities. And I live in Boston! You would think I lived on the Kentucky frontier or up in the wilds of Maine, for heaven's sake."

"Oh, well, I daresay she was misled by your father's books," said Vincent comfortingly. "They're all about Red Indians and such, so she probably thought that was the what-d'ye-call-it—the status quo in America, what?"

Constance looked at him very hard. She looked at him so hard that Vincent began to think he had said something amiss. "What I mean to say is, it's a natural assumption," he said apologetically. "If a person had never read anything but your father's books, he might think all there was in America was Red Indians and wilderness, don't you know."

Constance did not address this remark directly. Instead, she said, "I begin to think you are a fraud, Lord Yates."

"I beg your pardon?" said Vincent, startled.

Constance smiled. "I said I think you are a fraud, Lord Yates. From your appearance and manner of speaking, one would suppose you were the veriest court card. But I am beginning to think that is all window dressing. Indeed, what you say is often surprisingly to the point."

It would have been too much to say that Vincent was flattered by this speech. Still, he felt it showed an unusual perception. He began to think that Constance was not such a bad sort of girl after all. "I'm sure that's very kind of you, Miss Locke," he said. "But you mustn't get to thinking I'm a clever fellow like your father. I hope I've got my share of common sense, but where brains are concerned I'm not in his class at all."

Constance smiled and sighed at the same time. "Oh, Father! Certainly he is a clever man, and I do not think it would be overstating the case to call him a genius of sorts. But at the same time, he is quite capable of leaving the house on a cold day without an overcoat, or of absentmindedly giving a cabman a guinea instead of a shilling by way of a tip. When he spoke of coming to England, I knew I would have to come along with him, for he is quite incapable of attending to the details of traveling."

Vincent said leniently that geniuses probably had more important things to think about than tips and overcoats. "He's lucky to have a daughter like you along to look after him," he told Constance. "He told me you were invaluable to him, and it looks as though he wasn't overstating the case."

Constance flushed prettily. "You are altogether too complimentary, Lord Yates," she said. "If you keep on in that vein, I shall begin to feel even worse than I do now about having criticized you and your fellow aristocrats." She gave him a shy smile. "I hope you know that though I do hold the opinions I stated earlier, I did not mean my criticism *personally.*"

Vincent assured her he had not taken it personally. "And I hope when you've been in England a little longer, you might come to see that being born into the aristocracy don't automatically make a fellow a bully," he said. "We're not bad fellows, most of us, if I do say so myself."

Constance hesitated a little before responding to this speech. "Yes," she said. "I would agree with you up to a point, Lord Yates. I have met a number of titled people since coming to England, and most of them have been very charming. Some of them, too, like your sister, are excellent people in every way, moral, and well-mannered, and possessing character as well as charm. But others—"

"Yes?" prompted Vincent, as she hesitated.

"But there are others who—oh, how can I put it?— others who have manners and intellect, but seem to have no morals at all. Indeed, I have been quite shocked to see what passes for permissible behavior among the so-called upper classes."

Vincent felt very uncomfortable. He had always considered himself quite a clean-living fellow compared to some of his peers, for his vices were all relatively mild ones, and he had never pursued any of them to what he called excess. But he realized that in the eyes of this prim Yankee girl, they would appear shockingly lurid. And if he followed through on some of his recent thoughts concerning Mona, Constance would doubtless consider him quite beyond the pale. Even he had often disapproved of men who made love to other men's wives, and to Constance, such conduct would appear not merely deplorable but downright sinful.

Vincent cleared his throat. "I suppose there's some things that must strike you as pretty queer," he said. "Seeing as you've spent all your life in the States."

"Yes, indeed," said Constance emphatically. "That's not to say we haven't our share of vice and immorality in America, for we do, of course. But in America it isn't practiced so *openly*. And neither is it condoned by persons whose position ought to make them arbiters of public morals."

Vincent, being unable to think of anything to say to this, said nothing. Constance gave an apologetic laugh. "Oh, dear, I am back to haranguing you again, aren't I, Lord Yates? I had much better go to Hyde Park and air my opinions there. Someone was telling me earlier that there is a place in Hyde Park where anyone may stand and speak his or her views, and that large crowds sometimes gather to hear the oratory."

"Aye, so there is," said Vincent. He was still feeling uncomfortable after Constance's remarks on vice, but he did his best to keep his voice and manner on an even keel. "But I don't mind if you air your opinions to me, Miss Locke. They're dashed interesting, 'pon my word. Only thing is, I can't help wishing you'd let me get you a glass of punch or something to refresh you. Stands to reason you must be getting thirsty after so much talking, what?"

Constance smiled, then began to laugh. "Lord Yates, you shame me," she said between bursts of merriment. "Not only do you bear with my impertinent remarks in the most patient and long-suffering way, you offer to succor me with punch afterwards. This is generosity indeed!"

Vincent smiled at her. "So may I get you the punch?" he asked.

"You may indeed," she said, smiling back at him. "And whatever I may have said earlier against England and the aristocracy, I take it all back—in regard to you, at least, Lord Yates. You are a credit both to your title and birth!"

# Four

After Vincent had fetched Constance the punch, he remained talking with her for some time. Their conversation did not return again to serious questions of morality and social justice, but instead ranged lightly over a variety of subjects, from Constance's experiences with English cooking to Vincent's attendance at a recent royal levee.

Vincent was relieved to be subjected to no more uncomfortable reproaches. Yet Constance managed unwittingly to impart another barb or two before they parted ways. After listening to his account of the Prince Regent's levee, she had shaken her dark head.

"I don't doubt it's a wonderful spectacle to witness," she told him. "But still it seems strange to me that grown people should devote their lives to such nonsense. Oh, I don't mean you, Lord Yates," she added, misinterpreting Vincent's frown. "I know pomp and pageantry cannot occupy the whole of your time. You are a landowner as well as an earl and doubtless have your duties as well as your pleasures. That is as it should be, for both are necessary, and the one gives satisfaction to the other. But people like your Prince Regent, whose whole lives are spent in one long quest for pleasure—truly, I question what satisfaction they can really find in it."

Vincent knew the words were not directed toward him, but he felt their sting nonetheless. "Prinny ought to have satisfaction enough, by Jove," he said, striving for a light note. "Seeing how much of the nation's exchequer he's depleted!"

"But that's just the point," said Constance. "If he had earned the money, he might take an honest satisfaction in spending it, but as he has earned nothing, no amount of money can ever be enough for him. Work has been called the curse of man, but I think rather it is a blessing, if not an actual necessity. People *need* to work, not merely to earn a living but to maintain their own self-respect. That is one of Papa's maxims, and I firmly believe he is right, especially after coming over here and seeing a little of your so-called high society. It strikes me strongly that most of the excesses I have seen among fashionable people—the drinking, the gambling, the intrigues, and so on—are simply efforts to allay boredom, neither more nor less."

Vincent mumbled something in reply; he hardly knew what. Constance continued, her fine dark eyes fixed on his. "You will say it is none of my business, and of course you would be right, but still I can't help feeling what a waste it is. Many of the people I have met in English society appear to be men and women of talent and ability, yet that talent and ability is largely, if not wholly, wasted. In my opinion, it's as much a misallocation of resources as if a stand of valuable timber were left to rot away on the ground, or a piece of valuable farmland allowed to turn sour through improper husbandry."

Vincent was struck by Constance's words, yet they made him uncomfortable. He suspected she would think his own talents and abilities were among those being wasted. Yet what talents and abilities did he have? He wasn't a clever man, as he assured himself; the only exceptional ability he had ever shown was in playing the fool. Still, the idea nagged him for the remainder of the time he was with Constance. And when he finally took leave of her and went home, after having thanked his sister for her hospitality, he carried the idea with him to contribute to the growing dissatisfaction he was feeling with his life.

Constance had no idea she had inspired such an emotion in Vincent's breast. To her, he was just another smug, self-satisfied Englishman who thought his small island the center of the civilized world. She had to admit to herself that he was more charming than most Englishmen, with a wit that belied his somewhat foppish appearance. But his viewpoint was the standard English one. It stood to reason this must be so, and Constance wondered why she had spent so many words trying to convert him to her own point of view.

*You would think I would have learned by now to keep my tongue between my teeth,* she told herself ruefully. Since coming to England, she had several times been betrayed into voicing opinions that would much better have been kept to herself. It was, she acknowledged, a fault of temper that she ought to strive to correct. She was inclined to get on her high ropes when people patronized her, and there had been a great many people to patronize her since coming to England. The women, especially, had made her feel ignorant and uncouth. Constance supposed she was both these things, but she was determined not to appear in any way apologetic about her colonial origins. So she had taken to wearing a cockade in her hair, the better to emphasize her allegiances, and she had not hesitated to freely criticize those English institutions that seemed to merit it.

Yet it struck her tonight that such conduct was unworthy of her. It was one thing to make a sharp answer when someone criticized her or her country, but quite another to take the offensive. What if a few English ladies had patronized her? For every one who had done so, there had been twenty like Lady Beatrice who had been nothing but kind. She had been wrong to allow her resentment to express itself so generally. And she had been especially wrong to visit it so violently upon poor Lord Yates, who had never done anything personally to deserve it.

It was in vain that Constance told herself that Vincent was a member of the aristocracy she despised. He might come from a race of tyrants, but anyone could see he was not a tyrant himself. Remembering his guileless smile and self-deprecating humor, she was inclined to think him almost supernally good-natured. Whether or not she chose to acknowledge him superior in his rank and title, she could not help but admit that he had shown himself superior in his manners.

The thought was a rankling one for Constance. She did not like to admit that any English person could be superior to her in anything that mattered. Yet she could not deny that her behavior that evening had fallen short of the ideal. What had possessed her to launch a verbal attack upon a perfect stranger? Constance supposed that, piqued by her earlier conversation with the patronizing young lady, she had visited her pique upon the next available target. But though such behavior might be natural, it was also unjust, as unjust in its way as the hereditary aristocracy she had been reviling.

This was a thought to make Constance squirm. It certainly made her toss and turn that night as she lay in bed thinking over the events of the day. The hotel where she and her father were staying was a comfortable, old-fashioned one, and she had never had the slightest fault to find previously with either its beds or its pillows, but tonight the one seemed uncommonly hard and the other uncommonly lumpy. Constance rolled from side to side, vainly trying to find comfort. The discomfort was in her heart and mind, however, and thus not amenable to such measures.

She wished now that she had not said the things she had said to Vincent. They had been true things as far as they went, but still she wished she had not said them. Any intelligent person knew there was more than one way of looking at things. Her opinion might be a valid one, but she had no business trumpeting it forth as though it were the only one worth having. She had been intolerably didactic and narrow-minded in her judgments. It would be no wonder if Vincent now despised her as an ignorant, unmannerly colonial.

For some reason, the thought of Vincent despising her was to Constance the most uncomfortable idea of all. She had been prepared to despise him, seeing that he represented all the things she deplored about England, and instead she had ended up liking him. To be sure, he was not an intellectual gentleman, like some she had met since coming to London. Owing to her father's celebrity, she had met quite a number of the leading lights of the London intelligentsia, including a well-known poet, two popular novelists, and a famous biographer. But all these men, on close acquaintance, had proved to possess serious flaws of character. The poet had drunk like a fish; both novelists had been intolerable egoists, and the biographer had shocked her by trying to steal a kiss one evening while they had been sitting together talking. It was very queer, when she thought about it. She had always claimed to value honest merit and to despise men who held high position solely through an accident of birth. Yet when brought face-to-face with an English earl—a man who fulfilled the latter category if anybody did—she had ended up liking him, far better than those men who had succeeded on their own merits.

*It's poor taste on my part, to be sure,* Constance told herself wryly. It was some comfort to remember that she had liked Vincent not because of his title, but in spite of it. Furthermore, though he was admittedly no intellectual, neither was he devoid of wit. He had managed to deflate quite a number of her overblown sentiments in a quiet, unobtrusive way. And unlike the poet, the novelists, and the biographer, he had done it while maintaining the most perfect courtesy throughout.

*Ah, well! There aren't many men like Papa, who combine genius with charm of manner,* Constance reflected philosophically. *One is usually obliged to pick one or the other.* She thought affectionately of her fiancé William back home. He was certainly no genius, but he had charm of a sort, or she would never have engaged herself to marry him. What was more, he had the careful, conscientious New England temperament that Constance admired. They had been engaged two years now, and in another year, if all went well, his business would be on such a solid footing that they could finally afford to marry. The thought gave Constance much satisfaction. Of course it was hard to have to wait, but on the other hand she was not sorry to have another year to study, travel, and see the world before she had to settle down to marriage and wifehood.

William had quite understood. Although sorry to see her put the width of the Atlantic between them, he had agreed that the opportunity to see England and the Continent was one not to be missed. He had promised to write to her while she was away, and she was to write him in return. Thus far she had received only a single short note from him, but now that she and her father were settled in London, his letters would probably be more frequent. Constance herself had already written William three long letters describing her experiences in England thus far, and she confidently expected that those letters would soon bring a reply.

To amuse herself, she imagined how she would describe her meeting with Lord Yates to William. A very witty account might be made of their conversation, she thought. But she found, on further reflection, that she preferred not to mention the matter after all. William might not think her behavior so bad, because he shared her prejudice against hereditary aristocracy, but Constance was unwilling to publicize the fact that she had behaved so rudely to Lord Yates. She had as well a curious disinclination to turn him into a figure of fun. He might be in some ways ripe for it, with his quizzing glass and his "Whats?" and "by Joves," but she had liked him, and it seemed wrong to ridicule him when he had been so pleasant and good-humored. As a result, Constance made up her mind to say nothing to William about Vincent. Likely she would never see him again, and the hour or two they had spent talking could have no importance in the overall scheme of her life.

This was Constance's view of the subject. A few miles away, in his bedchamber in his handsome town house, Vincent was partaking of a very different view.

The hour or two he had spent talking to Constance had been in the nature of a revelation. It was not that he agreed with everything she had said. In some of her statements, he felt she had been guilty of exaggeration and in others of oversimplification. Taking it altogether, however, he had been impressed by her insight—or perhaps it would have been more accurate to say he had been discomfited by it. For in the course of their conversation, Constance had made several remarks that shed a strong and uncompromising light on his own character.

In particular, her remark about boredom being at the root of the excesses of English society had struck a chord with Vincent. She had mentioned specifically drinking, gaming, and adulterous intrigues. Much as he would have liked to deny it, Vincent had to admit he had flirted with all three of these vices. Indeed, for a time he had been quite enamored of drinking and gaming until he had grown bored with each of them in turn and moved on to other pastimes. And though he tried hard to convince himself that he had never been guilty of indulging in adulterous intrigues, he knew in his heart that since meeting Mona that morning he was guilty of the intent if not the deed. The thought made Vincent writhe with a curious sense of shame.

It did no good to tell himself that he and Mona loved each other, and that their love justified whatever might result from it. Somehow Constance's words had cut through the romantic mist with which he had tried to shroud his intentions, and he saw them as they really were. He knew with sudden conviction that his feelings were inspired not so much by love as by simple boredom.

He craved the excitement and romance of a love affair—
an excitement and romance that were presently lacking
in his life. And was it not likely that Mona's motivation
was the same? He remembered the discontent that had
flickered across her face several times during the course
of their conversation. She had been married long
enough for the bloom to be off her romance with Sid,
and now she was craving something new. No doubt such
feelings were perfectly natural, but Vincent suddenly
found he wanted nothing to do with them. He had in-
dulged in some foolish behavior in his life, and some
which might be called reckless or dissipated, but he had
never done anything of which he was really ashamed. It
might be straining at a gnat after swallowing a camel, but
he made up his mind that he did not want to start now.

It was a little mortifying to reflect that this decision
had come about because an underbred Yankee girl had
taken him to task for the shortcomings of English society. But try as Vincent might to discount Constance's
words, he could not rid himself of the conviction that
she was, at bottom, correct. Of course he did not care
what Constance thought of him. There was no reason
why he should care, seeing that she was a foreigner and
a stranger to him. There was no probability of their
ever meeting again. Indeed, Vincent felt he did not
even want to meet her again. The experience of seeing
himself through her eyes, though doubtless beneficial
in the long run, had been highly unpleasant in the
here and now.

So Vincent did his best to put Constance out of his
mind, although he could not put the words she had
spoken out of his heart. When he received a note from
Mona the following day, containing the promised
invitation to her "intimate" party, he promptly sent
back a courteous refusal.

*That's that,* he told himself, as he handed the note to a
footman and bade him carry it to Lady Carlyle. *And I believe it's just as well. Only what the deuce am I going to do with
myself now?*

# Five

In the days that followed, Vincent spent much time and thought trying to decide what he was going to do with himself.

He had to do something, that was certain. Although his former melancholy had not returned in full force, he could feel it hovering in the background, ready to attack the moment he let down his guard. Thus far he had evaded it by keeping his days full to bursting and allowing himself no time for reflection. Yet all the while he had the feeling that if he ever slowed down even a moment, he would be overcome by a sense of the futility of it all.

There was, at least, no difficulty in staying busy. With the near approach of Easter, the social whirl of the Season had begun, and Vincent might have attended half a dozen parties a day if he had wished. Invitations to opera parties, card parties, dinner parties, drums, routs, balls, and assemblies arrived in a steady stream, along with informal notes from friends inviting him to cockfights, prizefights, and gatherings at Tom Cribb's Parlor. Vincent plunged into the social maelstrom, accepting as many of these invitations as he could, but he still had the sense of marking time. Perhaps it was because Constance's words kept recurring to him at inopportune moments—as he was trying to enjoy a performance at the opera, for instance, or when standing about in some elegant drawing room, drinking punch and trying to make conversation. He feared that if Constance could see how he was occupying his time, she would consider him in the same class as the Prince Regent. Of course he did not share the Regent's vices, for he had ceased excessive drinking and gaming years ago and had eschewed adulterous intrigue altogether. But still there was no doubt that his life nowadays was devoted almost wholly to the pursuit of pleasure.

That being the case, it was curious how little pleasure he was finding in it. Vincent could not decide if it was he who had changed, or society as a whole. All he knew was that he was finding his fellow society men and women very insipid and unsatisfying. They were finding him the same, to judge by their comments. "You're very dull tonight, Vincent, old boy," one of his friends told him, when they were standing together one evening at a more than usually dull rout party.

"Yes, 'pon my soul, I haven't heard a word out of you all evening," chimed in another. "And this is a damned dull party, too. We could use a few jokes to break up the monotony."

"I'm in no mood for jokes," Vincent replied shortly. It was beginning to annoy him that everyone expected him to say something funny every time he opened his mouth. He could appreciate good jokes as much as the next man, but he wasn't a buffoon to be getting them up for the public entertainment.

*Though God knows everyone thinks I* am *a buffoon,* Vincent added gloomily to himself. *Almost everyone, that is.* He remembered Constance's words the evening of the party. *She,* at least, had been able to tell he had some intellect. It struck him suddenly that he would not have minded seeing Constance that night. Not only was she a woman of discernment, she was witty, charming, and dashed good company. *But if she was here, it's ten to one she'd only blast me for wasting my talents, like she did last time,* Vincent reflected with a fresh access of gloom. *Just as well she ain't here, I s'pose.*

Nonetheless, he found himself thinking about Constance a good deal as the evening wore on. There was something piquant in the memory of her, even in spite of the sting her words had left. He wondered if she and her father had embarked on their tour of the Continent yet. *Trix would probably know,* Vincent told himself. *I might drop her a line and ask her if they're still in London. But no, there's no point in doing that. Likely Miss Locke wouldn't want anything to do with me, even if she is still in Town.*

But though Vincent had assured himself on this point, he still found himself thinking about Constance throughout the evening. She was on his mind as he bade farewell to his hostess and went out to his carriage. Before he reached it, however, he was hailed by an urgent voice behind him.

"My Lord Yates!"

It was Mona. She had apparently just arrived at the party, for her carriage was standing at the curb with the footmen just remounting their perches. She wore an ermine-lined cloak of deep blue velvet, flung back from her shoulders to reveal a dress of cerulean-spangled gauze. Her golden hair was dressed in an elaborate arrangement of plaits and curls, set about with sapphire pins. To Vincent, at first glance, she looked as lovely as anything he had ever seen.

A second glance showed certain flaws in the picture, however. He had never had any particular objection to cosmetics, but it seemed to him that Mona had made such a liberal use of powder and paint that evening as to hardly look human. Her eyes, too, had a feverish glitter that did not seem either natural or healthy. She stood looking at him a moment, her bright, restless eyes running over his face.

"Imagine meeting you here, my lord," she said at last. "I had thought you must be out of town. It's been weeks since we met in the park, and you have not yet called on me."

Though she smiled as she spoke, there was an edge to her voice that made Vincent choose not to respond to her words directly. "Oh, nobody in his right mind'd miss the Prescotts' rout," he said lightly. "Pity I'm just leaving. If I wasn't, I'd ask you to stand up with me for a set."

"Oh, but you cannot leave now, my lord!" protested Mona. "Not when I have just arrived!"

"'Fraid I must," said Vincent. He spoke with real regret, but it wasn't so overpowering a regret as he would have felt in other circumstances. For one thing, he had been thinking about Constance only a moment ago, and her remarks about illicit intrigues were still strong in his mind. For another, there was something about Mona tonight that he found off-putting. The unnatural brightness of her eyes; the heavy rouge and powder on her face; the overpowering scent of attar of roses that emanated from her person: all were as unlike as possible from the sweet, fresh-faced girl he had known before. She seemed almost like a stranger and, in spite of the calculated allure of her toilette, a not wholly attractive stranger at that. When she laid a hand on his arm—a pretty hand in a neat-fitting kid glove—Vincent shrank from it as though it had been a predatory claw.

"Sorry I can't stay," he muttered. "I've got another engagement and mustn't be late."

Mona's eyes narrowed, making her appearance yet more alarming. "Another engagement?" she repeated. "What engagement could you have this late, my lord? It cannot be the Hurleys' ball, for I have just come from there myself, and they told me you had been there and come on to here."

This speech served to further alarm Vincent. Her words made it clear that she had been making inquiries about him, if not actively tracking him down. In desperation he chose the first excuse that came into his head. "M' sister," he said, "Promised Trix I'd drop in on her tonight. Aye, and I'm late already, by Jove."

To Vincent's relief, Mona accepted this excuse. "I see,"

she said. "If that is so, then of course you must not disappoint Lady Beatrice. But I own I am disappointed not to have more of a chance to talk to you." She slanted him a look through her lashes. "When will I see you again?"

To Vincent, this was a question both unwelcome and awkward. He hesitated, and Mona, seeing his hesitation, frowned again. "You must know I have been expecting you to call on me anytime these three weeks, my lord," she said. "Cannot you come tomorrow? Or better yet, come Tuesday." She lowered her voice to a suggestive murmur. "Sid is to leave for Newmarket Tuesday morning, and he will not be back until the following afternoon."

Vincent saw the pit yawning at his feet. He made a desperate leap for safety. "Well then, there's no use my coming Tuesday, is there?" he said brightly. "Mean to say, I'd rather come when I can see you both and kill two birds with one stone, don't you know. Been an age since I've seen old Sid."

Mona stared at him, clearly astounded by his stupidity. Vincent took advantage of the moment to bow and wish her a good evening. He then beat a hasty retreat to his waiting carriage and gave the order for home in accents of heartfelt relief.

On the way home, Vincent sat with furrowed brow, brooding over the interview just past. Even reliving it in memory made him uncomfortable. A few weeks ago, when he had fancied he was in love with Mona, he had felt guilty enough, but strangely enough he felt even guiltier now. After careful thought, Vincent decided it was because he had been not been honest with Mona. He had initially welcomed her advances merely as an antidote to boredom, not because he loved her. Although he was inclined to doubt that her feelings for him were any more real than his for her, he was sure her pride at least must have been hurt by his rejection. And that was all his fault, because he had chosen to deceive himself about his own motives.

Vincent tried to tell himself that the deceit had been an unspoken, unintentional one, but he knew that was no excuse. Lying to Mona through his actions was no better than lying with words. Besides, when he thought of it, he realized he had lied to her with words as well. Just that evening he had told her he had an engagement to see his sister. Of course it had been a white lie to spare her feelings because he did not wish to spend the evening in her company, but somehow it made him feel almost as badly as his other, more serious deception. It seemed to show, in fact, that dishonesty was a chronic condition with him. He reflected bitterly that Constance, while rating him for the immorality of his class, had little known the extent of it.

Then it struck him that his statement to Mona need not be a lie. Although he did not have a positive engagement to call on Beatrice, there was no reason why he might not drop by and pay his respects. Turning the idea over in his mind, Vincent found himself becoming quite enthusiastic about it. After all, he had been thinking only that evening that he might write his sister to ask for information about the Lockes. Calling on her would be a quicker way to get the information, and it would also go a long way toward squaring his conscience in regard to Mona. If she were to ask Beatrice if he had called that evening, Beatrice would be able to tell her honestly that he had.

So Vincent pushed open the trap in the roof and shouted to his coachman to drive to Lady Beatrice's instead of going home. As they approached his sister's house, Vincent, peering anxiously through the carriage window, was relieved to see that the reception rooms on the main floor were still illuminated. It had occurred to him belatedly that Beatrice might be out, or that she might have already retired for the night. But the butler, on answering his ring, confirmed that Lady

Beatrice was at home, and before long Vincent was being ushered into the parlor, where his sister sat at her little rosewood desk, busily writing out what appeared to be a letter.

At his appearance, Lady Beatrice dropped her pen and stared as if she saw a ghost. "Vincent! I did not look to see you this evening," she said.

"I'm not intruding, I hope," said Vincent. He stooped to pick up the fallen pen and restored it to her with a bow. Lady Beatrice accepted it with an absent-minded word of thanks. She was still regarding him with surprise and wonderment.

"Hope I'm not intruding," Vincent repeated, giving her a self-deprecating smile. "I wouldn't have disturbed you this late, but it looked as if you was still up, so I just took a chance and rang the bell."

"Oh, you're not intruding," said Lady Beatrice. "To speak truth, I am very glad to see you, Vincent." She indicated a chair near the fireplace, dropping into another beside it as she spoke. "Your arrival is very opportune, for there is a favor you can do me if you will, and your coming here has saved my writing you to ask it."

"A favor?" repeated Vincent curiously as he seated himself in the chair. "What sort of favor were you wanting?"

Lady Beatrice looked guilty. "Nothing very much. Only I am afraid you will think it a great bore. Indeed, if I could think of anyone else to ask, I would have done so. But Harold is laid up with the gout right now, so *he* cannot help me, and the other peers I know would regard it as even more of an impertinence than you would. Then, too, you did seem to get along quite well with Miss Locke the other night, so I thought—"

"Miss Locke!" repeated Vincent. He had been trying to think of a way to bring Constance's name into the conversation, and now he found it introduced without even trying. "Miss Locke?" he repeated in a rising voice. "You mean to say your favor involves Miss Locke?"

"Yes, it does," said Beatrice, looking more guilty than ever. "You don't sound pleased, Vincent. I suppose it is not surprising, for of course Constance is hardly the sort of girl to appeal to you. But I had thought at least you did not dislike her. You seemed to get along with her quite well at my party, or so it appeared to me."

"You're right, I did," said Vincent. "Thought she was a jolly nice girl. Enjoyed talking to her very much."

Beatrice looked bemused. "She said the same thing about you! I can't imagine what you two found to talk about. There never were two people more different, I daresay. Why, I am sure you cannot have two ideas in common."

"More than you'd think, Trix," said Vincent, nettled. "Not everyone thinks I'm a cipher like you do."

"Oh, I don't think you're a cipher, Vincent. It's only that you are not the least bit intellectual. But if you find Constance agreeable, then the favor I ask will not be such a great one after all. She is wanting to see the British Houses of Parliament, and since you are a member of the Lords, I thought you would be the ideal person to take her there. You would be better able to show her around Westminster than an outsider would. As I say, I know Harold would have been glad to do it, but he is laid up with the gout, and heaven knows when he will be better."

Vincent nodded. Harold, Lord Evers, was Lady Beatrice's husband and chronically afflicted with gout. "I wouldn't mind taking Miss Locke round to Westminster a bit," he said. "When was she wanting to go?"

"As to that I couldn't say, Vincent. She does not even know such a visit is in question, you see, for I thought I would rather mention the idea to you first and see how you felt before saying anything of the matter to her. But I know she wants very much to see Westminster, for she has said so on several occasions. I would like to gratify her wish if I could. She is such a charming girl—not so taking as her father, perhaps, but very amiable when one comes to know her."

Vincent assented to this statement in a reserved manner. He went on to ask a few questions about when Constance might like to make her visit and what particularly she wished to see. When presently he took leave of his sister, it was with the understanding that he would escort Constance to Westminster sometime during the coming week.

# Six

In the days that followed, Vincent found himself looking forward to his engagement with Constance with almost equal parts of eagerness and anxiety.

It had been several weeks since he had seen her. He preserved a clear memory of her lively charm, but he also remembered the abuse she had showered upon him. He did not suppose she would abuse him this time, for they had parted friends, and in any case she would be unlikely to abuse a man who was doing a favor for her. But still he felt absurdly nervous at the idea of seeing her again. So nervous did he feel, in fact, that it occurred to him to wonder if it was wholly fear of her tongue that accounted for it.

Could he, in fact, be developing feelings for her? Vincent considered the idea but soon discarded it. He had spent barely two hours in Constance's company, and that was hardly enough time to develop romantic feelings in his opinion. Then, too, her manners on the occasion he had met her had hardly been ingratiating. It was true she had apologized for her insults, but still it seemed unlikely that he would develop a *tendre* for a girl whose first impulse on meeting him had been to revile him.

The thing that really argued against his having a *tendre* for Constance, however, was the fact that she wasn't pretty. True, she had fine eyes and a certain distinction of manner, but that was hardly enough to captivate a connoisseur of female beauty like Vincent, Lord Yates. It stood to reason that any woman who won his heart would have to be a Diamond of the First Water.

So Vincent was able to set aside the notion that he was becoming in any way enamored of Constance. She was merely a pleasant diversion, an interesting girl who was something out of the common way. Still, a pleasant diversion was nothing to sneeze at, given his present state of disaffection. As a result, he could not be blamed if he found himself anticipating their outing with more than usual eagerness. On the morning of the appointed day he rose early, took extra care with his toilette, and set off to meet Constance with sensations of liveliest anticipation.

Constance was anticipating their meeting quite as much as he. She told herself it was because she welcomed the opportunity to erase the bad impression she had made at their first meeting. Indeed, for several days after that meeting she had been able to think of little else and had only managed to make peace with herself in the end by reasoning that Vincent's path and hers were unlikely to cross in the future. It could matter little what kind of an impression she had made on a person she would never see again.

Now it turned out she *was* to see him again. That being the case, it was natural that she should be experiencing a certain amount of excitement and anxiety. But to Constance, her excitement and anxiety seemed disproportionate to the occasion. After all, she still disapproved of Vincent on principle, and it wasn't as though she really cared what he thought about her— did she? Constance told herself firmly she did not. But when, the day before the proposed expedition to Parliament, she went out and bought a new hat and pelisse; and when, the morning of the day itself, she actually sent for a hairdresser and had her hair professionally arranged for the first time in her life, she could not help suspecting she was not so indifferent to Vincent's thoughts as she was trying to make believe.

This, of course, was unacceptable. Constance gave herself a stern lecture as she sat in her and her father's hotel sitting room, waiting for Vincent to arrive. *It's ridiculous that I should prink and primp for him,* she told herself. *He is a pleasant, good-natured gentleman, but I don't fancy I'm in love with him, or anything of that sort. For one thing, he's not in the least the sort of man who appeals to me. For another, I'm engaged to Will back home.*

Despite these salutary reminders, Constance still felt absurdly nervous at the prospect of seeing Vincent again. For at least the twentieth time, she got up and went to the looking glass to inspect her reflection. What she saw satisfied her, insofar as her own reflection ever could. There was no fault to be found with the dashing little cap of bronze-green velvet slanted over one eye, or in the clusters of curls fresh from the hairdresser's hands. Her face, however, was another matter. It was, as Constance reflected ruefully, a face both too thin and dark for beauty, with a mouth a little too wide and a nose a little too prominent. "Just like Father's," Constance soliloquized, as she turned her face to inspect her profile. "It's a very fine nose on *him.* If only I were a boy, I wouldn't mind it a bit. But unfortunately I was born a girl, and so I must make the best of it."

With a philosophical sigh, Constance turned her attention to her appearance below the neck. Here, at least, she had no criticism to make. Her bronze green pelisse was the highest kick of fashion, as all the fashion magazines assured her. Back in Boston, she had always made it a point to be neatly and appropriately dressed, but she had never cared whether she was following the latest modes. Since coming to London, however, it had been borne in upon her that her dress was plain to the point of dowdiness, at least when compared with the toilettes of most of the women she was associating with. Initially she had told herself this did not matter, and that she had a mind above fashion, but when she had learned she was to accompany Lord Yates to Westminster, she had discovered that she was not so high-minded after all. She had been quite unable to resist the urge to go out and obtain the fashionable attire that would make her look like everyone else.

This thought made Constance so uneasy that she turned away from the glass. It seemed wrong that she had gone to more effort making herself fine for Lord Yates than she ever had for anyone else in her life. Even for Will, her fiance, she had never taken such pains with her appearance. And who was Lord Yates to merit so much effort?

"Who indeed?" said Constance aloud. She told herself sternly that it would be more true to her principles to strip off her fine feathers and put on the oldest, shabbiest clothing that she owned.

Fortunately, she was not compelled to follow through with this advice. Even as she turned it around in her mind, a manservant rapped on the door and announced that Lord Yates was there to see her. He then stepped aside to reveal Vincent, clad in an exquisitely tailored blue coat, buff-colored pantaloons, and gleaming Hessian boots.

There was a tentative smile on his face as he regarded her. "Hullo there," he said, removing his hat and executing a bow of effortless grace. "Fine day, what? It's a pleasure to see you again, Miss Locke."

"And it's a pleasure to see you again, sir," said Constance. She had to fight down a rising shyness as she returned his greeting. Somehow she had forgotten just how handsome he was. He might be—probably was—a brainless fop, but he was also a very attractive man, with an air of worldly ease that intimidated her. *This won't do*, Constance told herself, and made an effort to summon her wits about her once more.

"It was so kind of you to offer to take me to see Westminster," she told Vincent. "I am all ready to go, only I must just say good-bye to Father first. He is in the next room, working on an essay. A newspaper back home has contracted him to write a series of essays about England while he is here, and he must get this one off by the next mail."

Vincent bowed again to show polite acquiescence, and Constance slipped away to make her adieux to her father. When Mr. Locke learned that Vincent was in the next room, however, he insisted on coming over to shake hands with him. "Glad to see you again, Lord Yates," he told Vincent genially. "I enjoyed talking to you very much the other night. So you're taking this girl of mine to look at your Parliament buildings, are you?"

"That's right, sir," said Vincent respectfully. "If you've no objection."

Mr. Locke laughed heartily and said he didn't suppose it would matter if he did have an objection. "If Connie's made up her mind to do something, do it she will, though the sky should fall," he said, smiling fondly at his daughter. "Fortunately, I never have to worry what she's about. My daughter's a sensible girl with all her wits about her."

"Lord Yates and I must be on our way, Father," said Constance hastily. She was oddly mortified by her father's speech. It was not that she minded being called a sensible girl, for she hoped she *was* a sensible girl, but at the same time she could not help thinking it sounded a dull thing to be. A thousand times better to be called a charming girl, a taking girl, a *pretty* girl. But of course she could never be any of those things, she assured herself.

Vincent, meanwhile, was assuring Mr. Locke that he would take the greatest care of Constance. "I'm sure you will, though I don't suppose she's likely to come to any harm where you're going," said Mr. Locke, smiling. "I've seen your Parliament buildings a number of times since coming to London, and they're more impressive even than I'd been led to believe. I wouldn't mind taking a look inside myself sometime."

"Perhaps you would care to accompany us, sir?" said

Vincent politely. "No reason why you couldn't come along if you've a mind to."

Mr. Locke declined the invitation, however, saying he needed to finish his essay. Vincent was secretly much relieved. For several days he had been looking forward to having Constance to himself for the space of a few hours, and after seeing her today his eagerness had been compounded. *Why, she isn't plain at all,* he told himself with astonishment, studying her covertly as they went down the stairs. He wondered how he could have thought her plain before. Her features might not conform to the classic ideal, but there was charm in every angle of her face and in every line of her figure, from the plume on her little bronze green cap to the slender slippers peeping beneath the flounce of her dress. So Vincent thought, at any rate, and he looked at her again and again as he led her out through the hotel vestibule and into the waiting carriage.

Once seated in the carriage, however, he found himself in a predicament. It was clearly his duty to strike up a conversation, seeing that they were destined to spend the next two or three hours together, but he was afraid to speak to her—afraid of sounding like a fool. Already he felt he had shown a singular lack of wit and originality in his speech. The only remark he had made thus far, apart from exchanging greetings, had been a trite comment about the weather.

He stole a sideways look at Constance. Anyone could see she was a clever girl just by looking at her. She had grown up in the same household as a literary genius and had doubtless been accustomed to mingling with the best in American society. Now, here in London, she had been associating with England's leading lights for the past few weeks. How must he appear to her in contrast?

*About like a tailor's dummy, I expect,* Vincent told himself gloomily. *No brain and less conversation, by Jove.*

Still, he knew he must speak sooner or later. Already

the silence was becoming oppressive. Constance did not seem to be aware of it, for she was looking out the window, seemingly interested by the views she saw passing there. But even as Vincent was thinking these thoughts, she turned her head and encountered his eye. For a moment her own eyes held his gaze, then she opened her lips and spoke.

"You must be thinking me the most impertinent female on earth," she said.

Vincent was so astonished by this statement that his tongue was freed from its paralysis. "'Deed, no, Miss Locke," he protested. "I don't think you the least impertinent, 'pon my word. Why on earth should I?"

"Need you ask?" said Constance ruefully. "After my performance the other night, you must have carried away a fine impression of me! And now, to add insult to injury, you find yourself saddled with me today, engaged to show me Westminster Hall when I am sure you would rather be doing almost anything else."

With perfect sincerity, Vincent assured her there was nothing else he would rather be doing. "And you're wrong to say I've been saddled with you," he added. "I *wanted* to take you to Westminster, by Jove. Didn't my sister tell you so?"

Constance nodded, glancing at him from beneath her plumed cap. "She said you were happy to take me, but I feared that was only politeness on her part and on yours. Truly, sir, I never would have said a word about Parliament if I had thought she would take it upon herself to gratify my whim. And when she had told me she had spoken to you, and that you had engaged to take me to Westminster yourself—well, I thought I should sink through the floor. After the things I had said to you! It makes me quite ashamed to think of them."

"Don't know why it should," said Vincent firmly. "Mind you, I didn't agree with everything you said, but that's not to say there wasn't some truth in it. If the shoe fits, what?"

"No, no, Lord Yates! You shall not excuse my ill manners that way. Considering what you have done and are doing for me, for you to make excuses for my bad behavior is to heap an unbearable number of coals of fire on my head."

Vincent, in a musing voice, said he had always supposed any quantity of coals on the head would be an uncomfortable state of affairs. Constance gave him an amazed look, then burst into laughter. "You have a great facility for putting your finger on the ridiculous, Lord Yates," she said between bursts of laughter. "I have heard that verse quoted from the Bible all my life, and yet I never really reflected on what a curious contradiction it seems. I wonder why it would be considered a Christian thing to put coals of fire on someone's head? I must remember to ask Father and see if he knows."

Vincent said he would like to know, too, and for her to please to tell him once she got to the bottom of it. He was happy to see the conversation running along so nicely. He was also happy that he had made Constance laugh. She looked very attractive when she laughed— quite pretty, in fact. He essayed to make her laugh again, telling her about a clergyman he had seen once who had accompanied his sermon with such sweeping gestures that he had ended by falling out of the pulpit. Constance did laugh, though she also shook her head over the story.

"I must say, I have been disappointed in the sermons I have heard since coming to England," she said. "Some of them have been very fine, but nothing I have heard thus far can compare with our own home clergyman back in Boston."

It was on the tip of Vincent's tongue to offer to take her to the Chapel Royal and see how the sermons there stood up against the native New England product. Just in time he caught himself. What was he doing? He had not attended divine services in years, and his private feeling had always been that they were a bore to be avoided rather than a treat to be embraced. So he held his tongue and merely listened as Constance described the churches she had attended since coming to England. He was amazed at how much interest she took in the subject. It was obvious that churchgoing and religion were very important to her, and so animated and articulate was she upon these subjects that he began to feel a certain interest in them himself. It had never occurred to him that a holy service might be as worthy in its way of critical attention as a play or an opera. But at the same time, he began to have the same uncomfortable feeling he had had during their previous conversation, the feeling that Constance was reproaching him for his style of life without in the least meaning to. Fortunately, before he was able to grow too uncomfortable, they arrived at Westminster, and the conversation was necessarily given a different direction. As he assisted Constance out of the carriage, Vincent reflected with relief that he could better hold his own in a discussion of politics than religion.

# Seven

The trip to Westminster proved a great success.

Vincent had not really known what Constance wanted to see when she had said she wanted to see Parliament. He had supposed, vaguely, that a turn about Westminster Hall from the outside and a look inside from the gallery would satisfy her. But it turned out Constance was interested in everything: not only in seeing it, but in learning about it. So lively was her interest in all she saw that Vincent found himself becoming interested, too. He had always taken Parliament for granted as a dull but necessary institution; but now, seeing it through the eyes of this odd Yankee girl, he found himself appreciating it as both a symbol of English law and the forge where that law was hammered into being. He did his best to answer all Constance's questions, and when she expressed a wish to examine the hall more closely, he enlisted the help of a sympathetic attendant and smuggled her down (strictly against the rules) to inspect at firsthand the Chamberlain's box, the Chancellor's seat, and the benches where the Commons sat.

"It's much more imposing than I imagined," she told Vincent, as they looked around the hall. "I confess I came prepared to look down my nose at it, but I find I am impressed in spite of myself. I suppose you sit down here with the other lords, because you are a peer?"

Vincent gave a self-deprecating laugh. "Oh, about

once every two years," he said. "I'm not one of your political fellows, y'know. In fact, the only time I've ever spoken was when I sat for the first time, after m'father passed on."

Constance gave him a surprised look. "Oh, yes? But I had supposed that on important issues, the attendance of every Member was indispensable."

"Oh, when there's anything really important being discussed, they can make up a House without my lending a hand," Vincent assured her. "'Deed, I expect most of 'em would say they could make it up a good deal better without me!" He gave another self-deprecating laugh. "I'm not at all a brainy fellow, y'know."

Constance did not join in his laughter. Instead, she fixed him with a stern and disapproving gaze. "This is nonsense," she said. "Such statements may impress your friends, Lord Yates, but they don't impress me. You have a perfectly adequate quantity of brains. If you choose not to sit with your fellow peers and do your legislative duty, it's only because you're too lazy or otherwise disinclined to do it, not because you're not fit for it."

Vincent was stung by her words. "Well, I like that!" he said. "I wouldn't think you'd care whether I do my legislative duty or not, Miss Locke. After all, you told me the other day that you don't approve of hereditary offices!"

"That is quite true," said Constance. "I *don't* approve of hereditary offices. But for better or worse, you live in a country that operates with a hereditary legislative body, and since you are yourself a member of that body, duty would seem to dictate that you discharge the responsibilities of your office."

"But look here," argued Vincent, "I don't see that at all. You've just said you don't think it's right there should be hereditary offices. Well, maybe I agree with you. What then?"

"I don't believe for a minute you agree with me," said Constance, eyeing him askance.

"Well, say for argument's sake that I do. In that case,

wouldn't it be better that I not take my seat rather than take part in a system that's unjust?"

"No," said Constance. "If you really felt as I do, then your proper course would be to work for a change in the system through the proper legislative channels."

"But not all changes can be made through proper legislative channels," said Vincent. "Desperate situations call for desperate measures, y'know. There's situations where taking a stand is the only choice. Look at France, by Jove. And look at your own country. You didn't achieve independence from England by going through proper legislative channels now, did you?"

"The situations are not the same," said Constance firmly. "If there had been a way to achieve independence through legislation, then of course that would have been the best way. As it was, however, America had no choice but to revolt."

"Well, I'm thinking that's my best option, too. Given a choice between that and petitioning to abolish the House of Lords, I'm at least as likely to succeed at one as the other. So I'm revolting as of this minute. I'm renouncing all parts of the system of hereditary representation, and I vow I won't set foot in the House again until I've been elected there by popular mandate."

Constance bit her lip, then began to laugh, unwillingly. "Lord Yates, you are too absurd," she said. "You know perfectly well you don't mean a word of that."

Vincent gave her a conspiratorial smile. "To speak truth, I don't know whether I do or not," he said. "What I mean to say is, I never thought much about the matter one way or another." He went on, his voice growing serious. "'Strewth, Miss Locke, you've given me a deal to think about. All fooling aside, I'm thinking you might have a point about that business of doing my duty. I suppose it wouldn't hurt if I sat in on Parliament now and then, just to keep my hand in."

Constance said nothing. She continued silent as they

left Westminster together and went out to where the carriage was waiting. Vincent feared she was offended with him, and he decided he should not have joked about a subject she obviously took very seriously. But her reticence proved to be motivated by feelings quite different, for when at last they were seated in the carriage and Vincent had turned the horses toward the west, she raised her eyes to him and spoke in a resolute tone. "Lord Yates, you have given me a deal to think about, too," she said. "And among other things, you have just borne in upon me that I have been haranguing you again. And after I just got done apologizing for the last time! And after all the trouble you have taken for me today, too. Once again I find I am quite ashamed."

Vincent reached out to pat her hand. "Don't be ashamed," he said. "You meant what you said, didn't you? Well, then, why shouldn't you say it?"

"Because it was rude and impertinent," said Constance dejectedly. "And because I ought to show gratitude for your kindness. Instead of which I have been abusing you like a fishwife."

"You can't know much about fishwives if you think that!" Vincent told her. "In any case, I don't want your gratitude, Miss Locke. I'd a deal rather have your abuse, given the choice."

Constance studied his profile with curiosity. "Truly?" she said. "Why?"

"Because it's more of a compliment," said Vincent. "Anybody can earn gratitude from a lady, easy as winking. All you have to do is open a door for her, or help her with a parcel or something, and there, she's grateful. But to earn a lady's abuse is a higher sort of compliment. It—well, it shows she cares, don't you know."

Vincent was aghast as soon as these words were out of his mouth. He was sure Constance would be offended by the implication that she could care for him. Of course he had meant only that she cared for him in a disinterested way, as a kind of civic duty. It was ridiculous to suppose a clever girl like her could care for him in any other way.

He glanced sideways at Constance. She was looking out the carriage window again, as though absorbed by the passing landscape. It appeared almost as though she had not heard him. The bronze green plume on her cap curled coquettishly around her cheek—a cheek that was a little pinker than it had been a moment before. Still, when she spoke at last, her voice was perfectly composed.

"It's true I should like to see you realize your potential, both as a man and as a member of your country's government," she said. "You are, if I may say so, Lord Yates, altogether too modest about your own abilities."

Vincent turned a startled gaze on Constance. She was still looking out the window, however, and did not meet his gaze. He studied her a moment, conscious of a rising sense of pleasure. The compliment she had paid him was hardly a fulsome one, but something in it touched him like no compliment he had ever received before. And there was a further pleasure to be found in looking at her. Her slim, upright figure in the pelisse of bronze green; the long lashes lying on the soft curve of her cheek; the dark curls clustered about her neck: all struck him as highly satisfactory. Before he knew what he was doing, he spoke again, impulsively.

"Must I take you right back to your hotel?" he asked. "Or have you a little time? What I mean is, I'd like to take you driving a bit if you haven't any other engagement."

These words brought Constance's head around to look at him. She studied him a moment, then slowly shook her head. "I am afraid I have no time to go driving today," she said. "Father will be expecting me back at the hotel. But I thank you very much for the invitation."

Vincent took her refusal philosophically. He had been pretty sure she would turn him down. Still, he was not sorry he had asked, for it had seemed important somehow that he make the effort, even if the effort was doomed to failure. He let it out a scarcely perceptible sigh. Glancing again at Constance, he found she was looking at him once more. She quickly looked away when she encountered his gaze, however. "I'm sorry," she said, still with averted face.

"For what?" said Vincent, surprised.

"For not being able to go driving with you." Constance threw him a fleeting glance. "I would like to, but I simply can't."

Vincent, who had never supposed she could, found this speech encouraging rather than otherwise. "I see," he said. Cautiously he added, "Another time, perhaps. Or perhaps there is something you would rather do than go driving?"

Constance gave him a long look. To Vincent, it appeared almost as though she were trying to make up her mind. "In truth, my lord, my time is very occupied at present," she said. "I am kept busy helping Father, you know, and I have other occupations as well."

This sounded like an evasion to Vincent. He was quite sure that however demanding Constance's other occupations might be, she still could have found time to go driving with him if she had wanted to. "I see," he said with forced cheerfulness. "Shouldn't be surprised, of course. No doubt you've so many invitations to parties and such that you've hardly time to draw breath."

Constance shook her head decidedly. "No, it's not that. People have certainly shown great kindness to Father and me, and we have been invited to more parties than I can keep track of. But for myself, I find a continual round of parties night after night unfits me for anything else. I do still attend one now and again when someone I like—such as your sister—is giving one. But for the most part, I prefer to spend my evenings in more productive ways."

"Like what?" asked Vincent curiously.

Constance was silent a moment. "Well, in attending concerts, for instance," she said. "I am very fond of

music. And plays—Father and I have attended Drury
Lane regularly since coming to London. And I recently
heard about a series of lectures being sponsored by Mr.
Cather, the poet. I have been thinking of subscribing to
them, since it appears Father and I will be staying here
in London at least till the beginning of June."

"Lectures, eh?" said Vincent. "What sort of lectures?"

"Their subject is to be ancient history. A different ancient civilization will be discussed each week, with the
first dealing with ancient Egypt, the next with ancient
Assyria, and so on."

There was a short silence while Vincent thought this
over. "You enjoy that sort of thing, do you?" he said at
last. "Lectures on ancient history?"

"Yes," said Constance firmly. "I do."

Vincent cleared his throat. "Well, then—I don't suppose you'd care to attend 'em with me?"

Constance turned startled eyes upon him. "With
you!" she exclaimed.

"Aye, with me," said Vincent doggedly. "You say
there's to be lectures every week. Well, I'd like to go
along, if you'll let me."

Constance regarded him a moment in silence. "I can
hardly believe you are in earnest, Lord Yates," she said
at last. "I am sure you can have no interest in ancient
history."

"I haven't up till now," said Vincent honestly. "But
you never know till you try, what? Mean to say, I might
as well give 'em a go and see if there's anything in 'em."

Constance shook her head. "It's kind of you to offer,"
she said. "But I think I must decline, Lord Yates. I am
sure you would be most dreadfully bored."

"Well, if I am, that's my lookout, isn't it?" argued
Vincent.

Once more Constance shook her head. "I know you
mean well," she said. "But really, I cannot allow you to
sacrifice your own interests for mine in such a manner. It
would be better for me to attend the lectures by myself."

There was a short silence, then Vincent spoke again in a reflective voice. "You say the lectures are by subscription?" he said.

"Yes," agreed Constance.

"That means they're public lectures, what? Open to anyone who buys a ticket?"

"Yes, " said Constance, looking a trifle wary now. "That is correct."

"Well, then, I don't see that you can stop me from going if I want to," said Vincent triumphantly. "I can't make you go with me, of course, or sit with me, either, but there's nothing keeping me from buying my own ticket and coming on my own, as far as I can tell."

Although he spoke with bravado, he could not help eyeing Constance a bit apprehensively after making this speech, fearing that she might be angered by his presumption. To his relief, however, she only laughed. "You are one too many for me, Lord Yates," she said. "Of course I cannot stop you from attending the lectures if you are really set on it."

"Then you don't mind if I come?" said Vincent anxiously.

"Of course not," said Constance, smiling at him. "As you have justly pointed out, you have a right to come if you want to. And if you do really want to come, there's no need to persist in this farce of independence. As long as we both are going, we may as well go together."

Vincent was delighted by this concession. He listened carefully as Constance described when and where the lectures were to be held and how one went about obtaining subscriptions. When they finally parted at Constance's hotel, it was agreed between them that he would escort her the coming Thursday to a lecture on Ancient Egypt.

# Eight

For nearly twenty-four hours after parting from Constance, Vincent remained in a state of elation. It had been a hard-fought battle to win the right to escort her to the lectures, and he could not help exulting over his victory. But by the following morning, his exultation had begun to subside, and he began to feel his victory might be a Pyrrhic one.

What, after all, had he won? The right to attend a series of lectures on ancient history. And he had always considered ancient history a dead bore, when he bothered to think of it at all. The only reason he had wanted to attend the lectures, as he now admitted, was because he wanted to be with Constance. He had already begun to realize there was something about Constance that attracted him strongly.

But could any woman, however attractive, be worth spending six evenings listening to lectures on ancient history? And if there *was* a woman in the world who was worth such a sacrifice, was he certain that woman was Constance?

Vincent, in considering these questions, found he was far from assured on either score. He was willing to admit that he was attracted to Constance, but it was absurd to suppose he could ever have serious intentions about a plain American bluestocking who raked him over the coals whenever they met. It was true she wasn't as plain as he had first thought her; in fact, she had looked quite

pretty today when he had been taking her through Westminster Hall. Still, by no stretch of the imagination could
she be considered a Diamond of the First Water. And of
course the future Lady Yates must be a Diamond of the
First Water as well as British-born and a member of the
aristocracy. Thus it followed that he could not possibly
have serious intentions about Constance Locke. It must
be that he merely fancied her as a flirt. His intentions
were in no wise dishonorable, of course. All he wanted
was a little light flirtation that would be stimulating to
both parties.

*But if that's the case, why the deuce am I taking her to lec-
tures?* was Vincent's logical response to this argument.
He could think of no unlikelier venue for flirtation
than a fusty lecture hall. Probably he would not even be
able to talk to Constance during the lectures, let alone
flirt with her. In truth, his cause would likely be dam-
aged rather than advanced by such an expedient, for it
was ridiculous to suppose he could sit patiently
through six evenings of lectures. In all probability he
would fall asleep in his chair or otherwise disgrace
himself. And then Constance would see him for what
he was, a brainless Tulip who wasn't fit to tie the shoe
of an intelligent, cultured woman like herself. Of
course she must learn the truth sooner or later if they
continued to see each other, but on the whole he
thought he would rather postpone the evil hour.

So, what with one thing and another, Vincent came to
the conclusion that it had been a mistake to insist on
taking Constance to the lectures. He ought to have invited her instead to some purely social function, where
he stood half a chance of making a decent impression.
Of course it was probable that she would have refused
such an invitation, just as she had refused his invitation
to go driving in the park, but in that case he ought to
have given up the whole business as a lost cause. Instead,
he had been like a gambler throwing good money after

bad, with the result that he had ended up staking his all on a candle that was assuredly not worth the game.

Though Vincent reached this conclusion early in his reflections, he never even thought of trying to back out of his engagement with Constance. He had committed himself to attend the lectures with her, and a commitment was a commitment, as he told himself. Strangely enough, however, as Thursday approached, he kept forgetting that he thought ancient history a bore and found himself regarding the evening ahead with as much anticipation as he had ever a party or ball.

Constance, too, was anticipating the evening ahead, although not with an easy mind. She could not imagine why Vincent had been so insistent on accompanying her. He had admitted he had no previous interest in ancient history, and one had only to look at him to know he would be as out of place in such gatherings as a ruby in a rag basket. He was Vincent, Lord Yates, man of fashion, madcap prankster, and renowned sportsman, and the idea of his sitting tamely through a lecture on ancient history was perfectly ludicrous.

Constance knew all about Vincent by this time, for since making his acquaintance she had been at pains to learn more about him. Everything she had learned had only reinforced her initial impression that he was a superficial aristocrat with no higher purpose in life than amusement and self-indulgence. True, he wasn't exactly a profligate—not even his worst critic had implied that—but likewise no one had suggested that he had any interest deeper than the latest play, the latest fashion, or the latest prizefight.

So what could he mean by choosing to attend a series of lectures with her, Constance Locke? It was ridiculous to suppose it was her company that attracted him. She wasn't conceited enough to believe there was anything about her that would attract Lord Yates. During the previous week, she had gone walking in the park with Lady Beatrice, and Lady Beatrice had pointed out to her a beautiful blonde woman in a fashionable barouche who sat near the Serpentine, surrounded by admirers. "That's Lady Carlyle," Lady Beatrice had told Constance. "I expected at one time she might become my sister-in-law. But the affaire went off somehow, like all Vincent's affaires seem to. Where women are concerned, he seems incapable of any serious or settled passion."

Constance preserved a clear memory of the lady in the barouche with her furs, her silks, and her crowd of admirers. If Lord Yates could not develop a serious or settled passion for such a beauty as that, then it stood to reason he would have no use at all for plain Constance Locke. Of course looks were not everything in a woman, but for such a man as Vincent, Lord Yates, they were probably all that mattered.

In any case, as Constance reminded herself, after the rag-mannered way she had comported herself during their two previous meetings, her intellect and personality had doubtless appeared as unappealing to Vincent as her face.

The only thing she could suppose was that Lady Beatrice had somehow heard of her desire to attend the lectures and prevailed upon her brother to offer himself as an escort. Of course it was kind of them to go to so much trouble on her behalf, but Constance felt she would rather not accept such charity. She resolved to find out during the course of the evening whether pressure had been brought to bear on Vincent to accompany her. If this proved to be the case, then she would lose no time freeing him from his commitment. She wanted no unwilling cavalier. Doubtless she could prevail on one of the women of her acquaintance to accompany her to the remaining lectures, if it was improper for her to go by herself.

Constance could think of at least a half-dozen women whom she felt sure would be willing to attend the lectures with her. Oddly enough, however, the prospect of attending the lectures with a person of her

own sex seemed rather flat compared to the prospect
of attending them with Vincent. It was this phenomenon that made Constance uneasiest of all. For if she felt
excited at the prospect of attending the lectures with
Vincent, it could only be because she was, in some measure, susceptible to him as a man.

Try as she might, she could not rid herself of a conviction that she did possess some degree of such
susceptibility. It wasn't just that she liked him, for anybody must like him, Constance felt, remembering the
charm of his smile and his droll, self-deprecating wit. But
she feared there was an element in her feelings for him
that went beyond mere liking. When she had asked him
that afternoon why he regarded a lady's abuse as a
higher thing than her gratitude, he had looked directly
at her and responded, "Shows she cares." A tingle had
gone down her spine at the words, so that she had been
forced to look away to hide her confusion.

Of course that incident was little enough in itself.
But if she had no feeling beyond liking for him, then
why had she failed to tell him she was engaged? It was
a plain fact that she had not said one word about
William while in his company. It might be egoism to
suppose Lord Yates cared whether she was engaged or
not, but in that case it appeared she must be an egoist,
for something in her shrank from the idea of telling
him. Setting her lips, Constance summoned up an
image of William back in Boston. He was trusting that
she would be true to him while she was in Europe with
her father. She would be a beast to betray his trust,
even in so small a thing as this. It followed that she
must lose no time in acquainting Lord Yates with the
fact that she was engaged. Once that was done she
would be safe, for if by some freak he did regard her as
a possible object of gallantry, he would then know
there was no hope for it. And she, knowing he knew,
would be safeguarded both from any advances on his
part and any weakness on her own.

As an additional safeguard, Constance sat down and wrote William a letter before going out with Vincent that evening. She tried to envision William as she wrote, sturdy and square-shouldered with dark brown hair, honest brown eyes, and not an ounce of levity in his makeup. For a young man he was almost unnaturally serious. Constance liked him that way, as she assured herself, although she had sometimes regretted his inability to appreciate a joke. But that was better than making all life a joke, she reminded herself, frowning down at the half-filled paper. Lord Yates was by all accounts a famous jokesmith. Realizing belatedly that she was now thinking of Vincent rather than William, Constance resummoned her image of William to mind and once more addressed pen to paper. Still, she found her mind returning to Vincent again and again as she wrote of her activities during the past week.

There was the trip to Westminster, for instance. Vincent had certainly figured largely in that, yet when she started to describe it to William she found herself avoiding any mention of the man who had escorted her there. Of course William would not have known who Vincent was or cared if he did know, but just as she had shrunk from mentioning William to Vincent, so did she shrink from mentioning Vincent to William.

At last Constance became so much annoyed by these feelings that she brought the letter to an abrupt end and went out for a walk in an effort to clear her head.

Her head proved unresponsive to this treatment, but the exercise did serve to relax her slightly, not to mention bringing a pretty color to her cheeks. Surveying her appearance in the glass as she put the finishing touches on her toilette for the evening, Constance felt she looked very well indeed. She was wearing a muslin dress of white figured in green, with green morocco slippers. It was a tolerably becoming toilette—not so becoming as her new mulberry evening dress, but she felt sure the other women patrons at the lecture would not be wearing evening dresses, and besides, she distrusted her impulse to make herself fine for Vincent. It seemed more than likely that such an impulse had its roots in a desire to impress him, and she was not going to give way to it.

Yet when Vincent arrived to take her to the lecture, she could not help wishing her appearance were more worthy of such a distinguished escort. He, too, had eschewed formal evening dress, but so perfectly tailored was his topcoat of blue Bath cloth, so exquisitely knotted his neckcloth, and so perfectly glossy his boots that Constance felt dowdy beside him. When he bowed and greeted her with the words, "You look dashed pretty this evening, Miss Locke," she felt sure he was merely being polite.

As it happened, however, Vincent was *not* merely being polite. With surprise and pleasure, he reflected that Constance grew better looking each time he saw her. At Westminster a few days before, he had decided she was passably pretty; now he realized she was downright handsome. What was more, her distinction was one that went beyond any superficial charm of feature or coloring. It was something in the way she carried herself, and in the direct way her fine dark eyes met his, that gave evidence of a strong and attractive personality.

In the company of so much distinction, Vincent felt tongue-tied once more. During the drive to the lecture hall, he sought desperately for something to say. "I'm not much of a dab at ancient Egypt, I'm afraid," he confessed as they drew near the building where the hall was located. "I hope I won't be out of my depth tonight, what?"

"Oh, I shouldn't think so," said Constance. "It stands to reason most of the audience will not know a great deal about the subject. I don't know much about it myself, to speak truth."

"Don't you?" said Vincent in accents of surprise.

"No," said Constance. She smiled at him. "You look

surprised, Lord Yates. Have I given you the impression that I am one of those obnoxious people who know everything about any subject under the sun?"

"No, indeed," Vincent said fervently. "I wouldn't be here if you were one of those sort of people, by Jove."

Constance studied him. She wondered just what sort of a person he did think she was. But she was too shy to ask, and in any case they had arrived at the lecture hall and there was no time for further questions. Vincent assisted her most carefully in dismounting from the carriage, and together they went into the hall.

The lectures had drawn only a moderate audience. Some few dozens of people were sprinkled about a hall that would have held several hundred. The audience sat in little groups talking among themselves or, in the case of a few who had come alone, sat looking shyly about them. There was little enough to see from Vincent's point of view. The hall itself was a shabby room with pink plastered walls, faded green baize hangings, and a raised platform at one end on which stood a cheap dealwood lectern. The audience that filled the hall was somewhat shabby, too. A few months before Vincent would have dismissed them as a parcel of Cits and dowdies, but now he regarded them with interest, wondering what could have impelled such a heterogeneous gathering of people to pay out six shillings each for the pleasure of hearing about ancient Egypt. There were at least a dozen whom Vincent felt would have been better off spending the money for clothing, and at least one who looked as though she should have used it to buy food.

When the learned professor who was to give the lecture presently appeared on the platform, Vincent regarded him with interest, too. He looked a pleasant man, plump and full of good humor, not at all the lean and ascetic scholar Vincent had been expecting. "I say," he whispered to Constance, "he don't look much like a

professor, does he? Not like the ones I had up at Oxford, at any rate."

"No, but he has the reputation of being very knowl-
edgeable," Constance whispered back. "Besides, you of
all people should know better than to judge a man by
his appearance, Lord Yates."

"Aye, to be sure," said Vincent. "At least—what d'ye
mean by that?"

Constance gave a low gurgle of laughter. "I mean,"
she said, "that anyone looking at you would wonder if
you had wandered into this gathering by accident and
were merely too polite to get up and leave again."

Vincent felt hurt by her words. There was certainly a
novelty in finding himself in a lecture hall when he could
have been attending a ball or a play, but condescension
toward his fellow lecture-goers was the least of his emotions. If anything, he had been regarding them with
respect, for he felt if he were starving or shabby he would
never have been willing to emulate them by parting with
hard-earned money for the privilege of mere abstract
learning. Yet Constance's words seemed to indicate she
thought he was taking an aristocratic view of the pro-
ceeding and looking down on those around him. Or did
she merely think a man of such trifling character had no
place in such an intellectual gathering?

Constance was regarding him quizzically. "I hope I
have not offended you, Lord Yates," she said. "But you
must admit that to find a blue-blooded earl at such an
event as this is a trifle unexpected."

"I wouldn't admit anything of the kind," said Vincent
with warmth. "There's nobody who belongs here more
than me. What I mean to say is, there's probably nobody
here who's so ignorant about ancient Egypt. It stands to
reason I need swotting up more than the rest of you."

Constance regarded him a moment with parted lips.
"Lord Yates, you are an example to us all," she said at
last. "I begin to think I would do well to emulate your
humility."

"Lord, no," said Vincent in some confusion. "What I mean is, you've nothing to be humble about."

"Oh, but I do! I may know a little more than you on the subject of ancient Egypt, but there are hundreds of other subjects concerning which I am far more ignorant. And I daresay I should not be half so humble about it as you, if someone laid it to my account." Laying her hand on Vincent's arm, she smiled at him beseechingly. "Do forgive me. I keep making assumptions about you, and I ought to know by now you are a law unto yourself. Indeed, you are nothing like I expected an earl to be."

Vincent, looking into her eyes, felt a warm glow suffuse his being. "Well, you're nothing like I ever expected an American lady to be, by Jove," he said.

Constance smiled. "Am I not? But you know you must not judge all American ladies by me, Lord Yates. Even back in Boston, I am accounted something of an eccentric."

"I don't think you're eccentric at all, by Jove," said Vincent. "I think you're *wonderful*."

There was a brief silence, during which Constance looked at him and he looked at her. Finally she gave an uncertain laugh. "That is a great compliment, Lord Yates," she said.

"It's the truth," said Vincent. Emboldened by a certain something in Constance's eyes, he reached out, took her hand between his, and kissed it.

Constance said nothing, but only regarded him with wide eyes. The silence stretched between them until a voice from the platform announced that Professor Augustus Weatherly, eminent authority on ancient history, was about to begin his first lecture.

Constance gave a little sigh. "The lecture is about to begin," she told Vincent unnecessarily.

"Aye, so it is," assented Vincent. He was still holding Constance's hand in his, and he felt strangely and inexplicably happy.

Constance attempted to draw the hand away from him. "The lecture is about to begin," she repeated. In a tone that strove to be lighthearted, she added, "I must beg you not to pay me any more distracting compliments until after it is over, Lord Yates. They make it very difficult to concentrate upon ancient Egypt."

"I won't," said Vincent. Again Constance made an effort to repossess her hand. This time he let it go, reluctantly. She at once settled herself in a very upright posture, fixed her eyes on the platform, and folded her hands in her lap.

Vincent studied her profile anxiously. "You're not offended?" he whispered.

"Heavens, no," whispered Constance back, giving him a quick smile. "Why should I be offended?"

Reassured, Vincent settled back in his chair. Constance's reactions were a mystery to him, and he recognized clearly that where a girl like her was concerned, he was as ignorant as upon the subject of ancient Egypt. But his ignorance of the latter was about to be remedied, and he was willing to trust that, given time, the former might be elucidated also.

# Nine

All in all, that evening proved a milestone in Vincent's life.

He had not expected to find the lecture a bit interesting. As far as he was concerned, Constance's company was the sole attraction, and sitting through the lecture was the price he had to pay for it. But when the chubby professor mounted the lectern and began to speak of the civilization that had arisen on the banks of the Nile thousands of years ago, he found himself growing unexpectedly intrigued.

It was not that the subject was made clear to him in the course of one evening. As the professor explained, the little that was actually known about the ancient Egyptians was a mere spark in the darkness that still enshrouded most of their culture. Still, what little was known Vincent found fascinating. He listened with absorption as the professor discussed the pyramids and the Sphinx and the elaborate ritual of mummification. This last subject, especially, caught Vincent's interest. It struck him that the first earl, in building his mausoleum, had merely taken a page from the ancient Egyptians' book in his efforts to build a stronghold against the nullifying force of death. With amusement, he reflected that some intrepid explorer thousands of years hence might stumble across his own bones and make speculations regarding his own culture in the same way the professor was doing about the Egyptians'.

In this manner, a couple of hours passed without Vincent being at all aware of it. He forgot about the fact he had come to be with Constance and grew so absorbed that he came close to forgetting she was there at all. Yet at the same time, the sense that she was with him added greatly to the enjoyment he felt. It was a refreshment to turn his head and see her there, to catch her eye when the professor described some droll incident and see his own amusement mirrored there. With pleasure he reflected that she was his companion for the evening—his, Vincent Yates's, and no other's. That was a privilege that any pharoah might envy, he reckoned. He was sorry on every account when the professor brought his lecture to a close and stepped down from the platform amid tumultuous applause. Vincent, clapping as loudly as ever he had applauded an aria or a ballet, looked down at Constance. She, too, was applauding, her face lit up with enthusiasm.

"That was wonderful!" she told Vincent. "I don't believe I ever heard a more interesting lecture."

"Nor I," said Vincent. He wanted to add that it was a jolly good lecture, by Jove, but somehow the words stuck in his throat. He simply did not possess accolades high enough to express the way the professor's talk had made him feel. It wasn't only that he had learned a great deal about the ancient Egyptians; it was that he had had such a good time doing it and had had a brief taste of something that satisfied the restless disquiet of his spirit. He almost felt as though that evening had opened a new world to him—not a material world so much as a world of possibility.

But of course it was impossible to put such a feeling into words. He was Vincent Yates, whom everyone knew to be the least intellectual of men. He was sure his friends and acquaintances would have found the idea of his being moved by a lecture on ancient Egypt exquisitely ridiculous. And since he had no wish to sound ridiculous, especially to Constance, he resolved to keep his feelings to himself. Without putting the thought into so many words, he was aware that Constance's opinion was beginning to carry a great weight with him, and he wanted desperately to remain high in it. So when she turned to him on the way out of the hall and asked, "Did you really enjoy the lecture, Lord Yates? Come now, I want your true opinion," he answered lightly, "Aye, to be sure. It was jolly interesting, I thought."

Constance gave him a long look in which it seemed to Vincent there was a measure of disappointment. "I see," she said. After a moment's pause, she added, "I thought you looked as though you were enjoying it. But of course I could not be sure. I was half afraid you were merely being polite."

"Not at all," said Vincent. "I *did* enjoy it. In fact I enjoyed it so much so that I was sorry to see it end."

"Were you?" said Constance. "So was I." She said no more until they were seated in the carriage once more. Then she spoke again, in a low voice. "I can't tell you what this evening has been to me, Lord Yates. I never would have supposed a mere lecture could be so fascinating—so engrossing. It wasn't just that Dr. Westerly made the ancient Egyptians seem real to me. It was more the way he tied the past and the present together, so that I suddenly saw things differently—as if I were an actor in a play that had been going on for centuries."

"But that's just how I felt," said Vincent, astonished. "Exactly like that, by Jove."

"Truly?" said Constance.

It was dark inside the carriage, but even in the darkness Vincent could see the skepticism in her eyes. "Yes, truly," he assured her. He hesitated, then went on with abrupt frankness. "I expect you'll think it's foolish of me, but when the professor was talking about those old kings who were laid to rest in their pyramids, I couldn't help thinking of the mausoleum at my seat in Kent. A lot of my ancestors are buried there, and it's always seemed to me a barbarous kind of place . . ."

With these words, his tongue was loosened. He went on to describe for Constance the family mausoleum, and how its brooding presence on the landscape had lately come to seem a reminder of his own mortality. She listened in silence, her eyes fixed steadily on his face. "You'll think it a foolish thing, no doubt," he concluded with an apologetic smile. "Any fellow with a particle of sense knows he's got to die sometime, but there's times I feel I'd rather not have the fact shoved in my face continually, don't you know."

Constance nodded. "I can understand," she said. "There are some truths that one would prefer not to look in the face."

"Aye, that's it exactly. It's part of being an earl, I suppose." He smiled at Constance. "Of course you'd say that as an earl, I have little enough to trouble me in any case!"

He supposed Constance would agree with this statement. She did not, however, and neither did she return his smile. Instead she said soberly, "It's becoming increasingly clear that I know nothing about what being an earl means, Lord Yates. Perhaps you will undertake to enlighten me, just as the professor has enlightened us this evening about ancient Egypt."

Vincent looked at her, saw she was serious, and was swept up in a sudden wave of enthusiasm. "I'd be glad to," he said. "I wish I could show you Larkholm, by Jove. If you were willing to come visit me there, you could see the first earl's mausoleum for yourself. Do you think there's any chance you and your father might be able to make a visit down south before you leave England?"

"Why, I don't know," said Constance. She sounded interested, but then her voice suddenly went flat. "No, I am afraid not. I thank you for the invitation, but I am afraid it will be impossible."

Vincent made the requisite polite expressions of disappointment. They were wholly inadequate to the way he

was feeling. The idea of showing Larkholm to Constance
had appealed to him strongly, and he was very loath to
let it go. Still, he could tell from her voice and manner
that she had set herself against visiting him. He wondered if it was because some real obstacle prevented her
from coming or because she simply did not wish to
come. She had seemed to be seriously entertaining the
notion at first, but then she had turned him down flat.

Had he said something amiss, or had she misunder-
stood the nature of his invitation? But no, he had
mentioned her father accompanying her, so she must
know there was nothing dishonorable in his intentions.
Unless, of course, she was so ignorant of noblemen as
to suppose he was like one of Mrs. Radcliffe's Gothic
villains, who would consider any woman fair game for
seduction. But Vincent was pretty sure this was not the
case. He thought it more likely he had said something
that had offended Constance. Still, he couldn't imagine what it was. She had shown no sign of offense
previous to his invitation. He could only assume it
wasn't the custom in America for young men to invite
young women to visit their homes, even when they
were properly chaperoned by a parent.

So Vincent said nothing more about Constance visiting Larkholm. Instead he began to talk about the
lecture again. "If the next one's as good as this one, it'll
be something to look forward to, won't it? Will it suit
you if I pick you up at the same time next Thursday?"

Constance hesitated before replying. Vincent, looking at her, felt a dreadful certainty that she was about
to decline his escort the following week. But when she
spoke, it was to confirm their engagement rather than
refuse it. "The same time will do very well, Lord Yates.
I, too, am looking forward to next Thursday."

Vincent was so much relieved by her words that he
said nothing more. He had not realized what a crushing blow it would have been if she had declined the
engagement. That evening had meant a great deal to

him, and he wanted to think it had meant something to her, too—at least enough that she would not mind repeating the experience. He could see clearly that something was troubling her, but apparently it was nothing that made her want to eschew his company entirely. For that he was profoundly grateful, and in his humility, he wanted nothing more.

Of course something *was* troubling Constance. That something was her engagement. She had promised herself that she would tell Vincent about it that evening. Several times she had been on the brink of it, but each time she had drawn back. She told herself that the evening had been a very enjoyable one, and she wished to do nothing to spoil it. Yet when she examined these feelings, she saw how irrational they were. Telling Lord Yates about her engagement could not spoil the evening unless he had begun to care for her in a way that was inappropriate.

*Hardly a probable contingency*, Constance told herself. But when she remembered the way he had kissed her hand, and the way he had looked at her once or twice during the course of the evening, she could not rid herself of an uneasy conviction that the improbable might after all be coming to pass.

*Nonsense*, Constance told herself. *I mustn't take his gallantries seriously. It's only because I have so little experience with men that I am mistaking flirtation for serious courtship.* But try as Constance might to convince herself that Vincent was only flirting with her, there was something in her heart that refused to believe it.

*Well, if I don't believe it, then that's all the more reason why I ought to tell him now*, Constance told herself. But this reasoning did not appeal to her any more than the other had done. And when she tried to delve deep into her innermost feelings and understand the motives behind her reticence, the motive that sprang first and foremost to mind was one she shrank to consider.

So Constance shut the door of her mind on the whole

issue, then locked and barred it. For this one evening, she told herself, she would simply enjoy herself and let events take their course.

Alas, her conscience was not of a type to follow such a laissez-faire policy. Even as she agreed to meet Vincent the following Thursday, a small voice inside her was whispering that it was her duty to excuse herself from attending any more lectures in his company.

*But I told him I would attend the lecture series with him,* Constance reminded herself. *That's a kind of duty, too. It would be breaking my word to refuse him now.* This was undeniably true and a sop to her conscience, but still she continued to feel uneasy in her mind. As a result, she was rather silent on the drive back to the hotel, giving Vincent his own cause for uneasiness. But when he had safely conveyed her to her room, wished her a polite good evening, and told her he was looking forward to next Thursday very much, she gave him her hand and said, "Yes, so am I." And after he had gone, she went to the window and stood watching until she saw his carriage drive off down the street.

# Ten

In the days that followed, Constance did unceasing battle with her conscience.

It had become clear to her that she was developing a strong partiality for a member of the British upper class—that class of whom she disapproved on principle. And if appearances were to be believed, he was developing one in return, or at least putting on a very good imitation of it.

This, of course, was unacceptable. She was engaged to marry another man—a good, hard-working, honest man, as Constance reminded herself. On that account alone, it was wrong to let herself be drawn to another. And to such another, too! A British earl, born with a silver spoon in his mouth and (no doubt) an inherited contempt for colonials like herself. The whole thing was so ridiculous that it was laughable. Constance felt the situation was too serious to admit of laughter, however. She could not doubt she felt something for Vincent that went beyond friendship. If she *had* doubted it, all she would have had to do was shut her eyes and recall the moment he had kissed her hand and told her she was wonderful.

*No one ever called me that before,* she reflected wistfully. *And he said it as if he meant it—as if he really thought I was wonderful.*

It was useless to tell herself that Vincent had merely been flirting with her. Probably he had been, but his flirtation had turned her head nonetheless. Likewise it was useless to tell herself that she ought to despise him because of his rank and position. The problem was that she knew him now, and the mere fact that he was a nobleman (though still deplorable) was no longer enough to make her despise him. And when she tried to dismiss him as a well-dressed aristocrat with hardly a brain in his head, her heart rose up so fiercely in his defense that she took warning and eschewed that particular line of argument. He might not be an intellectual genius, but he had mind and imagination enough not only to argue with her as an equal, but to make her see points of view she had never been able to grasp before. Of course they were different in many ways—as different as two people well could be, Constance told herself. Yet there was a bond of sympathy between them just the same, a mutual accord and understanding that had evinced itself early in their acquaintance and had grown stronger with each subsequent meeting.

That, in itself, would not have been such a bad thing. Accord and understanding were things one could feel even toward a platonic friend. But Constance was beginning to suspect that the emotions she cherished toward Vincent were not strictly platonic. If they had been, she would not have reacted to his presence in such a distinctly physical way. When he touched her, something inside her responded in a way she had never experienced before with any other man—not even with Will, her fiancé.

Constance found this dismaying, but she was determined it should make no difference in her conduct. She had, she reminded herself, a duty to Will over and above her duty to anyone else. And part of that duty entailed repressing anything she might feel toward Vincent that was not consonant with mere friendship. It might even be that she had a duty to break off relations with Vincent altogether, although things seemed to Constance not yet so serious as to warrant this drastic step. Thus far he had done nothing more than kiss her hand. "And likely he would not even have done that if he had known I was engaged," Constance muttered to herself. "I must tell him about my engagement. I *must.*"

Once he had been told, Constance felt certain her difficulties would be at an end. As soon as Vincent knew she was engaged, he would no longer look at her in that delightfully intimate way and call her wonderful. And if by some chance he *was* the sort of man who went around kissing girl's hands and calling them wonderful, even when he knew they were engaged, Constance felt he would no longer represent the slightest danger to either her heart or her peace of mind.

As it was, however, such peace of mind as she possessed was distinctly ruffled. It was further ruffled the next morning, when a bouquet of red roses was delivered to her with Vincent's card. Looking ruefully at the roses, Constance told herself again she must lose no time telling Vincent of her engagement. Perhaps he would have sent the roses even if he had known about it, but as it was, she felt she had obtained them under false pretenses. It took away the pleasure she would have otherwise felt in receiving such a magnificent gift. So Constance told herself; but still she could not repress a certain pleasure knowing that Vincent had sent her flowers, whether in misapprehension or not. She even went so far as to snip one of the roses and press it between the pages of one of her father's books, an act of sentimentality of which she was quite ashamed.

*It's only till Thursday,* she told herself. *After Thursday, it won't matter. There won't be any more roses once I tell him about my engagement.*

In this way, she found herself simultaneously dreading Thursday and looking forward to it as the end of her difficulties. She was resolved in any case to tell Vincent about her engagement. But when Thursday evening actually arrived, and Vincent was ushered into her hotel sitting room, looking staggeringly handsome in his olive

topcoat and biscuit-colored pantaloons and wearing a
smile that lit up his whole face, Constance felt a shrink-
ing distaste for the duty that lay ahead of her such as she
had never felt for any duty in her life.

It was a fortunate thing that Mr. Locke was there to re-
lieve the awkwardness of the moment. He shook hands
with Vincent, saying it was a pleasure to see him once
again, and expressing appreciation for all Vincent had
done for his daughter. "Constance tells me you've been
attending these ancient history lectures with her, sir," he
told Vincent. "She said the one on Egypt was very interesting. Let's see, what's tonight's subject to be?"

"Ancient Assyria," said Vincent promptly. "I'm looking forward to hearing it very much, by Jove. Jolly
interesting characters, those ancient Assyrians."

Constance slanted an oblique glance at him. He
sounded sincere, yet she could scarcely believe that any
gentleman who looked the way he did could have a serious interest in ancient Assyria. He was the best-looking
gentleman she had ever known: the best-looking and the
best-dressed, too. It followed that anyone who looked so
much like a fashion plate could hardly have a serious
thought in his head.

She would have been amazed to know that in the
past week, Vincent had not only thought a great deal
about the lecture that evening but had gone so far as to
study up on it in advance. He had asked his sister to
loan him a book on ancient history, a request that had
quite staggered Lady Beatrice, but she had come
through handsomely with a whole armload of books
dealing with ancient civilization. Vincent had glanced
through one or two of them in the past week, and
though he did not delude himself that he was now any
kind of expert on the subject, he felt better able to hold
his own in a gathering where everyone seemed to know
more than he did.

Constance, however, knew none of this. As a result,
she had trouble believing Vincent when he assured

her father that he found the ancient Assyrians "jolly interesting." She could also hardly believe she had worried so much about a mutual affection developing between the two of them. Stealing glances at Vincent's exquisitely tailored clothing, his elegant figure, and his handsome profile, she told herself she was a conceited idiot to imagine he could feel anything for her except perhaps pity. Tell him about her engagement? There was no need to tell him about her engagement. He would not have looked twice at such a girl as she was, even if she had been the last girl on earth.

The thought was hardly a cheering one, but it had a calming influence on Constance's nerves. With no need to worry about making any awkward revelations later in the evening, she was able to relax and converse intelligently about the coming lecture. To be sure, she still felt a little awkwardness now and then—when Vincent took her arm to help her in and out of the carriage, for instance. There was something so tender in his touch, something so frankly appreciative in his eyes when he looked at her, that she kept forgetting she had no cause to worry.

Arriving at their destination at last, they entered the lecture hall arm in arm. As before, there were a few dozen other people scattered around, many of whom looked curiously at them as they took their seats. Constance felt they must be wondering what a dowd like her was doing with such a Buck of the *ton*. She blushed crimson as she arranged her skirts around her and folded her hands in her lap. Then the professor came out and began speaking about the ancient Assyrians, and she was able to forget, for a time, the matters that were troubling her.

Ancient Assyria was just as interesting as ancient Egypt under the professor's tutelage. Constance was soon absorbed in accounts of Ninevah and Assur. But her absorption was not so great that she was unaware of

Vincent sitting beside her. He looked up to smile now and then, as the professor was describing the rites attached to the cult of Ishtar, and since Constance was now assured he could have no personal interest in a girl like her, she had no hesitation about smiling back.

It appeared, however, that her assurances had been misplaced. When the lecture was over and they were filing out of the hall along with the other members of the audience, Vincent cleared his throat and spoke. "A very fine lecture," he said. "Fine evening altogether, in fact." Clearing his throat again, he added, "You look dashed pretty this evening, Miss Locke. I've been meaning to tell you so all evening, but what with one thing and another I haven't got around to it."

Constance looked at him in amazement. She was wearing the same muslin dress she had worn last Thursday evening, along with the same green pelisse and plumed cap. She could not imagine that this toilette possessed any fresh charms for him, assuming it had ever possessed any in the first place. "You must be joking," she said.

For some reason, these words brought a flush to his cheeks. "Indeed I am not," he said emphatically. "Why should I be? I am quite in earnest, I assure you."

"Well, thank you, then," said Constance. "I'm sure I appreciate the compliment." There was a silence for a moment before she went on diffidently. "There is another thing for which I must thank you, sir. I am referring to the lovely roses you sent me last Friday. That was very generous of you—too generous, indeed. I hope you will not think of doing such a thing again."

Vincent studied her with a closer attention than Constance was wholly comfortable with. "Why not?" he asked. "Didn't you like them?"

"Oh, yes! I loved them. But it was too generous of you, as I say."

Vincent shook his head decidedly. "Not at all," he said. "It's little enough for me to do, 'pon my word. I'm only glad if they gave you pleasure. You've given me such a lot of it, don't y'know, letting me tag along like this and listen to these lectures. Sending you a few flowers is the least I can do in return."

"But I am doing nothing, really, Lord Yates. It's absurd to pretend you are under any obligation to me. As you pointed out yourself, the lectures are public ones, available to anyone who buys a subscription. And it's you who are paying for the subscriptions, mine as well as your own!"

Vincent helped Constance into the carriage and seated himself beside her before replying to this speech. "That's as may be," he said. "But to my mind, the balance of obligation is still on my side. It's you who are giving me your company, and I tell you plainly I consider that worth a deal more than the cost of a subscription or two."

He was looking at her as he spoke, and something in his expression made Constance drop her eyes hastily. "You are very kind," she said.

"I'm not kind at all," contradicted Vincent. "Only telling the truth as I see it."

"Yes, as *you* see it," said Constance. Summoning up a smile, she added, "But since you are the most generous and forbearing of men, I am persuaded you see the situation differently than most people would."

"Maybe so," said Vincent. He gave Constance a long look. "But I wouldn't want you to get the wrong idea. All this talk about my being the best and most generous of men—that's all gammon, y'know. I don't say I'm a bad fellow—I hope I'm not—but I'm not half so good as you make me out to be."

There was a pause during which all Constance could think to say was, "You have been very good to *me*, Lord Yates."

"Well, that's natural enough," said Vincent. "What I mean to say is, it's only right I should be good to you.

Because you're the best thing that ever happened to me, and that's a fact."

The silence that followed these words seemed charged with meaning. Constance was conscious of Vincent looking at her, but she could not bring herself to meet his eyes. A storm of contradictory emotions was swirling in her breast. Part of her wanted desperately to know what he would say if allowed to go on, and part of her wanted just as desperately to stop him. It was the latter part that won; summoning up a smile, Constance spoke. "That is a high compliment, Lord Yates," she said. "Years from now, when I am an old woman in Boston, I will remember your words and honor you for them."

Another silence followed this speech, but it was a different sort of silence than before. "Yes?" said Vincent at last. "Er—are you planning to go back to Boston soon? I had thought—"

Constance, determined not to hear what he thought, broke in quickly. "Oh, I shall not be going back to Boston immediately," she said. "But of course I must go back before very long. New England is my home, after all. My friends and relatives all live there—and my fiancé, too."

Her voice was little more than a whisper as she spoke these last words. There could be no doubt that Vincent heard them, however. He stared at her with an expression of mingled doubt and dismay. "Your fiancé?" he repeated. "You mean to say you're *engaged?*"

"Yes," said Constance miserably.

"Engaged to be *married?*" said Vincent, still obviously suspecting a mistake somewhere.

"Yes," said Constance again. She thought she knew how St. Lawrence must have felt, writhing on his gridiron.

Another silence followed. "I see," said Vincent at last. "Shouldn't be surprised, of course. Perfectly natural that you should be engaged. It's only that no one told me you was."

Constance hung her head. "Not many people here know about my engagement," she said softly. "I suppose I should have told you sooner, but I didn't think . . ."

Her voice trailed off, for she could hardly say what she had been thinking. In any case, it did not seem to matter, for when Vincent spoke again, his voice was composed. "There's no need for apology," he said. "Mean to say, you don't owe me any explanation. I'm sure I wish you and your intended all the best."

Constance murmured a subdued "Thank you." She wondered why she could not die on the spot. If only she had told Vincent about her engagement at their first meeting! That would have saved her the pain of an interview that was turning out even more painful than she had envisioned. Looking at Vincent's face, she had the unhappy sense that she had murdered something—something innocent and beautiful.

Vincent, meanwhile, had continued speaking. "It's no wonder you're looking forward to getting back to Boston," he said. "Anyone would be, in your situation. But you say you're not going back immediately?"

"No, Father and I plan to spend several more weeks in London, then go north to Scotland and the Lakes. After that, we plan to see something of the Continent. Probably we will not return to Boston until autumn," said Constance. She found it impossible to meet Vincent's eye.

"Then you'll be here to attend the rest of the lectures with me?" he said.

This was the last question Constance would have expected. Somehow, when she had told him she was engaged, she had taken it for granted he would not want to attend the rest of the lectures with her. But now it sounded as though they had been his only concern. "Yes," she said cautiously. "Of course I would be glad to attend the rest of the lectures with you, Lord Yates—if you really want me to."

"Well, of course I do," he said, as though any other possibility were out of the question. "Shall I fetch you next Thursday at the same time?"

"Yes, please," said Constance.

There was no time for further conversation, for the carriage was even now stopping in front of the hotel. Constance was glad it was so. But as she took leave of him in the hotel vestibule and went upstairs, her head was buzzing with questions. And it continued to buzz long after she had extinguished the lights and gone to bed.

# Eleven

Having done her duty and told Vincent about her engagement, it seemed to Constance that her conscience ought to be easy. But still it continued to trouble her, until there were times when she wondered if she had done the right thing to tell him after all.

There was no logic in such doubts, of course. If he were developing real feelings for her, then it was undoubtedly her duty to tell him about her engagement. A decent girl did not encourage a man to declare himself when she could not return his affections. And of course she could not return his affections, except in a friendly way. The situation was perfectly clear-cut, so clear-cut that Constance was at a loss to explain why she felt so troubled about the way things had turned out.

She was haunted by the memory of Vincent's face when she had told him of her engagement. It was the expression of someone who had just suffered a devastating loss. Recalling it made her feel a sense of loss herself. Constance tried to tell herself this was irrational, and that there was no way a love affair between two such different people could have prospered, even if there had been no engagement to act as a bar between them.

*Indeed, I don't even know for certain that he intended anything serious,* she reminded herself. *He might not have been going to declare himself at all. And even if he was, it*

*might not have been marriage he had in mind. I am hardly
the kind of woman a man such as he would choose to marry.*

But though Constance could acknowledge the truth
of such statements with her head, they had no effect on
her heart. That contrary organ remained firmly inclined in Vincent's favor. It insisted on aching in
sympathy over the blow she had dealt him, and so
strongly and persistently did it ache that Constance
began to have the uneasy sense that even in this she was
being disloyal to Will. Yet she told herself she could not
help the way she felt. This was assuredly true: Try
though she might to feel glad that she had done her
duty by both Will and Vincent, she found she could not
feel glad at all, but only very sorry.

Part of the problem was that Vincent was here with
her, while Will was thousands of miles away. Back in
Boston, where she saw and spoke to Will on a daily
basis, she had never for a moment wavered in her loy-
alty to him. But here, with the rolling depths of the
Atlantic between them, she was gradually losing the
sense of him as a man and coming to think of him
more as an idea—an idea to which she owed her loy-
alty, but one which could not command it with the
same concrete urgency. It did not help that Will had
written her only a handful of letters during the time
she had been in England. Constance had read those
letters over countless times, trying desperately to revive
the feelings of love and respect with which she had entered into her engagement and which she had
confidently expected to last all her life. But the letters
seemed more formal than affectionate, their personal
references few and far between. They might almost
have been the letters of a stranger.

Of course this was not Will's fault, as Constance told
herself. Not everyone could be a first-class letter writer.
In any case, she had not chosen to marry him for his
epistolary skills, but rather for those steadfast qualities
of character that she esteemed above all else. In her

present mood, however, she found surprisingly little comfort in reflecting on Will's steadfast character. He might represent safe anchorage for her troubled heart, but at present that anchorage was obscured by a mental fog that not only made it difficult to find but almost made her doubt its very existence. She could no longer even seem to summon up a clear picture of Will in her memory.

Constance was horrified to find herself in such difficulties. She had never supposed she was a fickle girl or an irrational one. Yet if such behavior was not fickle or irrational, Constance could not say what it was. She could only read over Will's letters and hope that when she was back in Boston with him, all her doubts and fears would be removed. As it was, however, she continued to fret, plagued by doubts and fears from which there seemed to be no relief.

Vincent, meanwhile, was suffering quite as much as Constance with even less hope of relief. The news of her engagement had shaken him to the very core. In fact, looking back over the thirty-five years of his life, he could not think of any event that had struck him more painfully. The death of his father had been a grievous loss, to be sure, but since his father had been ill for some months preceding his decease, it had not come as a real shock. Indeed, given his sufferings, the eleventh earl's death had seemed as much a release as a loss to his friends and family.

But there was no similar comfort to be gained from the knowledge of Constance's engagement. That news had struck Vincent like a crushing blow. And in the days that followed, insofar as he could feel anything apart from an overwhelming misery, he felt only surprise that on hearing the news, he had not broken down on the spot.

As it was, he had betrayed his feelings, but only for a moment. Constance might have seen that he was surprised, but he felt satisfied that she could not have guessed the extent of his shock. All the comfort Vincent possessed was centered around this fact. He was glad to think he had saved her knowledge of the blow she had dealt him. She was a woman of character and integrity, and it would doubtless grieve her to know she had caused him pain, however unwittingly. Still, there was little enough comfort in this thought. The days that followed were very dark ones for Vincent. He went nowhere and did nothing, but only remained in his rooms, staring into the fire or flipping idly through the books on ancient history that his sister had lent him.

He could not explain why he felt so stricken. Of course he loved Constance; that much had become clear to him over the weeks he had known her. Likewise, it was clear to him that he wanted to make her his wife. He could not imagine a state of existence more blissful than to go through life with her by his side.

But even before he had learned of her engagement, he had had no real expectation that she would marry him. He knew well her opinion of hereditary aristocrats, and holding the views she did on that subject, it stood to reason that she would be reluctant to marry into a group she so detested. Even without that obstacle, there were plenty of others to stand between them. He was an ordinary man of middling intelligence who had been content up till now with idling his life away. Constance was good and clever and *beautiful*—for it seemed to Vincent now that she was as beautiful as any woman he had ever known. Naturally such a girl would think twice about marrying an idler like himself. He had intended to ask her just the same, of course, but his hopes were hardly sanguine.

Now, however, all hope was at an end. Constance was engaged to a man back in America, and she might as well have been dead so far as any hope that he himself might marry her was concerned.

So Vincent told himself bitterly. It wasn't so much the fact that Constance wasn't going to marry him, for he had never had any real expectation that she would marry him in the first place. But the thought of some other man marrying her—some underbred Yankee clodhopper—was simply intolerable. The mere thought made Vincent grind his teeth with rage. Yet he knew in his heart that his rage was as impotent as his love and just as misplaced. There was a time he would have dismissed all colonials as crude and underbred, but that was before he had met Constance and her father. Together they had shown him that Americans could be just as cultured and educated as native-born English people. Probably Constance's fiance was cultured and educated, too; it stood to reason that he must be, if she had chosen to marry him. Nothing but the best was good enough for her, and even that was hardly good enough.

Vincent hoped the unknown fiancé appreciated his good fortune. But no, it wasn't good fortune, as he reminded himself. Constance would never have bestowed her affections at random. If she had chosen to marry this American fellow, it was because he had qualities that made him worthy of her love.

This reflection, far from making Vincent feel better, only made him feel worse. He knew very well that his own qualities were of an inferior sort. If only he had been a different kind of man—a man such as Constance could have loved and esteemed. There had been times recently when he had felt it was not too late to effect some change in that direction. He could never be a genius or a paragon of virtue, but he thought he could see his way clear to making something more of his life. Indeed, under the influence of Constance, he had already made considerable strides. He had taken to attending Parliament regularly and speaking now and then on questions that interested him. He had begun studying his bailiff's reports from Larkholm instead of merely tossing them aside unread. He had personally interested himself in several matters concerning his estate and tenantry rather than leaving it all in the hands of his agents. He had finished reading *Moccasin Tales*, which had inspired him with a desire to visit America; *The Valley of the Nile*, which had filled him with a desire to visit Egypt; and *The World of the Greeks and Romans*, which had made him burn to visit Greece and Italy.

The fact was that since meeting Constance life, which had seemed dull and narrow to the point of suffocation, had suddenly blossomed forth with new possibilities. There was a whole world out there that he had never dreamed of, a world beyond the narrow round of social ritual that was fashionable London.

It was not that associating with Constance had taught him to scorn society. In an odd way, he found himself enjoying it more than ever, because he was seeing it in context now. As though for the first time, he saw the men and women around him as human beings like himself, people with hopes and dreams and fears. He looked at them with new interest when he met them, listened with new attention when they spoke, and found himself seeing new aspects to their personalities he had never noticed before. It was surprising what a difference this had made. But now Vincent felt as though this new world was lost to him. None of it seemed of any use without Constance. In fact, nothing seemed of any use. There were times when he wondered whether he ought not simply put a period to his existence and be done with it.

But even in his darkest moments of depression, he never entertained such thoughts for long. They seemed somehow a reproach to Constance, a reproach that she in no way deserved. Vincent might take a morbid pleasure in envisioning her weeping tears of regret over his lifeless body, but he recognized in his heart that such imaginings were simply silly. It was not Constance's fault if she loved another man. Likewise, it was not her fault if he had squandered the best years of his life in pleasure-seeking and folly. In a dim way, he could see that if his love for Constance meant anything at all, it ought to inspire him despite this blow to his hopes.

And so, gradually, Vincent began to pick up the pieces of his life. By the time the following Thursday had come around, he was able to make himself go out a little into society, to tend to his duties as legislator and landowner, and to recommence the program of reading and studying that he had begun a few weeks before. All the while, however, the thought uppermost in his mind was that he would see Constance that evening at the third lecture on ancient history.

It would be the first time he had seen her since learning of her engagement. Would he be able to hide his feelings so as not to make her uncomfortable? Vincent hoped so. It never entered his head to worry whether he himself would be uncomfortable. Given the way he felt about Constance, there was no way he could be anything else. As Vincent reflected with morbid amusement, passing an evening in her company was rather like presenting a starving man with a table of food he was forbidden to touch. Still, even if he were forbidden from touching, he might still enjoy the crumbs of companionship that would fall to his lot. So Vincent told himself, and the thought was some slight comfort. He went to pick up Constance at the hotel that evening in what was, all things considered, a tolerably calm and philosophical frame of mind.

Constance, on the other hand, was feeling the very reverse of calm and philosophical. She tried on every dress in her wardrobe at least twice, put her hair up and pulled it down half a dozen times, and exhibited every other symptom of feminine disquietude in the process of preparing herself for the evening.

All the while she was doing it, she reminded herself that it could not have mattered less what she looked like. Vincent would not care, for he knew about her engagement now. If by some chance he persisted in caring even in spite of her engagement, then she didn't want to encourage him in it. But she kept finding reasons why she needed to wear her new mulberry evening dress and India shawl that evening rather than the dress and pelisse she had worn during the first two lectures. And when she had finally settled in favor of the evening dress (having found a nearly invisible spot on the green and white muslin that justified setting it aside), she still found herself prey to nerves and disquiet.

When the knock finally came on the door announcing Vincent's arrival, Constance felt as she supposed the late Marie Antoinette must have felt when notified that the tumbrils had come for her. The ordeal that lay immediately before her might be a terrible one, yet it seemed almost a relief after the long drawn-out strain of worry that had preceded it.

Yet when at last Vincent stepped into the room, greeting Constance with his usual diffident smile and polite, "How d'ye do?" she wondered why she had built his coming into such an ordeal. It could never be an ordeal to spend time with Vincent. There was something so comfortable and unassuming about him, something so very dear and familiar. And yet withal he was every inch the earl: handsome, distinguished, and exquisitely courteous. He helped Constance with her shawl as though it were a fur-lined cloak and handed her into his waiting carriage as though she were a queen.

Constance, no Royalist, felt she ought not to be unduly impressed by these civilities. But she could not help reflecting that it was rather nice to be treated as though one were something precious—something *wonderful.*

It was just as well for Constance's peace of mind that Vincent did not put this idea into words. Indeed, by the time they arrived at the lecture hall, she was beginning to wonder if she had been making a mountain out of a molehill. Vincent was certainly solicitous of her comfort, but there was nothing overtly loverlike in his manner. Likewise, there was no sign that he was nourishing a broken heart. Perhaps the news of her engagement had not come as such a disappointment to him after all. Constance told herself she was a fool to suppose it ever had. But at any rate, she no longer had any cause to worry about hurting him. Everything was right now, and she could relax and enjoy the lecture.

She did enjoy the lecture, after a fashion. But all the while she was listening to the professor talk about ancient Greece, she was conscious of an undercurrent in her thoughts—a decidedly Vincent-related undercurrent. It did not seem she could let the subject alone, but must keep continually returning to it, even though it appeared to be settled in a satisfactory manner.

Vincent, for his part, was obliged to exercise the utmost self-control to avoid looking at Constance instead of the professor throughout the lecture. He thought he had never seen anything lovelier than the sight of her in the mulberry dress. Its rich color set off the dark beauty of her hair and eyes, while its flowing draperies accented the slim grace of her figure. He found pleasure in looking at her—a bittersweet pleasure, to be sure, but pleasure nonetheless.

The fact was that all the lectures he had read himself during the past week had had their effect. He had accepted the fact of Constance's engagement and was now trying to make the best of it. It was still not a happy fact for him, but seeing that it was one he could not change, he found he could even think of her fiancé in America without undue bitterness. After all, he reasoned, it was he who was with Constance this evening, not the unknown fiancé. He meant to get all the good out of her he could while he had her to himself. How he was to go on after she returned to America he did not care to think. He could only trust that the evils of that day would be sufficient unto the day and try as far as possible not to think about them.

At any rate, there were plenty of other things to think about at the moment. The professor's lecture that night was as interesting as any of the others, dealing as it did with the subject of the ancient Greeks. In itself, it provided Vincent much food for thought. Listening to the professor discourse about the Trojan war, he found for the first time that he could appreciate the roots of that ancient conflict as he never had in his schoolboy days of struggling with Homer and Virgil. The idea of two nations going to war for possession of a single woman no longer seemed foolish or far-fetched. With sorrowful amusement, he reflected that if he had been King of England, he would have been quite capable of waging war with the United States for the privilege of possessing Constance.

Still, he reminded himself that such a campaign would have been worse than useless. Constance was not to be won by the mere fact of possession. It was her heart he wanted, and such a prize was not for him to achieve by means of warfare or anything else.

*Besides, if I were a king, it's ten to one she would despise me even more than she does now,* he reminded himself wryly. *It's bad enough that I'm an earl, one of the aristocrats she despises.*

He sighed at the thought, so audibly that Constance turned to look at him. Vincent, looking back at her, felt such a surge of love and longing that for a moment he knew an urge to cast discretion aside and declare his feelings aloud for all the world to hear. If Constance had gone on looking at him, he might have done that very thing, but fortunately for him, she quickly averted her gaze and turned her eyes back to the professor. Vincent hardly knew whether to feel relieved or disappointed. Of course it would have been disastrous to have declared himself to Constance at such a time and place, but he could not help feeling it would also have been a considerable relief to his feelings.

Such relief was denied him, however, so he, too, returned his attention to the professor. He took care not to so much as glance in Constance's direction during the rest of the lecture, feeling that he could not afford such another near slip. As it was, he knew he was walking a fine line to sit through three more lectures with her when he felt so passionately about her. He thought it just as well not to extend the temptation any further.

Constance, meanwhile, was beginning to realize that she, too, was walking a fine line. Indeed, she was not altogether sure it would not have been more accurate to say she was playing with fire. When she had looked at Vincent, and he had looked back at her, she had felt shaken by emotions too powerful to express in mere words. Or was it merely that the words were ones she did not wish to acknowledge? In any case, she wanted nothing to do with such powerful and inconvenient emotions. She made a point of attending strictly to the professor after that, with never a look toward Vincent. But she was as aware of him sitting at her side as though she had looked at nothing else. Her nerves were all a-tingle, and she felt strangely flushed, as though the drafty hall had suddenly become a Turkish bath.

# Twelve

On the way out of the hall, Constance spoke. "There are only three lectures left," she said. "The Persians next week, and then the Phoenicians and the Romans."

"Yes," agreed Vincent. Thoughtfully, he added, "But there's other lectures, of course. The professor spoke of doing a course on English history this fall."

"Yes, but I won't be here," said Constance.

The words seemed to hang in the air between them. Vincent glanced at her, then away. "When exactly are you returning to America?" he asked. "I know you said before that it wouldn't likely be until autumn."

"No, probably not. Father wants to stay in London at least until the end of May, and then go north. After we have seen something of Scotland and the Lakes, we intend to cross the Channel and see France, Switzerland, and Italy. I don't know exactly how long we will spend there, but it stands to reason it will be at least two or three months before we return to America."

Vincent nodded absently. "Your fiance's a patient man," he said. "I don't know if I could be so patient myself." He cleared his throat. "Must be difficult, being separated from him so long."

"Yes, it is difficult," said Constance. She spoke in a constrained voice, for this was the last subject she would have chosen to discuss with Vincent. Fortunately for her, he said no more about it but began to talk instead about the evening's lecture. Constance was relieved, yet at the same time oddly resentful. She felt that he would not have been able to talk so calmly about the ancient Greeks if he were feeling what she felt.

When they reached the hotel, Vincent helped Constance from the carriage. He was about to accompany her inside when a voice hailed him from behind. "Good evening, Lord Yates!"

It was Mr. Locke. He was clad in evening clothes, hatted and great-coated and looking as though he had just returned from an evening at the theater. This in fact proved to be the case, for Mr. Locke explained he had just been taking in the latest play at Drury Lane.

"It's good to see you again, sir," he told Vincent, shaking the latter's hand warmly. "I'm glad I met up with you. Would you care to come upstairs and have a bite of supper? I'm feeling peckish myself and thought I'd order a bite of something before turning in for the night. Come now, do join us, Lord Yates. I'm sure Constance and I would both be glad to have you."

Vincent glanced at Constance. She did not say anything, but her expression was far from encouraging. "Don't know," he said. "Mean to say, it's growing rather late. Wouldn't want to put the two of you out, what?"

Mr. Locke assured him he would not be putting them out at all. "Why, the night's still young," he said, showing Vincent his watch. "It's not even midnight yet. As for putting us out, I think I speak for both Constance and myself when I say we'd welcome your company, hey, Constance?"

There was a brief pause and then Constance said, "Yes, of course," in a constrained voice. "Do please join us, Lord Yates," she added in a more natural tone. "Since you and I have been attending these lectures, my father has said several times he would like to improve his acquaintance with you."

This was all the encouragement Vincent needed. He fell in with Mr. Locke and Constance, and together the three of them entered the hotel and went up the stairs to the Lockes' rooms.

Constance excused herself to remove her shawl and gloves, and Mr. Locke, having ordered the supper, seated himself before the sitting room fireplace and beckoned Vincent to the seat beside him. "I didn't think much of the play at Drury Lane tonight," he observed. "One of these newfangled modern pieces. I'd as soon stick with Shakespeare." He shot a smile at Vincent. "Or with Sophocles! I suppose you heard a good deal about the Greek playwrights tonight, seeing that your lecture was on the ancient Greeks."

Vincent agreed that he had and added that he now had some notion of why the Greeks included a chorus in their plays. "Which is more than I could understand when I was in school," he said ruefully. "I'm ashamed to say I never appreciated half the clever things the Greeks did until tonight. Mean to say, there's a statue by Praxiteles in my Great Hall. One of my ancestors got it in Greece when he was there on his Grand Tour, and I doubt I've ever looked at it except to wonder why he bothered to cart the moldy old thing home. The next time I see it, however, I'll look at it with a bit more respect."

"You've a statue by Praxiteles?" exclaimed Mr. Locke, half rising out of his chair in excitement. "Why, man, that's a treasure—a priceless treasure."

"I know it is, now. But I assure you that before this evening, anybody might have bought it from me at a penny a pound and I'd have thought I was getting the best of the bargain, what?"

Mr. Locke shook his head. "It's often that way," he said. "We little esteem what we have always possessed." To Constance, who had just reentered the room, he said, "My dear Constance, Lord Yates has just been telling me the most amazing thing. He says that he has a statue by Praxiteles in his home!"

"Has he?" said Constance in a reserved voice. "I

cannot say I am at all surprised, Father. A man in Lord
Yates's position doubtless possesses innumerable treasures, the like of which would make rustics like you
and me open our eyes."

Vincent looked as though he were going to make
some protest to this speech, but Mr. Locke beat him to
it. "To be sure, my dear Constance, but a statue by Praxiteles is something beyond even the common run of
treasures," he said reprovingly. "I must confess that I
would like very much to see it."

""Deed, and you're welcome to see it, sir," said Vincent. "But unfortunately it's at Larkholm, my estate in
Kent." He looked uncertainly at Constance, but she
seemed very busy rearranging the fire irons. After a
moment, he went on again with a touch of hesitation.
"Of course Kent's not so far from London as all that.
If you was willing to make the trip, I'd be more than
happy to put you up. In fact, I suggested to Miss Locke
a few weeks ago that you and she might care to come to
Larkholm, but she seemed to think it wasn't possible."

Mr. Locke looked surprised. "Indeed? I would not
have thought there was any objection to our making a
trip to Kent." He looked at Constance, and so did Vincent. She bit her lip, then addressed her father with a
forced smile.

"Now, Father, you know you have spoken of leaving
London at the beginning of June to visit the Lakes and
Scotland," she said. "After that we were planning to go
to France and Switzerland and Italy. That leaves no
time for visits to Kent."

"But, my dear Constance, there is no earthly reason
why we need go to the Lakes and Scotland precisely at
the beginning of June. They will be there later if we
want to visit them. It merely means pushing our plans
back a few weeks, that is all. I for one would very much
enjoy visiting Lord Yates's home."

Constance frowned and threw a quick glance at Vincent. "Father, I fear you are not being very considerate,"

she said. "It would mean a great deal of trouble for Lord Yates to have us come visit him. And you know you practically invited yourself."

"Only after I had invited you first," said Vincent swiftly. "Mind you remember that, Miss Locke." Turning to Mr. Locke, he added, "I'd like very much to have you and Miss Locke both visit me, sir, but I'll understand if it isn't possible. If your plans for the summer are already made, I wouldn't want to disarrange them."

He could not resist looking at Constance as he spoke. Her brow was furrowed and her lips tightly compressed, and Vincent could easily see she was not in favor of the trip. Still, he found himself wishing all the same that she might come. He found himself actually praying about it, saying over and over to himself, *Please let her come,* with the utmost fervor. As a reformed man, he supposed he ought really to pray that God's will be done, but he had never wanted anything in his life so much as to see Constance at Larkholm.

Mr. Locke, meanwhile, was looking indecisive. "I am sure both Constance and I would like nothing better than to visit you in your home, Lord Yates," he said. "But it occurs to me that my daughter may be right. It would mean a great deal of trouble for you, and we wouldn't want to put you out."

"You wouldn't be putting me out," said Vincent. "Any more than I am putting you out now, by sharing your supper." He smiled at Mr. Locke. Mr. Locke smiled back but shook his head. "Ah, but that's a small matter in comparison," he said. "Perhaps you have other plans for the beginning of June. I know a great many English people go to watering places then, or to the seashore."

"No, I always go to Larkholm at the beginning of June," said Vincent. "Have to be there for the fete, don't you know."

"The fete?" repeated Mr. Locke.

"Aye, the Larkholm fete. Every year on the sixth of June we get up a big party with dancing and fireworks and what-not. All of our tenants are invited, and the neighborhood gentry as well. And since I'm Earl of Yates and Larkholm, it's my job to play host to the whole party. Feudal sort of business, what?" He gave Constance an embarrassed smile.

She did not return the smile, but merely regarded him with an inscrutable expression. Mr. Locke, however, was looking interested. "I would enjoy seeing your fete, sir, as much as your statue," he said. "Such old-time English traditions interest me very much. However, if you have such a large and elaborate party to organize, I doubt you will be wanting house guests. I am sure Connie and I would be in the way."

"No, you wouldn't," said Vincent earnestly. "We always have a party down from London for the fete—at least a dozen or so relatives, and friends, and general hangers-on. A couple of guests more or less won't make any difference at all. 'Deed, sir, and I'd be very glad if you could see your way clear to coming—you and your daughter." He looked again at Constance.

Mr. Locke looked at her, too. "Well, Constance, what think you?" he asked. "It seems to me there is no good reason why we may not accept Lord Yates's invitation."

There was a pause while Vincent waited with bated breath. Finally Constance spoke. "You must do as you think best, Father," she said. "If you think it best to accept Lord Yates's invitation, then I am sure I have no right to think otherwise."

Vincent let out his breath in a long sigh. He had hard work not shouting for joy. It did not matter that Constance's consent had been wrung from her with obvious reluctance. It did not even matter that she was still engaged to that offensive Yankee back in Boston. He did not expect anything to come of her visit. He merely wanted to have the pleasure of seeing her at Larkholm, and of postponing for a few more weeks the parting that must separate them forever.

Given the circumstances, this was more than Vin-

cent had dared hope for. It put him in such a good
mood that his appetite, which had been largely in
abeyance for the past week, made a revival, and he
was able to do full justice to the supper when it arrived. Constance helped him and her father
generously to roast rabbit, bread and cheese, biscuits,
and apple tart, but took little for herself despite their
joint urgings. Vincent could see she was still disturbed
over the prospect of visiting Larkholm. He was sorry
for it, but he told himself that she had no cause to be
reluctant. He had no intention of pestering her with
his attentions, or anything of that sort.

*Not but what I'd like to,* he admitted to himself, watching the play of firelight on her dark curls. Still, he
recognized that if his feelings for Constance were sincere, then he must put her wishes before his own. It was
clear she did not wish him to make love to her, and
Vincent therefore resolved that he would do no such
thing. But he resolved, too, that he would show her just
as good a time at Larkholm as he possibly could. He
wanted her to leave it with feelings of regret, even if she
could not accord its owner the same compliment.

# Thirteen

Constance, on the eve of her departure for Larkholm, was prey to grave misgivings.

On the one hand she could not help being glad that she was to see Vincent's home. She had never visited an English country house before, or indeed any house on the scale of Larkholm. Lady Beatrice had waxed lyrical about its treasures of art and architecture, and a guidebook that Constance had privately consulted made it sound like a positive palace. Republican though she was, Constance was not above being interested in palaces. In any case, she had an interest in seeing Vincent's home quite apart from its material beauties. It would, she thought, be interesting to see the home in which he was born, the place where his tastes and character had been formed. She thought she would like to see firsthand the influences that had wrought so unique a personality.

Yet she was uncomfortable at the prospect, too. Much as she wanted to see Larkholm, she felt uneasily conscious that the prospect of seeing Larkholm's owner attracted her more. And that was simply wrong, as Constance told herself. She was engaged to William back in Boston, and she had no business being attracted to another man. She had naively supposed that once she told Vincent about her engagement, she would be preserved from further temptation. Unfortunately, that did not appear to be the case.

It was true that since learning of her engagement, Vincent had maintained a courteous distance in his manner. He had never made further allusion to the feelings he had expressed on the night of the Assyrian lecture. They had attended the remaining lectures together in perfect amity and with no sentimental passages whatever. Constance could, in fact, find no fault at all with Vincent's behavior. It was her own behavior that vexed her, for she persisted in feeling drawn to him in spite of the urgings of her conscience.

To Constance, who had always prided herself on being above such moral equivocation, this departure from the norm was very disquieting. During her last weeks in London, she found herself unable to settle to anything. It was a relief when the day of departure for Larkholm came at last, for it gave her something to do. Even amidst the business of ordering a chaise and packing the last of her and her father's belongings, however, Constance was aware of undercurrents in her thoughts—undercurrents that only increased her sense of disquiet.

It did no good to tell herself that Vincent could attach no special significance to her visit. That might be so, but her own mind insisted on finding it very significant indeed. And yet, what significance could it have, given her future as Will's wife? Such time as remained to her between packing and dressing and breakfasting Constance spent on her knees, praying that she might be preserved from sin and error. And when, just as she was mounting the steps of the chaise, one of the hotel servants brought her a letter from Will, saying it had just been delivered in the morning's post, it seemed an answer to her prayers.

Thanking the servant, Constance seized the letter with the same enthusiasm a drowning man might have clutched at a lifeline. Yet when she broke the seal, she found it little enough in the way of a mainstay. A dozen hastily scrawled sentences, dealing wholly with Will's business and his hopes of obtaining a contract with a local businessman was the sum total of the letter's contents. There wasn't a word about missing her, or about their future together, unless you counted the closing salutation wherein he signed himself, "Yr sincerely attached."

Altogether, Constance found it a very inadequate cure for the doubts and fears that were afflicting her. But she reminded herself that to receive a letter from Will at all at such a time was miracle enough. She must not look for help from him or the Almighty when she was capable of helping herself.

*It only wants resolution,* Constance told herself. *I have always prided myself on having plenty of that. I won't give way to this nonsense, no matter what happens.*

Her conscience responded dampeningly that she wasn't at all likely to have the chance to do so. If Lord Yates had ever imagined he cared for her, he had doubtless come to his senses by now. His behavior at the last few lectures was witness of that.

*But that's all to the good,* Constance assured herself. *Doubtless I will come to my senses, too, in time. Anyone with a shred of common sense must see it's impossible that I should seriously care for a man in Lord Yates's position, or he for me.*

Nevertheless, she continued to fret as the chaise made its way south to Larkholm. She had no distraction from her thoughts, for Mr. Locke had fallen asleep almost as soon as the chaise began to move and sat with his head tilted forward on his chest, snoring gently. He roused when they paused to change horses and again when they stopped for nuncheon at an inn, but in the main his companionship was soothing only by example and not because it gave poor Constance any respite from her thoughts.

Larkholm was reached late that evening, after Constance had begun to feel she could not stand to be rattled in body and racked in mind any longer. The carriage turned between a pair of massive stone pillars, and Constance, peering through the window, could distinguish the figure of a lark upon the near one. By this, she deduced that she had reached her journey's end. *Journeys end in lovers meetings*, whispered memory with disobliging promptitude. Constance put the thought from her as hastily as though it had been a flaming brand.

"Wake up, Father: we're at Larkholm," she said aloud. "I expect we'll reach the house any minute now."

In point of fact, however, it was nearly an hour's drive through parkland and woodland before the chaise reached its destination. Constance, peering out the window once more, could just make out the outline of a towering baroque edifice rising darkly against the sky. Its central block stood stolid and square and crowned with towers, while broad arching wings curved out to either side. Moonlight glinted coldly from its myriad windows, though here and there one was lit from within by the warmer glow of firelight and candlelight. Still, the overall impression was hardly welcoming.

Constance shivered and looked about, vainly trying to find comfort amid these alien surroundings. Larkholm was situated on a rise of ground that sloped down to a lake in front. A smaller house stood nearby, surrounded by gardens. Constance supposed it to be the dower house where Vincent's mother now resided. Farther off she could see what appeared to be yet another house, its vast domed rotunda silhouetted against the rising moon. For a moment she stood admiring it; then, with a belated jolt of recognition, she realized it was not a house at all, but rather the mausoleum Vincent had spoken of on the night of the Egyptian lecture.

Constance shivered again. Although she had been sympathetic enough when he had complained about having this reminder of mortality thrust continually on his sight, she realized now she had not grasped the sheer weight of its presence. The wonder was not that he found such a reminder depressing, she felt. It was rather that he was able to bear its weight at all.

Beside her, Mr. Locke, stifling a yawn, was also looking about. "A handsome property," he observed. "Hard to believe it all belongs to one man, hey, Constance?"

"Yes," said Constance. She felt resentfully that Vincent had grossly misrepresented himself. How dare he act like an ordinary, appealing man when he possessed a private kingdom like this?

Just as she was thinking these thoughts, Vincent himself materialized suddenly in front of her. "Evening, Miss Locke, Mr. Locke," he said. "Welcome to Larkholm, what?"

Constance let out a little cry, then felt furious with herself for doing so. "Lord Yates, you startled me!" she said. "Where in the world did you come from?"

Vincent, with many apologies, explained that he had been out looking at his coverts. "I couldn't seem to settle to anything this evening," he said with an apologetic sidelong glance. "So I thought I'd go for a walk. Then I heard your carriage in the drive and thought I'd come over and be the first to greet you, don't you know."

Constance merely nodded. Privately, she felt a good deal unsettled. In part this was due to the suddenness of Vincent's appearance, but the way he was looking at her had something to do with it, too. Almost she could fancy that there was something more than mere friendliness in his eyes. Constance told herself it was only a trick of the moonlight, however. Averting her eyes, she addressed her father. "Your neckcloth's crooked, Father," she said. "Had I better not straighten it before we go into the house?"

Mr. Locke agreed that she had better and stood obediently still while Constance straightened his neckcloth. She was aware of Vincent watching, but took care not to meet his eyes. "There," she said with spurious vivacity, once the neckcloth was neatly tied. "Now, we are both fit to enter Lord Yates's Palace Beautiful."

Vincent made a noise that was half amused and half disparaging. "Larkholm's hardly that," he said. "Mean to say, it's got its points, but it's a dashed drafty barracks of a place when all's said and done."

To Constance, however, as Vincent ushered her and her father through Larkholm's enormous entrance hall, this was false modesty of the most egregious kind. Everywhere she looked was gilt and splendor and terrifying formality. The entrance hall took them into an even more cavernous reception hall with a sweeping double staircase and a stained glass skylight. Constance, observing the magnificence about her, felt increasingly insignificant as well as increasingly uncomfortable. She had a conviction that there was dirt on her face, and that her hat must be on crooked.

A glance at a gilt-framed mirror showed her she was wrong on both counts, but it also reflected her own nondescript face, looking very out of place amid the splendor of her surroundings. Averting her eyes from her reflection, Constance raised her chin a trifle and followed Vincent and her father through a set of double doors opening off the reception hall near the foot of the curving staircase.

This room did not strike Constance as being as oppressive as the part of the house she had already seen. The fire in the grate gave it a homelike touch the other rooms had lacked, and though exquisitely furnished and proportioned, it bore unmistakable signs of use and occupancy. An enormous tabby cat with a ragged ear lay on the hearth rug, washing itself with unhurried ease. Books and papers were strewn casually across the room's several tables, and a basket of clothes topped by what was unmistakably a worn-out stocking lay near an upholstered armchair.

Constance blinked a little to see such a homely sight in a room of such elegance. Then she became aware that an elderly lady dressed in rusty black had risen from the armchair and was regarding her with a curious gaze. In one hand she clutched a darning egg; the other held a stocking, which appeared to be the mate of the one in the basket.

Constance's first impression was that the woman must be some kind of superior servant. It seemed odd, however, that a servant would do the household mending in the family drawing room, and Constance, taking a second look at the woman, observed that though her attire verged on the shabby, there were diamonds glittering on her slender hands and a certain something in her mien that did not speak of servitude. Thus she was not wholly surprised when Vincent said, "'Evening, Mama. I'd like to introduce the Lockes to you."

He went on to make introductions while Constance and the dowager surveyed each other in a measuring way. On the whole, Constance found herself agreeably surprised by Vincent's mother. She had expected her to be a terrifying grande dame, draped in silks and velvets and too haughty to acknowledge a commoner like herself. Instead Lady Yates appeared to be an ordinary, rather shabby-looking middle-aged woman with manners as agreeable as her son's. She did, it was true, show flashes of an acerbic wit, but Constance was inclined to like her none the less on this account. "It's a pleasure to meet you, my dear," she told Constance, after Vincent had performed introductions all around. "My son's told me a deal about you."

"Has he?" said Constance involuntarily. She looked at Vincent, who looked away quickly with a reddening face. "I'm sure I am honored if Lord Yates has seen fit to mention me," said Constance, regaining her composure. "It happens I owe him a great deal, ma'am. Has he told you how he was good enough to accompany me to Professor Weatherly's lectures on ancient history?"

"Is that so?" said the dowager, with an inscrutable look at her son. "Well, it just goes to show one never knows." She made no effort to explain this remark, however, and to Constance's relief began to talk instead about the plans for the upcoming fete.

Constance listened with interest to the Dowager's descriptions of this event. It appeared that Lady Beatrice and her husband would be among those coming to Larkholm for the festivities. Constance was relieved, for she had known there were to be other guests at the fete and had feared that she and her father might find themselves odd men out among a party of strangers. This would be no hardship for her father, to whom a stranger was only a friend not yet made, but to Constance, who possessed a more reserved temperament, it would have been an awkward ordeal.

Even more than being among strangers, however, Constance had dreaded being alone with Vincent. Yet such a state of affairs seemed well nigh unavoidable, for she and her father were the first of the guests to arrive at Larkholm. Still, she resolved to avoid being tête-à-tête with him insofar as possible. If she stayed in her room until late in the morning and did not venture downstairs until her father was ready to go with her, she reckoned she might keep herself out of temptation's way. It was thus with consternation that she heard the dowager tell Vincent, "You'll have to see to it that Miss Locke ain't bored while we're waiting for the rest of the party to arrive. Perhaps you could take her out riding tomorrow if it's fine. You ride, don't you, Miss Locke?" she asked, turning to Constance.

Constance admitted that she rode, but protested that such exertion on Lord Yates's part was unnecessary. "Really, ma'am, there's no need for him to go to so much trouble on my account," she said. "I am quite capable of keeping myself amused, I assure you. And I am certain there are things he would rather be doing than taking me out riding."

"Maybe so, maybe not," said the dowager, with another inscrutable look at her son. "But I expect he was going out riding tomorrow anyway. He's become mighty diligent lately about checking up on his tenants and the state of the crops. You might as well accompany him as not."

Vincent said promptly that he would be delighted to take Constance out riding on the morrow. Constance, feeling it would be impolite to demur further, assented, and they arranged between them to meet after breakfast to tour the estate. Having listened with grim satisfaction to this exchange, the dowager rose to her feet, saying she was sure that her guests were tired and wanted to see their rooms.

To this proposition Constance also assented. She was feeling tired and bewildered, as if events had been one too many for her. Yet as she followed the dowager out of the drawing room, she carried with her a comforting impression that Larkholm might be a more hospitable place than she had dared hope. Flames crackled in the grate; the cat on the hearth rug seemed to wink a friendly eye at her as she passed from the room; and Vincent smiled and said, "I'll look forward to seeing you tomorrow, Miss Locke. 'Evening, and I hope you pass a comfortable night, what?"

# Fourteen

As it happened, Constance did pass a comfortable night, though at first glance it hardly seemed a possible thing. The room to which the dowager showed her was a sumptuous chamber, more suitable to royalty than a Republican like herself, Constance felt. The gilded bedstead was fully twenty feet high and nearly half as wide, hung with draperies of rose brocade edged with heavy gilt fringe. There was a table flanked by twin candlestands that appeared to be made of solid silver, and a magnificent fireplace of marble surrounded by a carved frieze of cherubs. Constance's modest collection of dresses hardly occupied a tenth of the cavernous wardrobe, while her toilet articles looked distinctly shabby laid out on the richly inlaid surface of the dressing table.

Nonetheless, the room proved more livable than Constance would have supposed. The magnificent fireplace drew beautifully and put out a heat very welcome on an evening that was unseasonably chilly for June. The bed was deliciously soft and made up with sheets delicately perfumed with lavender, and the maidservant who brought her hot water for washing was a friendly, rosy-cheeked creature with none of those awe-inspiring qualities Constance had supposed endemic among British upper-class servants. Altogether, she was pleasantly surprised by the quality of her accommodations.

She fell asleep in a more cheerful mood than she would have supposed possible twenty-four hours before.

She awoke early the next morning and lay looking up at the fringed canopy above her. She was at Larkholm now for better or worse, and though she still felt it would have been better not to have come, she felt also that she would have been sorry to miss it. Rising, she went to the window and drew aside the velvet draperies.

Dawn was just breaking, and a light mist hung over distant fields where she could dimly make out the shapes of cattle grazing. Just below her window was a close-cropped lawn sloping down to a wood. On its farther side was a formal garden surrounded with neatly trimmed hedges. It was a pleasant prospect, but Constance was not looking for pleasant prospects just then. She was trying to get another look at the family mausoleum she had seen the night before.

The windows of her room did not overlook the mausoleum, but by opening one of the casements and leaning out, she could glimpse it beyond the formal gardens. It did not look so sinister in the morning light as it had by moonlight. In point of fact, it looked rather beautiful. Still, Constance could appreciate why Vincent did not care to confront it upon arising first thing each morning. Drawing her head back in, she set about making her toilette for the day in a mood that was a trifle pensive.

Later, as she went down to breakfast, she was still in a pensive mood. She lingered a moment in the gallery to inspect the portraits of dead-and-gone Yateses that lined its walls. There were several past earls and countesses who struck her as resembling Vincent, though none were anywhere near so good-looking, she decided. She decided also that none of them partook of his whimsical personality. They were a singularly stern and humorless gathering apart from one merry-looking eighteenth-century countess who looked as if she had stumbled into the group by accident.

"You look a delightful creature," said Constance aloud. "But you don't look as though you belong here in the least. That makes two of us, for I don't think I belong here either."

She glanced around after speaking, afraid someone might have heard her foolish address. There was no one about, however, so she gave the portrait a conspiratorial smile by way of farewell and continued on her way downstairs. In an odd way, the smiling countess had given her a happier feeling about Larkholm. She felt as though she had found a kindred spirit, someone like herself, who did not belong amid all this stately pomp and splendor. It occurred to her to wonder if Vincent, too, might feel out of place in it.

She expressed the same sentiments, haltingly, as she and Vincent went out to the stables later that morning. She had changed her dress for a riding habit of dark red cloth and a black hat with a high crown and trailing veil. Vincent had on buckskin breeches, topboots, and a snuff-colored frockcoat. "Your home is lovely," said Constance. "But I wonder if it does not become rather stultifying after a time, to be always surrounded by such perfection? Everything is so exquisite, and manicured within an inch of its life."

Vincent was silent a moment, thinking this over. "Aye, it's not the most comfortable place to live," he said. "I suppose that's why I've never cared to stay here for more than a few weeks at a time, though it *is* my home."

"Yes, your home," said Constance. She gave a half-embarrassed laugh. "It still seems impossible to believe that it could be your home—that it could be anybody's home. It is all so grand."

Vincent looked apologetic. "It's what I was born to, y'know," he said. "What I mean to say is, I hadn't any choice in the matter."

"Yes, of course," said Constance. "I didn't mean to sound critical. But there, I daresay you are thinking of the things I said at your sister's party." She gave another embarrassed laugh. "I hope you can forgive me, Lord Yates. I didn't properly appreciate what a burden it must be to have six centuries of ancestors looking over your shoulder, as it were. Believe me, I appreciate your situation much better now I am here and seeing it for myself. It makes me more than ever ashamed of having read you such a lecture."

"Nonsense," said Vincent. "Told you before you needn't apologize for that. It did me good, what you said to me that night."

"How could it?" protested Constance. "It was most unjust."

"No, it wasn't unjust—not all of it, at any rate. What I mean is, there's things I can't help or change in my life without hurting a deal of folk who rely on me to keep 'em the same. But there's other things I *can* change, and yet I never thought about changing 'em before I met you."

He threw her a sideways look. Constance had the impression the conversation was straying onto dangerous ground. Still, she could not help asking, "Have I indeed influenced you, Lord Yates? I must say I find it hard to believe."

Vincent gave her another sideways look. "You can believe it," he said. "My mother was saying just the other day how much I've changed. I wish—but of course, it don't matter what I wish. There's no changing some things, no matter how much I might want to."

Constance looked at him. She felt she should not pursue this line of inquiry, but curiosity was too much for her. "What do you wish?" she asked. "What would you change if you could?"

Vincent gave her a direct look. "Well, for one thing, I'd change that engagement of yours," he said.

Constance felt her color rising. She wanted to look away, but Vincent's eyes held her own. "I know I shouldn't talk about it," he said. "It's one of those situations where the least said, the better. But I wish—I

wish like thunder—that you weren't already spoken
for."

Constance was horrified to find a kindred wish rising
in her own heart. She wanted desperately to be free:
free to answer the yearning she saw in Vincent's eyes.
Sternly she reminded herself that she was engaged to
Will, and that what she was feeling now was a temptation (infernal in origin, no doubt) that she was bound
to resist. Yet even as she was telling herself these things,
she found herself moving toward Vincent. The next
moment she was in his arms. There was nothing conscious or deliberate about it; it was as though she had
been drawn there, like a river following its inevitable
course to the sea.

It was only a moment that she surrendered to attraction, however. The next moment her conscience sprang
to life, and realization washed over her like a bucket of
cold water. With a gasp, she wrenched herself away.

Vincent was looking down at her with a bewildered
expression. "Constance?" he said.

Constance shook her head. To put into words what
she was feeling was impossible. At last she managed to
choke out the words, "I'm sorry."

"Oh," said Vincent. He looked at her for a consider-
able time without saying anything at all. Finally he said,
"I suppose we'd better be getting to the stables, what?
Mean to say, it's getting on for ten o'clock."

Constance hesitated, then nodded. There was nothing she wanted less than to go riding with him. She felt
he must be thinking she was crazy or (even worse) an
unprincipled flirt. Almost she wished he would take
her to task for her behavior. That would have at least
given her a chance to explain why she, an engaged
woman, had behaved as she had.

On consideration, however, Constance realized it was
just as well he had not demanded an explanation. There
could be no explanation for behavior so outrageous. The
best that could be done was to simply pretend it had

never happened. That was what he was doing now, and Constance supposed she ought to follow his example. But as she silently followed him down the path, she had the sense that she had opened a kind of Pandora's box, and that what it had contained could never be recalled.

In the stable, a couple of horses were saddled and waiting for them. Vincent helped Constance seat herself on a pretty bay mare, then swung himself onto the saddle of his own mount. Constance, who was only moderately at home on horseback, found herself rather glad of this circumstance for the first time in her life. Managing a strange horse on unfamiliar ground gave her something to think about besides the inquiry of her own behavior.

"Where shall we go first?" said Vincent, who managed his own mount as effortlessly as though it had been part of himself. "Is there anything in particular you'd like to see?"

Constance thought quickly. It clearly would not do to let herself be drawn by him to some isolated locale, where she might be tempted to throw herself into his arms again. "The village?" she hazarded.

"Aye, to be sure," said Vincent. "We'll go to the village first. There's a decentish old church there, and the mill's an interesting place, too. Been there for I don't know how many hundreds of years. Nothing I used to like better when I was a boy than to go and watch the corn being ground."

This gave Constance something else to think about. As she rode toward the village she stole glances at Vincent, trying to imagine him as a boy hanging about the mill to watch the corn being ground. For her own part, she had little acquaintance with mills, but the fact that he was associated with this particular one imbued it with at least a vicarious interest if nothing else.

When they reached the mill, however, and had tethered their horses beside the mill pond, Constance soon began to find it interesting on its own account. For one thing, it was a very beautiful place. Situated in a dell of ancient oaks with the mill pond behind, its ivy-covered stone walls blended as harmoniously into its setting as if it had grown there like the trees around it. Inside it was beautiful, too, in an austere and wholly functional way. Sunlight slanted down from the small-paned windows high in the wall and set a-dancing the thousand dust motes that floated in the air.

The miller, busy dressing his wheel, greeted Vincent as an old friend—almost, Constance would have said, as an equal. She would not have expected to find such an egalitarian attitude in England. Vincent then introduced the miller to Constance and asked if he might show her about. "Certainly, my lord," said the miller genially. "Show the young lady anything you like. I'll just finish this stone here, and then perhaps we can grind a few bushel of corn for her, so she can see the mill at work."

"I would like that very much," said Constance sincerely. Vincent gave her his arm, and they set off on a tour of exploration that ended on the raceway that stood above the wheel.

"I don't wonder you used to like to come here as a boy," said Constance, looking down at the water. "It's a lovely place."

"Aye, that it is," agreed Vincent. "But quite a contrast from Larkholm, what? I mean, one's all show, and the other's all for function, if you know what I mean. Maybe that's why I spent so many hours here as a boy," he added thoughtfully. "Beauty's well enough in its place, but it's nice to see things that serve a purpose, don't you know."

"According to my father, there's no such thing as beauty without function," said Constance, smiling. "You should hear him on the subject of women's dress! He says any dress in which a woman cannot walk at a decent pace or sit comfortably is the very reverse of beautiful. I'm not sure I agree with him, however.

When we went to St. James's, I saw many dresses that were perfectly splendid, yet I am sure they cannot have been at all comfortable to wear."

Vincent pondered this in silence for a moment. "Still, I see your father's point," he said. "Often wondered how some of the women of my acquaintance get around when they're so weighed down by frills and furbelows. It don't look comfortable, and to me it ain't beautiful, either. That's one of the things I admire about you, Miss Locke," he said, looking down at Constance. "You always look like a lady. Neat and well-dressed, and—well, elegant, don't you know."

Constance, who feared the conversation was about to take another personal turn, merely smiled by way of acknowledgement and quickly changed the subject. "Do you suppose the miller is done with his stone?" she asked. "I am quite interested in seeing how wheat is made into flour."

Vincent gave it as his opinion that he probably was, and together they reentered the mill. The miller was indeed finished with his stone and proceeded to demonstrate how it was used, while Constance watched with interest. Vincent watched, too, but in truth his eyes were more often on Constance than on the mill.

"I never knew there was so much to the workings of a mill," remarked Constance, when finally they took leave of the miller and went out to their horses. She paused to brush the dust from her skirts. "Gracious, I seem to have picked up a peck of flour at least! I suppose that's the worst of being a miller. It's rather a dusty profession."

To this statement Vincent gave an absent agreement. He seemed to be thinking of something else. He helped Constance into her saddle, then swung himself onto his own mount. Together they set off once more in the direction of the village.

The church, on the outskirts of the village, was quickly reached. It was a picturesque Gothic structure that Constance would have enjoyed seeing very much in the usual way. But since her conscience was still troubled by her earlier indiscretion, this visible reminder of God and religion made her feel worse than ever. She was silent as she looked up at the stone bell tower, and Vincent seemed to sense her distress. At all events, he did not suggest they enter the church, but merely pointed out a few of its exterior features, told her something of its history, and suggested they continue on into the village.

The village of Larkholm consisted of a dozen shops and businesses and several times that many cottages, all grouped together round a green with a common nearby on which a flock of geese held noisy congress. Vincent eyed the common moodily as they rode by. "That's a sore point with me right now," he told Constance. "My bailiff wants to take the common and put it under the plow. I can see his point, for it's some of the best land hereabouts, and most of the villagers hardly use it aside from raising a few cabbages or turnips, or as pasturage for their cattle. Still, it's been theirs to use as long as anyone can remember, and it seems rather a dirty trick to take it away from them, what?"

"I'm not sure I understand," said Constance. "Do you mean the common belongs to the village? And now your bailiff wants to take it away?"

"No, the common belongs to me. So does the village if it comes to that." Vincent explained how the villagers leased their cottages from Larkholm, and that traditionally the use of the common was one of the perquisites of their lease. "It gives 'em a place to raise a few vegetables if they want to, or pasture a cow, or fatten a pig or two. But as I said, my bailiff's been after me lately to enclose it and rent it out as proper farmland. Says all the landowners hereabouts are enclosing. Well, there's no doubt it's a more efficient use of the land, as far as farming goes. And of course it'd be a deal more profitable for the estate."

"But you don't like the idea?" asked Constance, as he paused.

"No, I don't," said Vincent. He looked at Constance apologetically. "I know you haven't any liking for old English ways and traditions. Likely you think this whole estate should be done away with and the common along with it. But I'd as soon stick to the old ways if I can. Not that I'm opposed to progress, you understand. Only it seems to me sometimes that progress does as much harm as good, especially if it's forced on folks against their will."

"But I agree!" said Constance. "I agree completely, Lord Yates. I can see how you would naturally think me opposed to your English ways and traditions, given the way I talked about them earlier in our acquaintance." She gave him a rueful smile. "But the longer I spend in this country, the more I come to think better of some of those opinions. Your country and mine are very different, and what suits one might not necessarily suit the other. And what is more to the point, I don't see the countrymen of either of our countries suffering long under a government that systematically disregarded their needs. The process of change may be slower here, but the Englishmen I have seen are just as independent in their way as Americans and just as intolerant of injustice."

She paused. Vincent was looking down at her with bemusement. "Indeed?" he said.

"Indeed, yes," said Constance emphatically. "And I will tell you something else, Lord Yates. When I first came to this country, I'd have said the best thing you could do with an estate like this one was to divide it up among the common people. But now I have seen it for myself, I can understand why you would want to preserve it as it is. It would be a terrible shame to see so much beauty pass out of existence."

"Aye," said Vincent. He was regarding her with a look of almost painful concentration.

"It makes me glad I am not in your shoes," continued

Constance. "If all this were mine, it would put me in the most terrible dilemma. My principles would be telling me I ought to do one thing, and my heart quite another. I don't know how I would ever decide what to do, or be happy in the decision once I had made it."

"Aye," said Vincent again.

It struck Constance that he was looking rather grim. "Forgive me, Lord Yates," she said. "I always seem to be asking you to forgive me, don't I? But indeed, I don't mean to preach you any sermons. You know your own business better than I do, and whatever you decide in regard to your village common, I am sure the decision will be the right one."

"Don't know about that," said Vincent gloomily. "Seems to me I'm as like to do wrong as right if left to myself."

He looked so unhappy that Constance found herself wanting to coax him into humor and make him smile again. She reminded herself that this was none of her duty, however. Still, as they rode through the village together, Vincent silent by her side, she was plagued by a sense of duty undone.

# Fifteen

From the village, Vincent and Constance went on to look at the home farm, the stock ponds, and several of Vincent's tenant farms. Constance found much in all these places to interest her. It was late afternoon by the time they started back to Larkholm. "Is there anything else you'd like to look at?" Vincent inquired as they rode side by side down the drive.

Constance hesitated, then nodded. "Yes," she said. "I'd like to see your family mausoleum. Up close, I mean, for I've only seen it from a distance so far."

Vincent looked startled, but nodded in his turn. "Aye, to be sure. We'll stop and look at it on the way home."

When they reached the mausoleum, Constance reined in her horse and dismounted. After a moment's pause, Vincent did the same. Leaving their mounts to crop grass on the lawn, they went inside together.

The interior of the mausoleum was cool and dim after the sunlit day outside. Its marble walls rose high above them to meet the domed ceiling, where painted figures of saints and angels looked down on them with grave, incurious eyes. Memorial marbles were placed at intervals along the walls, and here and there a brass plate was hung, sacred to the memory of some departed Yates.

"M'father," said Vincent, nodding toward one such plate. "And there's my Great-Aunt Sarah over there.

Poor lady, she didn't wanted to be buried here, but here she lies just the same. Caused a regular scandal at the time, it did. She'd put it in her will, y'see, saying she wanted to be buried in the churchyard of her home village. But m'grandmother wouldn't hear of it—she was still alive at the time, my grandmother, and a regular Tartar by all accounts. And in the end she had her way. They ended up putting poor Auntie here with the rest of the Yates. Seems a shame, don't it?"

"Yes, it does," said Constance. "Poor lady! One would think her final wishes might have been respected. Still, I trust it's no great matter to her now where her bones lie."

Vincent nodded. Constance glanced at him as they went around the mausoleum, reading the inscriptions on brasses. Once more his face bore a grave and distant look. *I can't imagine what it would be like,* Constance told herself. *When he described it to me back on the night we attended the Egyptian lecture, I thought I understood, but I didn't.*

Finally Constance said she had seen enough, and they emerged onto the lawn once more. As they came out into the sunlight, Vincent heaved a sigh that seemed to come all the way from his toes. He still did not look exactly cheerful, but his expression was less gloomy than it had been a moment before. "That's it," he said. "That's the family mausoleum. Cheerful place, what?"

"No, not cheerful, but certainly beautiful," said Constance. She was silent a moment, looking up at him. "I'm glad you showed it to me," she said. "I only hope I didn't harrow up your feelings too much in the process."

Vincent looked surprised. "No, though it ain't a place I care to spend too much time," he said. "Those empty spaces on the walls—well, they look pretty suggestive, don't you know. But I don't mind it so much as I used to. Mean to say, with you here . . ."

He broke off suddenly and turned away, seemingly very busy examining a patch of clover on the lawn. Constance, sensitive to a change in the atmosphere, thought it better to let the subject drop. "We'd better be getting back to the house," she said. "It's only a short way to the stables from here, isn't it? Well, then, let's walk and lead the horses rather than ride them. I've had enough of riding for the day."

Vincent acquiesced, and they set off across the lawn, leading their horses behind them. At the stables, they left their mounts in the care of a groom, then proceeded to the house. "Thank you for the tour, Lord Yates," said Constance as they entered the side door together. "I enjoyed seeing your property very much."

Vincent did not respond to this speech. Instead he said abruptly, "I wish you wouldn't call me that."

"Call you what?" said Constance with surprise.

"Lord Yates," said Vincent with a grimace.

Constance surveyed him with puzzlement. "But that's your name, is it not?" she said reasonably. "Why should I not call you by it?"

"Aye, it's my name, right enough," said Vincent. "But I know you don't like it. The 'lord' part, I mean. There's no reason why you should have to use it. I've got other names, y'know, and—well, I wish you'd call me Vincent."

Constance was silent a moment, mentally examining Vincent's request and trying to see if there was anything improper in it. On the whole, she thought not. It was true that calling him by his Christian name was a kind of familiarity, and after her behavior that morning it might be better to keep their relations on as formal a footing as possible. But it was likewise true that she had always disliked calling him "lord." Indeed, when she could not use his full title of Lord Yates, she had preferred to addressed him simply as "sir" rather than using the more servile "my lord" or "your lordship."

"Very well," said Constance at last. "I will call you Vincent if you prefer."

"I do prefer," said Vincent. Formally, he added, "And I hope you've no objection to my calling you Constance?"

"No, to be sure," said Constance, smiling. "Indeed, I think you already have called me that this morning."

*Now why did I say that?* she demanded of herself in dismay. He had called her Constance that morning after she had impulsively embraced him, an event she was trying very hard to forget. Without even looking at him, she knew he was regarding her intently. Constance's cheeks flamed. It was a relief when she perceived the dowager's slim and upright figure coming toward them down the stairs.

It appeared that the dowager had some news for them. After greeting them and asking if they had had a pleasant ride, she turned to Vincent. "Some other guests arrived while you were out," she said. "Sir Sidney Carlyle, and his wife."

Constance, whose hand was resting on Vincent's arm, felt him stiffen at these words. "Sid's here?" he exclaimed.

"And his wife," repeated the dowager.

Vincent said nothing, and after a moment, the dowager went on. "I've no objection to your inviting your friends here, Vincent. Indeed, I've no right to object, as you very well know. But to invite people here now, when the servants and I are so busy with the party preparations, and then not even to tell us about it—"

"But I didn't know they were coming," said Vincent. Distractedly he ran his fingers through his hair. "Mean to say, Sid knows we hold our fete about this time every year, and ordinarily I'd have sent him a card. But when I saw him at the club a few weeks ago, he gave me to understand he and Mona was going up to Scotland after the King's birthday. I didn't invite 'em here, either one of 'em."

"Indeed?" said the dowager skeptically. "Well, I always thought Sir Sidney a mannerless scapegrace, but if it's true he came here without an invitation, then his manners are even worse than I thought. However, since he and Lady Carlyle are here, I suppose there's nothing to be done. I'll put them in the blue bedroom, and give Cousin Edith the yellow when she comes."

Vincent murmured an absent agreement. Constance, regarding him closely, could see that the news of the Carlyles' arrival had disturbed him. Or was it possible this was merely acting? She could not help remembering what Lady Beatrice had told her about Vincent having once been attached to the former Lady Carlyle. Lady Beatrice had supposed the attachment had come to nothing, but what if she were wrong? What if it had merely been transformed into another and less savory sort of attachment?

This thought had no sooner occurred to Constance than she sought to banish it, however. It was none of her business what sort of attachment Vincent had for Lady Carlyle. Even if it was an improper one, she herself was engaging in behavior only a degree less improper by speculating about it. Far better that she refrain from soiling her mind with such prurient suspicions and simply assume the two of them were platonic friends.

Still, she could not help remembering how Vincent had reacted to the news of Lady Carlyle's arrival. It had not seemed like mere passing surprise but more like deep shock. *Well, I'll see them together tonight,* Constance told herself. *Perhaps then I can judge if there is anything between them.* Even without this motive, she was eager to see Lady Carlyle again, for at the park she had caught merely a glimpse of her from a distance. Constance was curious to see exactly what kind of woman had won Vincent's heart. Of course he claimed now to care for her, Constance, but Constance still found that almost impossible to believe. When he was there, looking into her eyes, she could not help believing it, but away from him it had the improbability of a dream.

When she went downstairs at the ringing of the dinner bell and beheld Lady Carlyle for the first time, the idea seemed more improbable than ever. Lady Carlyle was blond, blue-eyed, and dressed in the height of fashion. What was more, she was really beautiful. Constance could not approve of the amount of rouge and other cosmetics with which she had adorned her lovely face, but this veneer of artificiality clearly overlaid features of classic perfection. Beside her, Constance felt plain, dull, and insignificant.

Inspired by motives she had not cared to examine, she had worn her new mulberry evening dress down to dinner. This modest garment was wholly eclipsed by Lady Carlyle's dashing *décolleté* gown of silver *lamé*, however. And when Lady Carlyle complimented her on her toilette, saying she wished her coloring would allow her to wear mulberry, Constance was sure the words were pure condescension.

The two of them had been introduced by the dowager as they were all waiting to go into dinner. It had been immediately clear to Constance that she and Lady Carlyle were not destined to become fast friends. It was not that there was any real antagonism or ill will between them; it was simply that they had nothing to say to each other. Lady Carlyle asked her a few questions about America, and spoke of a relative of hers who had emigrated there some years before, but it was clear she had no real interest in the subject. Her eyes kept flickering to Vincent, who was talking to Mr. Locke about farming and economics.

When dinner was announced, Constance was a little embarrassed to find that she had been given the place of honor at Vincent's right, and that Lady Carlyle had to make do with the inferior position to his left. This she did with good grace, smiling and behaving toward Constance in such a friendly way that Constance was ashamed of not liking her better. But she could not forget that this was the lady whom Vincent's family had once expected him to marry. The idea depressed her, making her silent and stupid throughout the meal. The sight of Lady Carlyle's lovely face only increased her silence and stupidity. She was not surprised to overhear Lady Carlyle whisper to Vincent during the second course, "She seems a charming girl, but she hasn't very much to say for herself, has she?"

Vincent's reply to this speech was inaudible. Constance, watching him, could not determine what his feelings might be. He was gracious and attentive toward Lady Carlyle, but not effusive. Indeed, he was effusive toward Constance herself, making a point of helping her to roast lamb and veal cutlets and insisting she try the lemon dumplings.

Sir Sidney, on Constance's right, was less effusive, though he, too, was courteous about helping her to the different dishes. He was a lanky dark-haired man with a sun-browned face and very bright blue eyes. To judge from his conversation, sport comprised almost the whole of his existence. He spoke of hunting, shooting, and fishing with equal enthusiasm and confided to Constance that he would have been in Scotland that minute engaged in the latter pursuit had it not been for his wife's desire to attend the Larkholm fete.

"Nothing would do but Mona should attend this blasted party," he told Constance. "I told her it wouldn't be her cup of tea at all, but she was determined to come. So I decided I might as well come, too, and say hallo to old Vince. We can stay a week or two, then go on up to Scotland."

Constance nodded politely. She wondered why Lady Carlyle had been so set on attending the fete. She had not even received an invitation, if Vincent's words were to be believed. Constance wanted badly to believe him, but she could not rid herself of a suspicion that he still had feelings for Lady Carlyle.

*Well, what does it matter if he does?* she told herself reasonably. *It's not as though he is pledged to me in any way. Besides, I am engaged to Will back in Boston.* But instead of making her feel better, somehow this reflection only made her feel worse.

# Sixteen

When the dowager gave the signal for the ladies to re-tire, Constance's heart sank. She had not enjoyed the dinner, but she was dreading far more the hour or two she must spend alone in the drawing room with the other ladies. She did not want to talk to Lady Carlyle, and neither was she altogether comfortable with the dowager, although Lady Yates had thus far been very kind to her. Fortunately, before the three ladies had no more than seated themselves in the drawing room, the butler appeared to announce that Lady Beatrice had just arrived along with her husband and daughters. A moment later Lady Beatrice herself came sweeping into the room, a trifle dusty about the boots and bonnet but otherwise her customary elegant and energetic self.

"Good evening, Mama," she said, embracing the dowager. "And good evening, my dear Constance," she continued, turning to salute Constance affectionately. "How well you look! The air of Larkholm must agree with you."

"I think it must agree with everybody," said Constance. She felt a trifle shy, for Lady Carlyle was watching her with a jealous attention. Lady Beatrice became aware of Lady Carlyle just then, however, and gave her a friendly greeting in turn, saying she had not expected to find her at Larkholm.

"Oh, yes, Sid and I are here for the fete," said Lady Carlyle gaily, shaking hands with Lady Beatrice. "I have never attended one of the Larkholm fetes before, but I have heard a great deal about them and am so looking forward to it."

Lord Evers, Lady Beatrice's husband, came hobbling in just then, creating another diversion. Lady Beatrice informed the ladies proudly that his gout was much better and that she was trusting a stay in the country would quite set him up. He greeted the dowager and Constance with formal courtesy and acknowledged an introduction to Lady Carlyle with a polite bow. Lady Beatrice's daughters then entered the room, a couple of little girls of ten and twelve years, accompanied by their governess. The dowager greeted the governess kindly and gave her a cup of tea, then kissed her granddaughters and gave them each a cup of tea, too, heavily diluted with milk. Lord Evers and Lady Beatrice accepted tea as well, and by the time the gentlemen came in, the party was seated comfortably around the drawing room drinking tea and talking about the upcoming fete.

Constance was greatly relieved that Lady Beatrice had arrived. Not only was she a friend, she served to absorb the attention of the gathering—an attention that Constance had felt to be too much focused on herself. She was further relieved when, on the following day, several carriages full of other guests came rattling up the drive. With so many people about, it was easier to blend into the background: easier to excuse herself from situations where she was likely to be alone with Vincent. Meals, too, became easier, not only because conversation was more general but because Lady Beatrice, being of a higher rank than Lady Carlyle, had absorbed her place across from Constance at the table. Of course Constance still had Vincent at her left, but his duties as host kept him too busy to devote his full attention to her, and Lady Beatrice's presence served even more than Lady Carlyle's to keep his manner reserved and formal on those occasions when she did have his full attention.

Constance told herself that the worst of her difficulties were now behind her. There would clearly be no more opportunities for dangerous tête-à-têtes with Vincent. She could not help noticing, however, that Lady Carlyle seemed to have no objection to tête-à-têtes with him. She was always making excuses to go see what he was doing, and Constance overheard her once begging him prettily to take her riding about the estate. Becoming belatedly aware that she was eavesdropping, Constance withdrew before she heard Vincent's answer to this invitation. She wondered if he would assent to it. Would he take Lady Carlyle to the mill, too, and to the mausoleum? Somehow Constance did not like to think of his showing those places to anyone else. But that was clearly irrational, for he must have showed them to scores of people over the years. He would probably show them to many more, too, until at last he himself was laid to rest in the mausoleum.

"No," said Constance aloud. The thought of Vincent laid to rest in the mausoleum stabbed her like a knife. She could hardly bear to think of it, even though reason told her that such an event must be many years distant. He seemed to come of a long-lived race, to judge by the dates she had seen on the various funerary brasses.

*In any case, we all are human, and death is a necessary part of the human condition,* she reminded herself. But these reflections did not comfort her in the least. There was something more disturbing in the idea of Vincent's passing than the simple mutability of human life. She had a sense of time ticking away, of minutes and hours that were slipping past never to return. He was only here on this earth for a limited time, and so was she. The feelings she had been trying to repress since that morning came pouring over her in an irresistible flood. If Vincent had been there, she would have thrown herself into his arms and never let him go. He was dear to her. She loved him, and she could not bear to think of life without him. How could she marry Will, feeling as she did? And yet, how

could she go against her principles and jilt the man with
whom she had exchanged those solemn vows of love and
devotion?

"How indeed?" said Constance aloud. She had been
over this ground before, and nothing had changed. It
was ridiculous to think she could ever be happy with
Vincent if being with him meant abandoning her principles. Probably there was no question of her being
with him anyway. He had spoken of caring about her,
but that was likely just a delusion. It would subside as
soon as she had gone back to America and perhaps
even before then. It was evident that Lady Carlyle was
ready and willing to absorb his time and attention.

Constance began to pace the floor. Clearly it was
madness for her to remain at Larkholm when she felt
as she did about Vincent. She was putting herself in the
way of temptation every minute she was there. *But I
can't leave until after the fete,* she told herself. *The dowager
and Lady Beatrice would be hurt if I did not stay at least until
then. And they have both been so kind to me. No, I can't leave
until after the fete, but I'll make sure to go right afterwards,
even if it means leaving Father here and going back to London by myself.*

Having made this resolution, Constance felt a little
easier. The fete was only a few days away, and surely she
could manage until then if she kept herself firmly in
hand. Already the whole of Larkholm was in a fever of
activity. Tents had sprung up like mushrooms on the
green velvet lawn, servants rushed about with chairs
and tables and flower stands, and delectable smells
drifted up from the kitchens. The dowager strode
about like a general presiding over a battlefield, a sheaf
of notes in her hand and a preoccupied look on her
face. Vincent, too, appeared preoccupied, although
Constance fancied he was preoccupied more with estate business than party preparations. She had several
times seen him in consultation with a grizzle-haired
gentleman whom Lady Beatrice had identified as his

bailiff. On one occasion she had overheard words that seemed to show that the subject of enclosure was still under discussion. Constance wondered if Vincent had decided for or against the idea, but she told herself it was none of her business and nothing to do with her.

Following her resolution, she did her best to avoid Vincent in the days remaining before the fete. There were plenty of other things to keep her occupied. Larkholm had a magnificent library filled with rare volumes and furnished with most comfortable chairs. Mr. Locke had discovered it early on and spent most of his days there, reading and working on his travel essays. Constance helped him with this work and also went on daily long walks with Lady Beatrice. In the evening she played at loo, whist, and commerce with the other guests. But she had not the single-minded interest in gaming that many of the other guests did, and the sight of Lady Carlyle rolling her beautiful blue eyes at Vincent was painful to her. Oftentimes she would slip away early, pleading a headache or some other excuse.

On the very eve of the fete, having excused herself from the gathering with such a plea, she nearly ran over Lady Diana and Lady Julia, Lady Beatrice's daughters, who were standing outside the drawing room door. "I beg your pardon," said Constance. In London she had hardly ever seen Lady Beatrice's daughters, who had been kept out of sight and presumably hard at work at their lessons most of the time. Here at Larkholm, however, Lady Beatrice had allowed them a holiday, and Constance had frequently seen the two of them running about the house and gardens. In their different ways, she thought them both charming. The elder, Lady Diana, was a serious, precocious little creature, dark-haired like her father and seemingly wise beyond her years. The younger, Lady Julia, was a madcap minx who reminded Constance irresistibly of her uncle. She had the same fair hair, the same clear blue eyes, and the same ingenuous smile. She was not smiling now, however. Both she and

Lady Diana were looking alarmed and—if Constance were not mistaken—slightly guilty.

"I beg your pardon," repeated Constance. "Were you wanting to speak to your mother? I can get her for you, if you like."

Lady Diana shook her dark head and Lady Julia her fair one. "No, thank you, we weren't needing Mama," said Lady Diana in her serious little voice.

"We just came downstairs to see the company," explained Lady Julia. "By opening the door just a crack, we can see quite well."

"It's not eavesdropping," said Lady Diana hastily. "We're just looking, not listening."

Lady Julia nodded affirmation of this statement. "Grown-ups' talk is dull as dust anyway," she said. "I'd rather look at the ladies' dresses."

Constance could not help smiling at this candor. "Well, if you've seen all you want to see, then perhaps you'd better come upstairs with me," she said. "I imagine it's about your bedtime, isn't it?"

"A good deal after, I expect," said Lady Diana resignedly. "But it's too much to expect a person to go tamely to bed at eight o'clock when there's so much going on."

"With the fete and all," elaborated Lady Julia. "Tomorrow's the fete, you know."

"Yes, I know," said Constance.

"I am going to wear my new white muslin with the light blue sash," Lady Julia informed her with pride. "And Di has a new muslin, too, only hers is yellow. What are you going to wear?"

"To tell you the truth, I haven't quite made up my mind," confessed Constance. "There are two dresses I like equally well, and I can't decide between them."

"Why don't we come and help you decide?" said Lady Julia at once. "We'd help you decide, wouldn't we, Di?"

"Yes, to be sure," said Lady Diana with a vigorous nod. "We help Mama dress sometimes when she is going out for the evening. She says she doesn't know what she would do without us."

Since Constance really had been perplexed in the matter of her dress, and since she found a good deal of amusement in the girls' conversation, she was glad to accept their offer of help. She insisted first on going to the nursery to inform their governess of their proposed expedition, however. The governess received the news with resignation. "I expect it's no great matter if they stay up late this once," she said. "They're so excited about the party tomorrow that they're not likely to sleep much tonight anyway."

"I won't keep them more than an hour," promised Constance. Taking a civil leave of the governess, she led the two girls along the corridor to her bedchamber.

Lady Diana and Lady Julia were very impressed with this apartment. "Oh, they've given you the state bedchamber," said Lady Diana, looking about her with wide eyes. "That must mean you're very important. Nobody but very important people get to sleep here." She lowered her voice to a whisper. "Aunt Fitzwilliam was peeved because she usually sleeps here when she's at Larkholm. But Grandmother said that she gave the state room to somebody else, and Aunt Fitzwilliam had to sleep in the gold bedroom instead."

"I suppose it's because you're American," volunteered Lady Julia. "Seeing how far you've come, it stands to reason you'd get the best room."

Constance gave an absent agreement. She felt embarrassed to think she had been staying for over a week in Larkholm's best bedchamber and had not even known it. She had simply assumed all the rooms were on this grand scale. Had the dowager given her the state bedchamber for some such reason as the girls had suggested? Or had Vincent insisted it be given her? And if he had, what had the dowager made of his insistence?

Dragging her thoughts away from this subject, Constance turned toward her wardrobe. "My dresses are in here," she said. "I simply can't decide which to wear. I have never been to a fete before, you see. I had supposed one might dress as for a picnic, and in that case one would want something very simple. This white cambric, for instance."

Lady Diana and Lady Julia looked dubiously at the white cambric. "It's pretty, but perhaps a bit plain," said Lady Diana tactfully. "I think you would want something fancier than that. A fete isn't just like a picnic, you see. It's more like an outdoor ball with dancing, and a dinner, and fireworks afterwards when it gets dark."

"I see," said Constance. "In that case, this mulled muslin, perhaps?"

Lady Diana allowed that the muslin was better than the other, but neither she nor her sister showed much enthusiasm for it. "What else have you got?" asked Lady Diana, peering into the wardrobe. "Oh, what's this? What a pretty color!"

She had seized upon a poppy-colored gauze evening dress with short sleeves and a flounced hem. "That? That's an evening dress," said Constance. "I had it made in London, but I haven't had a chance to wear it yet."

"Well, I'd wear it tomorrow if I were you," said Lady Diana, and her sister nodded agreement. "It's much the prettiest dress you've got, and quite suitable, too."

"Very well," said Constance, smiling. She reflected that she could always slip upstairs and change into other clothing if she found the girls were mistaken about its suitability. Lady Diana, meanwhile, had gone on scrutinizing her wardrobe.

"What will you wear with the dress?" she wanted to know. "Have you a suitable shawl?"

Gravely Constance exhibited her India shawl. This met with Lady Diana's approval, but when she questioned her next about her jewelry she showed visible diappointment with Constance's response. "I'm afraid I don't have a great deal of jewelry," said Constance apologetically. "It will have to either be my locket, or this gold cross."

Lady Diana looked dissatisfied, but said she supposed the cross would do. At that point the conversation was interrupted by an excited cry from Lady Julia. "I know! She can wear my coral necklace. That would look perfectly lovely with her dress."

"So it would," said Lady Diana, surveying Constance with an appraising eye. "An excellent idea, Julia."

"But, my dear, I couldn't take your necklace," protested Constance, both touched and amused. "Likely you will want to wear it yourself."

Both girls shook their heads decisively. "No, she won't," said Lady Diana.

"I'm not allowed to wear it, not till I'm older," explained Lady Julia. "Not after I lost the pearl ring Aunt Fitzwilliam gave me. Of course it turned up later in the milk pitcher, but Mama said it would be better to wait to wear my more valuable things until I'm older."

"Older and more responsible," added Lady Diana, giving her a reproving look.

Lady Julia made a face at her sister, then gave Constance an endearing smile. "So seeing that I'm not allowed to wear my necklace, you might as well," she said. "It will look splendid with your dress. And coral's good luck, you know. Here, I'll go get the necklace so you'll have it ready to put on tomorrow."

Constance attempted to demur, saying she did not wish to be responsible for what was evidently a valuable ornament. But when it became clear that Lady Julia would be hurt by her refusal, she gave way with a relenting smile. "If you really don't mind, then I shall be honored to wear it. I can use all the good luck I can get," added Constance, thinking ruefully of her dilemma in regard to Vincent.

"Then you need to carry my lucky sixpence, too," said Lady Diana promptly. "I'll go fetch it."

As a result, when Constance came downstairs the

following afternoon, attired in her poppy-colored dress and with her hair twisted into a chignon, she was equipped with not only a coral necklace but a lucky sixpence tucked in her reticule. Yet she was in some doubt as to what, in her situation, might constitute luck. It was her intention to avoid Vincent as much as possible throughout the afternoon. Given the size of the party, she reasoned there would be no great difficulty about that. But she was conscious all the while of wanting to be with him—a longing that was fiercely at odds with her good intentions. As a result, her state of mind was rather divided, and when she joined her fellow houseguests on the lawn for the formal opening of the fete, her expression was so grave that Sir Sidney told her humorously she ought not to wear such a Friday face on a Saturday.

Constance smiled and excused herself, saying she was preoccupied. As she turned away, however, she heard Lady Carlyle whisper to her husband, "What a little Puritan she is! You ought not to tease her, Sid. I expect Miss Locke does not approve of such extravagant entertainments."

There could be no doubt that the Larkholm fete was as extravagant an entertainment as Constance had ever seen. Lady Diana had been right in saying it was more like an outdoor ball than a picnic party. The freshly mown lawn was as smooth and velvety as a carpet, while the gardens were a perfect riot of colorful blooms. Shaded by one of the gaily striped tents, an orchestra played *divertimenti* and *canzonetti*, while guests strolled about the lawns and gardens or patronized the different refreshment tents. One of these catered chiefly to the gentry and featured such dainties as lobster patties, salad, French pastries, and champagne; the others served heartier fare, such as meat pies, sandwiches, and cold joints, with plenty of beer and cider to wash them down.

In the very center of the lawn, an open-air pavilion was set up for dancing. Constance eyed it with morbid

interest as she walked about on her father's arm. She
wondered who would lead off the dancing with Vincent
that evening.

*Probably Lady Carlyle,* Constance told herself. She had
seen Lady Carlyle only a minute before, standing beside Vincent as he greeted a party of newly arrived
guests. To Constance, it looked as though Lady Carlyle
had deliberately positioned herself where she would
seem to be fulfilling the role of hostess. She had also
dressed herself so as to make the most of her considerable beauty. Constance thought her sky blue silk a
trifle fussy and overelaborate for an al fresco party, but
there could be no doubt that Lady Carlyle looked very
lovely in it.

Constance looked over her shoulder, both to get another look at the dress and to see if its owner was still
engaged in conversation with Vincent. To her embarrassment, she discovered that Vincent was looking
directly at her over the heads of the crowd. Hastily Constance averted her eyes and turned to her father. "Let's
go to the refreshment tent and get something to drink,
Father," she suggested. "It's warm here in the sun."

Mr. Locke was amenable to this idea, and they
wound their way amid groups of guests to the refreshment tent. Here they encountered Lady Beatrice, who
hailed them with delight, saying she had some people
she wanted to introduce to them. The people expressed themselves very pleased to make Mr. and Miss
Locke's acquaintance, but it soon became evident that
it was really Mr. Locke's acquaintance they wanted to
make. In a matter of minutes, Constance found herself
shifted to the perimeter of the group, as a larger and
larger crowd gathered to listen to Mr. Locke hold forth
in his usual witty manner. Constance was too used to
this happening to resent it much. She finished drinking her punch, then put down her glass and looked
about for something to do. Sir Sidney was standing
nearby, moodily contemplating a glass of champagne.

Upon catching her eye, he flashed a brief, cheerless smile. "Hullo, Miss Locke," he said. "Not feeling blue-deviled any longer, I hope."

"Oh, no," lied Constance. "I am having a delightful time."

As she spoke, it struck her that Sir Sidney himself was looking less than cheerful. Perhaps he sensed her thoughts, for he drew nearer to address her in a confidential tone. "Maybe that's true, but you don't look it, and I'm not feeling so very jolly myself. Just had a bit of a disagreement with my wife, don't you know."

"I'm sorry," said Constance. She *was* sorry, but at the same time she could not help wondering if the disagreement had something to do with Vincent.

Sir Sidney, meanwhile, had continued with his plaint. "It's a deuce of a thing," he said. "Mona and I get along famously most of the time, but every now and then she gets an unreasonable fit. We had words a bit ago, and I don't know where she's gone off to."

"I saw Lady Carlyle talking to Lord Yates just a minute ago," offered Constance. "Over by the dancing pavilion."

She was careful to keep her face expressionless as she spoke. Sir Sidney evidently did not share her apprehensions, for he looked relieved by her words. "Ah, well, if she's with Vincent, then she's all right," he said. "He'll take care of her. One of my oldest friends, Vincent, and a dashed good fellow. Known him long?"

With some reserve, Constance explained that she and Vincent had met in London only a few months before. "A few months, eh?" said Sir Sidney. "Now I wonder . . . I wonder."

With these words, he appeared to fall into a reverie. Constance waited patiently for a while, but in the end curiosity was too much for her. "What do you wonder?" she asked.

Sir Sidney came to himself with a start. "What do I wonder?" he repeated. "Oh, well, it's only that old Vince has seemed different here lately. Quieter, don't you know, and—well—different. And I wondered if anybody else had noticed it. But there, if you've known him only a few months, likely you wouldn't have noticed any difference."

"No," agreed Constance.

There was a short silence. "A good fellow, Vince," repeated Sir Sidney. "Up to every rig and row—down as a nail—a regular out-and-outer."

"Yes?" said Constance, to whom this was so much Greek. "I wouldn't know about that. I only know I have found him very pleasant company."

Sir Sidney slanted a quizzical look at her. After a moment he said, "Miss Locke, I wonder if you'd mind my asking a personal question?"

Constance would have liked to say that she would mind but she did not wish to offend one of Vincent's friends, and in any event, she had a strong curiosity to know what question Sir Sidney might ask. "I suppose I would not mind," she said doubtfully. "Only—is this not rather a public place for personal questions?"

To her relief, Sir Sidney immediately grasped her point. "Aye, it is a bit public," he agreed, glancing around the crowded refreshment tent. "Perhaps you'd care to walk around the grounds a bit? There's an acre or two of gardens, so we ought to be able to find a spot of privacy without too much trouble."

Constance agreed to this proposition, and together she and Sir Sidney left the refreshment tent. They threaded their way amid tents and flowerbeds and groups of laughing villagers clad in their colorful Sunday best, until they came to a stretch of open lawn with only a few couples strolling about. "Ah, this seems more private-like," said Sir Sidney. But even now they had reached a place of privacy, he seemed loath to speak, and in the end, Constance was forced to take matters in her own hands as before. "What question did you wish to ask me, Sir Sidney?" she asked.

"Question?" said Sir Sidney blankly.

Constance was beginning to feel irritated. It occurred to her that Lady Carlyle, though doubtless wrong in trying to attach Vincent, might nonetheless have some excuse for preferring his company to that of her own lawful lord. "You said you wanted to ask me a personal question," she said, trying to hide her irritation.

"Oh, aye, so I did," said Sir Sidney. "The fact is, I wanted to ask you if there was anything between you and Vince."

"Between me and Lord Yates?" said Constance, with well-simulated surprise. "What should there be between Lord Yates and me?"

"I don't know," said Sir Sidney. Apologetically he added, "I just wondered, that's all. As I said before, he's been so different lately. I rather wondered if it might not be a case of Cupid's arrows, don't you know."

"You think Lord Yates has fallen in love?" said Constance. She tried to speak matter-of-factly, though she could not keep a flush from rising to her cheeks.

Sir Sidney threw her another apologetic glance. "Well, I thought he might," he said. "And when it came right down to it, I couldn't think of anybody but you he'd be in love with."

Constance was astounded by this statement. Try as she might, she could not help questioning it. "With me?" she asked. "But why would Lord Yates be in love with me? There must be hundreds of ladies who would be glad to receive his advances if they could."

"Aye, no doubt about that," agreed Sir Sidney. "But the thing is, y'see, Vince has been on the town for a round dozen years and more, and I've never seen the least sign before that he was anything but heart-whole. Not once, in all the time I've known him."

"No?" said Constance, trying not to look as gratified as she felt by these words. "But that does not mean that he cannot have met somebody just recently whom he could care for. Someone besides me, I mean," she added quickly.

Sir Sidney shook his head. "Don't think so," he said. "Who else has he met? Mean to say, there's plenty of pretty girls around, but when you get down to brass tacks most of 'em are all cut from the same bolt. Vincent's a choosy fellow, for all he is so easygoing. It'd take somebody different to suit him, and somebody not just in the common style. And I can see you're that, Miss Locke. It's not just that you're a Yankee and all. You've got something—a quality to you—that sets you apart from most ladies."

"Do I?" said Constance, quite overcome by this disinterested encomium.

Sir Sidney nodded decisively. "What with one thing and another, I can see how you might be just the type to appeal to old Vincent. Besides," he added inconsequentially, "I've seen the way he looks at you."

There did not seem to be any answer to this. Constance said nothing, accordingly, and after a moment Sir Sidney went on. "Expect I'm speaking out of turn," he said. "You haven't asked me to meddle in your affairs, and neither has Vince. But I'm not completely blind to the time of day, though you may think it." He gave Constance a direct look. "I've made a mistake or two in my time, and though I'm willing to take my dose without squawking, I'd as lief not see Vincent make the same sort of mistake. I think a lot of old Vincent, as I said before. He's a very decent sort, and I'd like to see him do better out of life than I have."

Constance could not help being touched by Sir Sidney's avowal. It sounded from his words as though he was not as blind to his wife's activities as she had supposed. Yet his sole concern seemed to be for his friend's happiness. Still, she was in some uncertainty as to what Sir Sidney wanted her to do in that regard. If he thought a match between her and his friend was imminent and was appealing to her to cry off, then she could reassure him as to her intentions. If, however, he was actually trying to foster such a match, then she had no hope to offer him. She could only assure him that she, too, cared for Vincent's happiness and would never do anything to deliberately injure it.

This seemed her best course in any case, so she set out to reassure Sir Sidney, choosing her words carefully. "I do appreciate your concern, Sir Sidney," she said. "Your feelings do you great credit, I'm sure. I, too, think a great deal of Lord Yates and would never do anything purposely to hurt him."

Apparently this statement was all Sir Sidney had wanted. He nodded approvingly. "That's the dandy," he said. "You can't say more than that, and I wouldn't ask you to." Drawing out his watch, he consulted it briefly, then thrust it back in his pocket. "Nearly six o'clock," he remarked. "Times flies, don't it? Suppose I'd better be getting you back to the party."

"Yes, thank you," said Constance. Sir Sidney gave her his arm, and together they strolled back across the lawn.

# Seventeen

After her conversation with Sir Sidney, Constance found herself feeling more confused and less sociable than ever.

The party was in full swing now, with crowds of people gathered about eating, drinking, laughing, and talking. Constance, however, had no wish to eat, drink, laugh, or talk. She wished it were possible to withdraw to some secluded spot where she might put her thoughts in order. Although none of the things Sir Sidney had said had shaken her certainty that she was doing the right thing in regard to Vincent, they had shaken her peace of mind. She felt unhappy to think she might be hurting him. If Sir Sidney was right and Vincent was genuinely in love with her, then it stood to reason she must be hurting him. But was Sir Sidney right? Constance tried to hope he was not, yet there was a part of her that hoped he was. In fact it was an impossible muddle, as she told herself, and there was no way to reconcile all her hopes, fears, and desires. She was just contemplating whether it might be better to plead another headache and flee the party when she was hailed by a childish voice.

"Miss Locke! Hullo there, Miss Locke."

Constance turned and saw Lady Julia's small, spritely face peeping out from behind a nearby statue. "Hello, Lady Julia," she said, smiling.

Lady Julia emerged from behind the statue and came

over to where Constance stood. "You look very elegant today, Miss Locke," she said, slipping her hand familiarly in Constance's. "That dress is simply bee-yoo-tiful. And what a bee-yoo-tiful necklace you are wearing," she added with a conspiratorial smile.

Constance laughed and fingered the coral necklace. "It *is* beautiful," she agreed. "I am much obliged to its owner for loaning it to me. What were you doing behind that statue? Are you up to your old trick of spying on people again?"

Lady Julia shook her head. "No, I am playing hide-and-go-seek," she said, "with Diana and some of the other girls. But I can't find anyplace good to hide. It has to be in the gardens, you see, between the lake and the terrace and no further than the edge of the woods. Can you help me think of a place to hide?"

"I can try," said Constance. She was happy to have this simple, straightforward task to absorb her attention. As she set off hand in hand with Lady Julia, she told herself whimsically she would not mind finding a place to hide herself.

Larkholm's formal gardens had abundant places to hide, but Lady Julia explained that most of the really good ones had already been found by the girls in previous games. "I need someplace new," she told Constance, "somewhere Di won't think to guess. Do you think you could help me climb onto the roof of the summerhouse?"

"No," said Constance. "And it's just as well. The roof is so steep you'd probably fall off and hurt yourself. I don't see why you couldn't hide *inside* the summerhouse, though."

Lady Julia shook her head. "That's no good," she said. "There's nothing inside the summerhouse but a few old chairs. Di would see me as soon as she looked inside."

Constance, glancing inside the summerhouse, had to admit Lady Julia was right. "I have an idea," she said.

"Why don't you get under one of the chairs, and I'll sit on top of it? My skirt will hang down and hide you, so no one will know you're there. And I'll drape my shawl over the back of it, so it will screen you even if Lady Diana comes to take a closer look."

Lady Julia smiled beatifically. "That is a wonderful idea!" she said, and forthwith dived beneath the nearest chair. Constance sat down on top of it, spreading her skirts as wide as possible and draping her shawl over the back so as to provide maximum coverage. "Di will never find me here," whispered Lady Julia exultantly. "Oh, Miss Locke, you are a brick! How can I ever repay you?"

"You don't owe me anything," said Constance. "Remember I was in your debt to begin with, because I lent me your necklace."

"So I did," said Lady Julia in a pleased voice. "I'd forgotten about that. Has it brought you good luck yet?"

"Not so that you would notice," said Constance. Ruefully she thought about her conversation with Sir Sidney.

Lady Julia put out a small, grimy hand and patted her knee. "Well, never mind," she said consolingly. "I'm sure it will before the day's over."

She proceeded to relate in a whisper all the incidences of good luck that had befallen her when she had worn the necklace on previous occasions, prior to the unfortunate incident of the milk pitcher. Constance, listening with amusement, reflected that the necklace might possess a species of luck after all. She had been wanting to get away from the party to some quiet place and here she was, in a quiet place and being well entertained in the bargain.

Just as she was thinking these thoughts, Lady Julia suddenly broke off her speech. "I hear footsteps," she hissed. "Someone's coming. I'll bet a shilling it's Di. She mustn't know I'm here!"

"She won't if I can help it," Constance whispered back. She arranged her skirts still wider on the chair,

then folded her hands in her lap. Presently Lady Diana
appeared in the doorway of the summerhouse. "Hello,
Lady Diana," said Constance, trying to keep her voice
calm.

Lady Diana curtsied politely. "Hullo, Miss Locke,"
she said. "I'm looking for Julia. Have you seen her?"

"She was here earlier," said Constance truthfully.
"But I haven't seen her for at least ten minutes." She
felt the chair beneath her quiver, as though with sup-
pressed laughter.

"I see," said Lady Diana. She threw a cursory look
around at the wicker chairs and bare tile floor; then,
apparently satisfied, turned again to Constance. "Well,
I'd better be off in search of her." Curtsying again, she
left the summerhouse, and Constance heard her footsteps receding into the distance.

"I think it's safe for you to come out now," she told
Lady Julia.

"No, I'd better stay here awhile longer," Lady Julia
whispered back. "Just in case she comes back, you know."

Constance was glad to have an excuse to stay a little
longer in the summerhouse. The vines that grew over
its trellised windows made it pleasantly cool after the
sunlit garden, and its quiet was a balm for her troubled
soul. Lady Julia did not speak, being apparently intent
on listening for any sign of her sister's returning. The
minutes slipped past in tranquil progression, until suddenly a voice spoke out of nowhere. It seemed to be
coming from just on the other side of the wall where
Constance was sitting. "Don't see him, Mona. Suppose
we'd best be getting back to the party, what?"

Constance sat up, electrified. She knew that voice.
There was a silence, and then another voice spoke
which Constance had no difficulty in recognizing as
Lady Carlyle's, though it spoke with a seductive purr
she had never heard in it before. "Why need we go
back?" she said.

Another silence followed. Constance strained her

ears for Vincent's reply. When it came, he sounded both jovial and uncomfortable. "Oh, well, you know I can't stay away too long, Mona. I'm the host, don't you know."

"Of course, but no one will miss you if we stay here for a little while." The purr in Lady Carlyle's voice was more pronounced than ever. Constance felt the blood mount to her face as Lady Carlyle added, "We could slip inside the summerhouse here, and no one would know . . ."

"Sorry, but I can't stay, Mona." Vincent's voice still sounded uncomfortable, but he spoke with a finality that seemed to give Lady Carlyle pause. When she spoke again, it was in a different tone.

"Vincent, what on earth is wrong?" she asked. "Don't you care for me anymore?"

"Of course I care for you," said Vincent. Even to Constance's ears, however, the words sounded unconvincing, and Lady Carlyle seemed to find them at least equally so.

"I don't think you do," she said, and her voice held a distinctly petulant note now. "Oh, Vincent, I have missed you so. I've been longing for you to kiss me—"

Constance could stand no more. She arose from the settee, snatched up her shawl, and hurried out of the summerhouse. She had forgotten all about Lady Julia, and neither did she know or care if Vincent and Lady Carlyle saw her leaving. Her sole intent was to get away before she heard any more of the conversation—a conversation that was assuredly not meant for her ears.

As she emerged from the summerhouse, she heard Vincent make a startled exclamation. She did not look around to see whether it was her appearance that had caused it, however. Breaking into a run, she flew down the path until she had left the summerhouse far behind her.

At the edge of the lawn, Constance stopped. She was out of breath, and there was a stitch in her side that caught her breath painfully. But that pain was nothing beside the pain in her heart. She could not bear to think that she had misjudged Vincent, but the conversation she had overheard was suggestive, to say the least. There was no relief in telling herself that what Vincent did was none of her business and that she had no claim on him. It seemed her heart had laid claim to him in spite of having no right to do so. It was that circumstance, more than anything, that made the episode she had overheard so painful. She could not help caring for him regardless of his dealings with Lady Carlyle or the fact of her own engagement. In that moment, Constance recognized clearly the extent of her plight. She was in love with one man and engaged to another, and it seemed to her there could be no solace for her on this side of the grave.

The idea must have suggested a course of action to her mind, for the next thing she knew, she was standing at the door of the mausoleum. Pushing it open, she passed into its dim marble chill.

The angels and saints looked down at her from the ceiling with their wide, incurious stares. The funerary plates gleamed faintly in the fading twilight. Constance sank down at the base of a statue of a weeping Britannia and gave herself up to misery.

It took Vincent a little time to get rid of Lady Carlyle. He had had his suspicions in the first place when she had appealed to him to help her find Sir Sidney, but there had seemed no polite way to refuse her request. As Lady Carlyle's search led them into increasingly secluded spots, however—spots where Vincent knew Sir Sidney would never have strayed—his instincts began to give off alarm signals. Finally he had dug in his heels and told Lady Carlyle that they had better be getting back to the party.

"Why need we go back?" she said.

Vincent muttered something about his duties as

host. He did not like the way Lady Carlyle was looking at him. As on the night of the Prescotts' rout, there was something uncomfortably predatory in her gaze. "Don't you care for me anymore?" she demanded.

"Of course I care for you," said Vincent. Yet even as he spoke the words, he wondered if they were true. He did care for Mona in an abstract way, as he might care for any fellow human, but on a personal level he felt more repugnance than affection when he looked at her. It was all too plain that the search for her husband had been merely a ploy to get him alone with her. Vincent felt resentful at being used in this way. And now here she was asking him to kiss her! He stepped back and opened his mouth to speak, and at that moment someone emerged from the summerhouse at a run and flew down the path in a patter of footsteps.

"Who was that?" demanded Vincent.

"Does it matter?" said Lady Carlyle. She was looking at him in irritation.

Vincent did not answer. He moved around to the entrance of the summerhouse and looked inside. There he encountered the unexpected sight of his small niece scrambling out from beneath a chair.

"Julia?" he said incredulously.

"Oh, it's you, Uncle," she said, greeting him with artless pleasure. "I thought it might be Di." With puzzlement she looked around. "Where did Miss Locke go?" she asked.

"Miss Locke?" repeated Vincent. He had the sensation that his blood had suddenly turned to ice water.

"Yes, Miss Locke," said Lady Julia, still looking around in a puzzled way. "She was here with me, but then she left very suddenly, just a minute ago."

"Where did she go?" asked Vincent sharply.

Both Lady Julia and Lady Carlyle were looking at him in astonishment. "I don't know," said Lady Julia. "She left very suddenly, as I said. I don't know why. I was playing hide-and-go-seek, and she was helping me to hide. I thought she was going to stay with me until we were sure Di wouldn't come back. It's very odd."

Vincent did not think it odd at all. He could guess perfectly well what had happened, and why Constance had left so suddenly. The idea made him more disgusted with Mona than ever. When she laid her hand on his arm and said, "Really, Vincent, what does it matter?" he pulled his arm away and addressed her with cold formality.

"It matters," he said. Turning to Lady Julia, he added, "Never you mind, Julia. I'll go after Miss Locke and find out what happened. You don't happen to know which way she went, do you?"

Unfortunately Lady Julia did not know. Lady Carlyle, meanwhile, was surveying him with increasing disfavor. "But, my lord, you can't mean to say you intend to go off and leave me here?" she exclaimed. "Just leave me here, all alone?"

Vincent turned to his niece. "Julia, please see that Lady Carlyle gets safely back to the party," he said brusquely. Lady Julia nodded with wide eyes and open mouth. Having favored her and Lady Carlyle with a bow, he turned on his heel and strode away.

# Eighteen

Vincent had set off initially at a good pace. As soon as he was away from the summerhouse, however, his steps began to slow. He really had no idea where to begin looking. Constance might have gone anywhere: into the house, into the woods, or back to the party on the lawn. Yet when he had stood a little while, thinking, he turned and began making his way in the direction of the mausoleum. It was not so much thought as instinct that led him there, and his instincts were justified, for when he cautiously pushed open the door of the mausoleum, he could dimly make out a female form huddled near the base of a statue. "Constance?" he whispered softly.

A startled silence ensued as Constance turned her face toward him. "Constance?" he said again. "Is that you?"

"Who is it?" she said. Her voice had a quaver in it, but she repeated the question in a stronger tone. "Who is it? Who's there?"

"It's me," said Vincent. "Vincent Yates."

A short silence followed his pronouncement. Vincent's eyes, adjusting to the gloom, could now clearly see Constance. She was sitting on the floor at the foot of a statue of a weeping Britannia, hugging her knees and staring at him for all she was worth. "What are you doing here, Lord Yates?" she demanded.

"Looking for you," said Vincent.

"Oh," said Constance. The words had clearly taken her aback, but after a moment she raised her chin with an air of hauteur. "That's very kind of you, sir. But you need not have put yourself to so much trouble."

"Don't be silly," said Vincent. "Wanted to do it, by Jove. Been wanting to talk to you all day."

"Indeed?" said Constance with disbelief in her voice. "I would have supposed from seeing you earlier that you were very pleasantly occupied just as you were."

"No," said Vincent. Coming over beside her, he, too, sat down on the floor.

Constance immediately began to get up. "I had better be going—" she said.

"No," said Vincent again. Constance paused, looking down at him. Vincent reached up and caught her hand between his. "Please don't go," he said. "I know you overheard Lady Carlyle and me, there by the summerhouse, and I want to explain."

The hand between his stiffened. "There is no need to explain," said Constance coldly.

"But there is," said Vincent. "I can't let you think me any worse than I really am."

"What does it matter?" said Constance. There was hopelessness in her voice as she added, "I am sure it is none of my business what your relations are with Lady Carlyle."

"You're wrong there," said Vincent. "It's your business because I care what you think. I care about you more than I care about any other person on earth, by Jove. I daresay it's not very chivalrous to put the blame on a lady, but—well, in this case, that's where it belongs, and I'm dashed if I'll have it creating any misunderstanding that I can help."

Constance was silent. Taking her silence for encouragement, Vincent began to explain what had been his relations with Lady Carlyle in the past, and how he had begun to sense lately that she wished to put their relationship on another footing. Constance remained silent throughout the explanation. She appeared to be listening, but he found it hard to tell what she was thinking.

"You believe me, don't you?" he asked anxiously, at the conclusion of his narrative. "I'm a ramshackle kind of fellow and don't pretend I've been any kind of saint, but I wouldn't want you to think I'm capable of anything as bad as that."

Constance sighed. "What does it matter?" she said again, hopelessly. "I can't see that it makes a bit of difference whether you were trying to seduce Lady Carlyle, or she was trying to seduce you. It's all the same thing—so sordid and horrible."

"Beg pardon, but it's not at all the same thing," said Vincent indignantly. "Wouldn't you consider there was a bit of difference between a pickpocket trying to steal your purse, and your trying to steal his?"

There was a longish pause before Constance said reluctantly, "Yes."

"Well, then!" said Vincent. "It's the same situation with me and Lady Carlyle. Mean to say, if a pickpocket tries to steal your purse, you might be angry at him, and you might be a little angry with yourself, too, feeling you'd been careless in putting yourself in the way of having it stolen. But it wouldn't be the same as though you yourself was the thief. You'd have a clean conscience where that was concerned. And so it'd cut you pretty deep if your friends took it for granted you were guilty of thievery, too."

Once more Constance was silent. Vincent went on, his voice husky as he addressed her. "I know I'm a worthless sort of fellow. I've never pretended otherwise, and I won't pretend it now. But since meeting you—Constance, do you think I could say the things I've said to you and yet carry on a vulgar intrigue with my friend's wife? If you do, I can't blame you for thinking the worst of me."

A long silence followed. At last Constance cleared

her throat. "I don't—" she began, then stopped. After a moment she tried again. "I do believe you, Vincent," she said. "About you and Lady Carlyle, I mean. It made me sick, listening to what she was saying to you, but I heard what you said, too. I know you weren't encouraging her."

Vincent pressed her hand tightly in his. "Thank God," he said. "I don't know what I'd have done if you hadn't believed me. Pitched myself off the roof, I expect, and joined my sainted ancestors over there." He nodded toward a wall adorned with funerary brasses.

Constance gripped his hand. "Don't!" she said. "I can't bear to think about it—about your dying."

Vincent saw to his amazement that there were tears in her eyes. "My dear, are you *crying*?" he said. "I beg you won't waste your tears on me. I'd be no great loss to the world, I assure you."

Through her tears, Constance turned on him a look of fiery indignation. "Why do you say things like that about yourself?" she demanded.

"Because they're true," said Vincent. "Who'd be a ha'penny worse off if I stuck my fork in the wall? I doubt anyone'd even miss me."

"*I* would miss you," said Constance.

The words were spoken softly, but Vincent heard them just the same. He looked at her and she looked at him, and somehow, without any intermediate process, she was in his arms, and he was kissing her with a passion fueled by some dozen weeks of pent-up love and frustration. He forgot in that moment she was engaged to someone else. He forgot about Sir Sidney and Lady Carlyle. He even forgot that he was sitting in his family mausoleum, hardly a suitable locale for dalliance. Constance seemed to be forgetting the same things. At any rate, it was several minutes before she spoke again. "Oh, Vincent," she whispered.

"Constance," said Vincent, clasping her tighter in his arms. "I do love you, Constance."

"I love you, too," said Constance, and burst into tears.

Vincent was at first bemused, then contrite. He knew the complexities of their situation as well as she did, and when he thought about it, he could readily understand why she was upset. "Sorry," he said. "Suppose I shouldn't have kissed you like that." After a minute, he added diffidently, "Constance?"

"Yes?" said Constance, sniffling.

"You really do love me?"

"Of course I love you," said Constance indignantly. "Good God, do you think I would have kissed you if I didn't?" Her face changed. "But all the same, I shouldn't have kissed you." The tears began coursing down her face once more.

Vincent patted her on the shoulder. He was sympathetic to her plight, yet he could not help being buoyed up by the thought that she loved him. "It's all right," he said. "There'll be a way out of this muddle somehow. It'll all work out in the end, you'll see."

Constance raised an incredulous face to his. "How?" she demanded. "How on earth can things possibly work out? I feel so dreadful—so *smirched.*"

Vincent shifted uncomfortably. He did not like to think that kissing him had made Constance feel smirched. "Sorry," he said again. "Like I said, didn't mean to kiss you like that. It just sort of happened."

Constance nodded. "I know," she said desolately. "It wasn't your fault." Sniffing, she made an effort to wipe away her tears.

"If you ask me, I don't think that it's anybody's fault," said Vincent. "These things happen, y'know."

"But they *shouldn't* happen," said Constance. "Not to people who are civilized and—and moral." She looked wretchedly at Vincent. "Vincent, this was all a great mistake. You must try to forget it ever happened."

"Forget it ever happened?" repeated Vincent with disbelief. "My dear girl! You can't tell me you love me and then ask me to forget it ever happened."

Constance looked more wretched than ever. "I know I have been wrong," she said. "Very wrong, and very weak. You have every right to be angry with me. After all, I am engaged to another man."

"I know you are," said Vincent. "And it's hard lines on the poor fellow, as I'd be the first to admit. But if you meant what you said just now about loving me, then it appears to me you haven't any business marrying him in the first place."

Constance shook her head. "It's not as simple as that," she said. "Vincent, I can't give way to this—this folly. It's true that I love you, and you love me, but the idea that we could ever be together—Vincent, it's laughable. You must see yourself how impossible it is."

Vincent set his jaw stubbornly. "I don't see it that way at all," he said. "I'll admit it's a pity about the fellow you're engaged to, but an engagement ain't the same as being married. Mean to say, people break engagements every day, and no one thinks a penny the worse of 'em for it. If you've made a mistake, the honest thing to do is admit it."

Constance twisted her hands. "But what if *this* is the mistake?" she whispered.

Vincent thought he must not have heard her properly. "Beg your pardon?" he said.

"What if this is the mistake?" repeated Constance, more loudly. "Vincent, you know it's true what I said before. It's ridiculous that two people as different as we are should think of marrying. We aren't even from the same country. What do you think your family and friends would say if you married an American girl without any fortune?"

"If they knew you, they'd say I'd done better for myself than I had any right to expect," said Vincent promptly.

Constance shook her head. "Vincent, that's nonsense. You know they would say I had tricked or trapped you into marriage. A man like you should marry a beautiful girl from a noble family, not someone like me."

"And here I thought you was a Republican," said Vincent, with a mournful shake of his head. "Thought you didn't hold with the idea of nobility."

Constance flushed. "I *don't* believe in it," she said. "But your family and friends do. And nothing would ever convince them that I wasn't a female fortune hunter who inveigled you into marrying me against your better judgment. Especially when they learned I broke an engagement with a man back in America to marry you."

Vincent surveyed her in silence a moment. "There's that," he agreed. "No doubt there'd be some talk when it came to the point. But I hadn't supposed you were the kind of woman who would let a little gossip keep you from doing what you thought was right."

Constance raised her chin. "I'm not!" she said. "But neither am I the kind of woman who breaks promises. And the fact is that I am promised to marry Will back home."

"No, you're *engaged* to marry him," corrected Vincent. "There's a difference, y'know. A promise is one thing, but an engagement—well, it's as I said before. People break engagements every day."

"*I* don't," retorted Constance. "And I don't intend to this time. I gave my word, and I intend to keep it."

She looked at Vincent, and he looked at her. "I see," he said. Slowly he got to his feet and began to move toward the door.

"Where are you going?" said Constance, surprised. She had expected he would argue more—expected, even, that he might try to kiss her again. Of course that would have been wrong under the circumstances, but there was a part of Constance that wished desperately her scruples might be overcome by fair means or foul. In her heart she knew she could never be happy if it meant surrendering her principles, but that did not prevent her from wishing it might be done just the same.

Vincent paused to look back at her. "Going back to the party," he said. "Mean to say, it's the only thing I can do, since keeping your word's such a matter of pride with you."

Constance swallowed. "It is," she said. "But oh, Vincent, can't you understand?"

"I understand you care more for your pride than you do for me," he said. And with those words, he turned and left her.

# Nineteen

It was not until after Vincent had gone that Constance found the words to reply to his parting speech. "I don't care for my pride more than you!" she said. But he was gone, and not a soul remained to hear her apart from the long-dead Yateses crumbling to dust behind the mausoleum walls.

Although Constance had been quite oblivious to the presence of those long-dead Yateses while in Vincent's arms, the thought of them struck her unpleasantly now. Getting to her feet, she hurried outside. But once out on the lawn again, she dropped down on the nearest bench and began to think over the interlude just past.

Her emotions were still running so high that she could not think of it in any coherent way. All she could do was say over and over, "How could he?" and "It's not true!" and "I shouldn't have—oh, dear, oh, dear." Eventually, however, she calmed down enough to consider all Vincent had said. He had told her she ought to break her engagement with Will. He had implied that what she called principle was merely pride, and that her intention of standing by her engagement showed she cared more for her pride than for him. Were those things true?

*They're not true*, Constance told herself. She reminded herself that an engagement was a solemn covenant, not to be set aside on a whim. She reminded herself that

Vincent was an earl, an English nobleman steeped in
centuries of pomp and ceremony quite foreign to her
American upbringing. She summoned up an image of
Will, steadfast and faithful, waiting for her back in
Boston. All these things were powerful arguments for
her own point of view. But Vincent's charge that she
cared for her pride more than she cared for him still
pricked her, and after a while she was forced to examine it point by point to see if there was not, after all, a
grain of truth in it.

On examination, it proved to contain more truth
than Constance liked to admit. She might shrink from
the idea of hurting Will, but she shrank at least as
much from the thought of what he and everyone else
would say if she announced she were to marry Vincent.
Undoubtedly they would suppose she had done it
merely because she wanted to be a countess. To Constance, who had always prided herself on being above
such worldly vanities, this thought was wormwood and
gall. Likewise, she had all her life prided herself on
being a person whose word was sacrosanct. To renege
on her engagement would be to show her word had no
sanctity at all.

And then there was the fact that she had spoken
publicly against the English system of aristocracy. To be
sure, she had generally been less vehement in con-
demning it to others than she had been to Vincent, but
she was on public record as opposing it. What would
she look like now, if she announced that she had decided to renounce her principles and join the class she
had claimed to despise?

*Like a hypocrite—or like a fool,* Constance told herself
gloomily. Such a prospect was, she felt, enough to give
any sensible woman pause. *But that's not the only reason
I won't do it,* she assured herself. *What I said before was
true, too. We're so different from each other. He can't possibly
really be in love with me. It's just an infatuation. If I give him*

*time, he will recover from it, and one day he will acknowledge
I was right.*

She did not imagine that time would work the same
cure on her own feelings. Little as she might approve
of her emotions in regard to Vincent, there was a stamp
of the eternal about them that she could not help recognizing. Still, she hoped that with earnest application
she might be strengthened to do her duty by Will.
"Will," said Constance aloud. She hoped the name
might serve as a talisman against the despair that was
threatening to engulf her. But even when she concen-
trated on summoning up a clear image of his face, she
felt nothing but sadness and a sense of shame.

Nevertheless, Constance was not swayed from her resolve. She did not expect the path of virtue to be easy or
congenial. Yet she had never known a case where right
felt so hopelessly wrong, and wrong so unutterably right.
That moment when Vincent had kissed her had been
magic, pure and simple. Constance told herself, however,
that this very quality ought to make her wary. She had always been a sensible, pragmatic woman who had been
content to live without magic in her life. If magic were
beckoning to her now, she was certain that it could come
only at a price she could not in conscience pay.

Having settled this to her satisfaction, Constance fell
to considering her best course of action. It was clear
to her she could not stay any longer at Larkholm. She
must go, and the sooner the better. The question was,
could she persuade her father to come with her? He
had greatly enjoyed their stay at Larkholm so far and
had even mentioned the possibility of extending it.
Constance felt sure he would not be willing to leave
without more of an explanation than she cared to give.

*All I can do is try,* she told herself. *Tonight, after the
party is over, I'll talk to him. If I talk enough about the Lakes
and Scotland, perhaps I can convince him to cut our visit here
short without having to make any explanation.*

Unfortunately, there were still a good many hours

until the time she might talk to her father alone. The party was now in full swing, with most of the guests gathered in either the dancing pavilion or the refreshment tents. From across the lawn, Constance could hear the strains of a country dance mingled with bursts of laughter. She had the strongest possible disinclination to rejoin the party, however, and decided to remain where she was a while longer before making her way back. Perhaps, with luck, she would encounter her father or Lady Beatrice or some other well-disposed person to whom she could attach herself for the rest of the evening and thus while away the hours until she could make good her escape.

To her surprise, after she had been sitting a few minutes, she saw her father making his way toward her across the lawn. She rose at his approach and stood waiting until he was within earshot. "Hello, Connie," said Mr. Locke, hailing her cheerfully. "Having difficulties, are you? Lord Yates said you weren't feeling quite the thing."

Constance blessed Vincent for having given her an excuse so unexceptionable. "That's right, Father," she said. "If you don't mind, I think I will excuse myself and go to my room."

"Mind? Of course I don't mind. I am only sorry you should miss the party. It looks like being a lovely evening, and there are to be fireworks, they say. But of course if you are feeling poorly, it's better that you should rest." Regarding her with concern, he added, "It seems to me you have been feeling poorly rather often these last few weeks."

Constance looked at him fleetingly, then dropped her eyes. "Indeed, Father, I don't think the situation here at Larkholm wholly agrees with me," she said softly. "Would you mind very much if we cut short our visit here and went on to the Lakes?"

Mr. Locke looked momentarily taken aback, but to Constance's relief he did not question her proposal.

"Certainly, my dear. I'll regret taking leave of Lord Yates's hospitality, but if your health is in jeopardy then of course we must not linger. I see no reason why we may not be off as early as the day after tomorrow."

Constance nodded. She was glad to have won her point, though she would have preferred to leave sooner than the day after tomorrow. Still, she had no wish to create gossip by a too-sudden departure. It would be a trial to spend another thirty-six hours in Vincent's company, but she was confident that he was too much a gentleman to dispute with her any longer, now that she had declared her intention of standing by William.

There was only cold comfort in this reflection, however. And even cold comfort deserted her later that evening, as she stood at her bedchamber window watching fireworks blossom in the sky over the lawn. She might have been down there now, watching the fireworks arm in arm with Vincent. Instead she was up here alone, feeling more melancholy than she had ever felt in her life. And would she not always feel alone and melancholy? Even if she went ahead and married Will, she would hereafter be obliged to conceal some part of her thoughts and feelings from him—unless, of course, she could bring herself to make a clean breast to him about what had been happening to her these past few weeks.

As a trial, Constance sat down at her desk and wrote out a full account of her relations with Vincent. It looked terrible written out in black and white. Constance shuddered as she read it through, especially when she came to the part about that kiss in the mausoleum. How could she ever hope to be forgiven for such a thing? Even if Will could forgive her for it, she could not forgive herself. Seizing the letter, she tore it to shreds, then burned the pieces in her bedchamber fireplace.

"I must forget it ever happened," she told herself, as she turned away from the hearth. "I must not think of it anymore." But despite these self-injunctions, she continued to think, and ponder, and regret until long after the letter was reduced to ashes.

Vincent, meanwhile, was also prey to melancholy reflections. As he made small talk with his guests and endeavored to avoid Lady Carlyle, he was mentally reviewing the scene that had taken place between him and Constance and wondering what he could have said to make it come out differently.

He was almost convinced that nothing he could have said would have made any difference. Constance had made up her mind to marry her fiancé back in Boston, and it was clear that no remonstrance of his would shake her. And yet, just the same, he found himself going over and over their conversation, wondering what he could have said or done differently. It was impossible that she should belong to anyone but him. She had said she loved him, and had even gone so far as to let him kiss her. Yet whenever Vincent found himself buoyed up by these reflections, the memory of Constance's parting words sent his spirits plummeting into depression once more.

*She can't really love me, or she wouldn't treat me this way, by Jove,* he told himself. The thought made him feel both hurt and angry. He would, he thought, have been willing to do anything for Constance, even if it meant making a sacrifice of his pride. *Her* pride, however, had to be preserved at any cost. So Vincent reflected bitterly, yet when he thought of what Constance's pride meant to her, he began to see that there was some difference in their situations. It was easy for him to speak of sacrificing his pride, for he had never had any pride worth speaking of to begin with. He had squandered it all years ago, riding ladies' sidesaddles and hanging chamber pots on monuments.

Constance, on the other hand, had lived life in a

more estimable manner. Naturally she would hesitate to do anything that would lower her in the eyes of the world. And more especially would she hesitate when it meant lowering herself in another sense as well. *Always knew she was above me, by Jove,* Vincent told himself. Naturally he could not help deploring the scruples that kept her from him, but she would not be Constance if she did not possess those scruples. He began to feel sorry he had spoken to her so roughly. If she were not willing to sacrifice her pride, then he had no business reproaching her for it.

*I owe her an apology,* he told himself. His immediate impulse was to seek her out and deliver it without a moment's delay, but a little reflection showed him the impracticality of this scheme. Her father had returned to the party a short time before, saying she was feeling indisposed and had retired to her room. He could hardly follow her there—that is to say, he *could* follow her, but it didn't seem an advisable course. The party was in full swing; he would be wanted presently to lead off the dancing; and Constance doubtless would resent any attempt on his part to enter her bedchamber. Likely she had already had a bellyful of him that day. Indeed, when he considered it, he realized she would probably feel obliged to quit Larkholm before many more days passed. He knew her scruples well enough to be sure she would not remain in his home longer than she could help after what had happened between them in the mausoleum.

*Come what may, though, I'm not sorry I kissed her,* Vincent told himself. The memory of that kiss filled him with triumph even in the midst of his misery. It seemed to him a kind of hedge against mortality. He had kissed Constance Locke, and whatever life might hold—however long or short his span of years might be—no one could take that away from him. It was a comfort that could not fade. And well it was that he possessed it, for it was his sole comfort just now. A philosopher might have been amused by the irony that, among all the people gathered at Larkholm that day, there was not a cottager or cowman but possessed a happier spirit than the master of Larkholm himself.

# Twenty

As Vincent had expected, Constance lost no time shaking the dust of Larkholm from her feet.

The morning after the fete, at breakfast, Mr. Locke announced that he and his daughter were planning to journey north the following day. Vincent heard this news with gloomy resignation. He was quite sure Constance and not Mr. Locke had precipitated their departure. Likewise, he was quite sure it would do no good to try to persuade her that it was not necessary for her to leave. For one thing, he felt that it *was* necessary, assuming Constance meant to persevere in her engagement. Clearly it would be madness for them to continue to see each other if it only meant misery for them both. But even admitting the necessity of their parting, he felt he had to see Constance at least one more time and apologize to her before she left. Their interview the previous day had ended with his reproaching her in what he now felt to be an unreasonable and ungentlemanly manner, and that was not the image of him that he wished her to carry away with her for all time. So when the morning of the Lockes' departure arrived, and she and her father were waiting in the hall for the postboys to bring around their chaise, he drew her aside to address a few words to her in private.

Constance was very willing to be drawn aside. She had been avoiding Vincent since the fete, feeling it to be her duty, but like him, she found it intolerable that they should part without speaking. If nothing else, she felt she owed him thanks for his kindnesses past and present. Many times in her room during the past day and a half she had rehearsed what she would say to him, and now, finding herself tête-à-tête with him, she embarked on her speech with what composure she could muster. "I wanted to thank you, Lord Yates, for—" she began.

"Don't thank me," he said, cutting her short unceremoniously. "It's little enough I've done, and nothing compared to what I'd like to do, by Jove," he added with a twisted smile. "You must know that, Constance, assuming I've been talking to any purpose at all."

Constance flushed. She had been trying to convince herself he had been mistaken in his feelings and was probably relieved now that she had not accepted him. It seemed the best way to assuage the guilt she had been feeling. But now here he was, stating his feelings with the candor that was his most outstanding trait. It struck straight to Constance's heart with sensations exquisitely painful. "Don't," she said, turning swiftly away.

"I won't," he said. "Don't mean to pester you, Constance. Mean to say, I understand why you're doing what you're doing and all. Stands to reason you wouldn't want to marry a fellow like me."

These words brought Constance around to face him once more. "Why wouldn't I want to marry you?" she demanded. "Because if you mean to imply that it's only pride that's keeping me from it—"

"I don't," said Vincent quickly. "Wanted to apologize for having said that the other day. Mean to say, I've been feeling badly about it, and hope you'll find it in you to forgive me."

"Oh," said Constance weakly. After a minute she went on in a stronger voice. "Oh, but there's no need to apologize, Vincent. I've been thinking about what you said, and I can see it *is* pride, in part, that keeps me from accepting you. But that's not the only reason—or even the chief reason."

Vincent gave her another twisted smile. "I understand," he said. "Believe me, I understand, m'dear. There's a thousand good reasons not to marry me when you come right down to it."

"But you *don't* understand," said Constance. To her dismay, she found her eyes filling with tears. What was still worse, the chaise had just appeared in the drive, and her father was calling to her, drawing it to her attention. "I'm coming, Father," she called back, blinking away her tears. There was no time to exchange any further private conversation with Vincent, for she had to step directly into the fray, instructing the servants about loading their baggage and exchanging farewells with the dowager and Lady Beatrice. Vincent, too, wished her farewell, but in such a formal manner that Constance was sure he was offended. She looked at him wistfully through the chaise window as she took her seat inside.

"Good-bye, Lord Yates," she said, offering him her hand through the window. She could not bring herself to add some conventional remark about hoping they might meet again, so she merely repeated, "Good-bye, and thank you."

"Good-bye, Constance," he said. Taking her hand, he bowed over it, then stepped away from the chaise. Constance's last view of him was of a solitary figure, standing beneath the portico of his palatial home as he watched her and her father whirl away in a cloud of dust.

She spent the next few weeks touring some of England's most magnificent scenery in a most distressed and unhappy state of mind.

Vincent's state of mind was scarcely less distressed or unhappy. He believed he would never see Constance again. This belief haunted him, preventing him from obtaining any pleasure during the day or any peace at night. Worse still, he was prevented from expressing the misery he felt by his continuing duties as host. Some of his relatives were staying on at Larkholm for the summer, Lady Beatrice and her family included, and he had to continue to act the role of host despite his feeling anything but hospitable.

Before long, however, he found at least one of the party offered a certain consolation. His sister Beatrice was not only a friend of Constance's but a correspondent, as he soon discovered. With only a little encouragement, she could be brought to speak of Constance often and even read him bits from her letters. It was a question whether these bulletins brought Vincent more pleasure than pain, but he was willing to endure the pain for the pleasure of hearing about the woman he loved. Beatrice had as high an opinion of Constance as he did and was never tired of praising her wit, intellect, and character. As a result, Vincent found himself feeling more in harmony with his sister than had been the case at any time in their lives.

His nieces, too, he found to be a consolation. Previous to now Vincent had had little to do with Lady Diana and Lady Julia, for they had been mere infants during their previous visits to Larkholm, and in London he and his sister had little to do with each other. Now, however, he found himself taking an interest in the girls, especially when he found that they, too, were willing to talk about Constance. Lady Julia never tired of describing the clever way Constance had helped her hide in the summerhouse, and Lady Diana, in her gravely precocious manner, gave it as her opinion that Miss Locke was a very nice lady though she *was* an American. To this proposition Vincent gave a heartfelt assent, wishing all the while he possessed the right to present Constance to his nieces as a most desirable aunt-to-be.

Since it could not be, however, he tried to resign himself to his situation. He threw himself with redoubled

vigor into his work about his estate, and into an
upcoming election in which he was interesting himself
on behalf of his party. Now and then a small voice whispered that if Constance did not care for him, he might
as well go to the devil, but since he felt the promptings
of this voice had been at least a contributing factor in
Constance's decision to reject him in the first place, he
was in small danger of heeding it now.

Thus the summer passed in as blameless a manner as
any Vincent had spent. Looking back on it on an
evening late in August, after a day spent helping his
men bring in a successful harvest, he found a certain
amount of satisfaction in contemplating his achieve-
ments, but they brought him no joy. In a way, he felt he
was hardly better off than he had been that February
morning when he had stood at his bedchamber window and contemplated his final resting place.

To be sure, when he contemplated the mausoleum
now, he saw not a reminder of mortality but rather the
place where he had kissed Constance. There was bitterness even in that reflection, however, for he could
not help recalling how Constance had told him it had
made her feel smirched. As a result, Vincent found the
memory of it smirched, too. It seemed to him that
there was no comfort anywhere, nothing good or beautiful that had not some blot in it. Still, he tried to
struggle on, and to hide as well as he could his dejected
state of mind. There was one person at Larkholm who
was not deceived by his pretense, however. The next
morning, as he was standing at his bedchamber window, moodily contemplating the mausoleum for the
thousandth time, there came a tap at his door.

"Come in," called Vincent. He imagined it was a servant with his shaving water, or his valet with clean linen,
and so did not bother to turn around until an acerbic
voice told him, "You might at least wish a body good
morning."

"Mama?" exclaimed Vincent, whirling around. The

visitor was indeed the dowager. She stood there, garbed in her usual rusty black, carrying a loaded tray in her hands.

"Breakfast," she said briskly, seeing Vincent's look of amazement. "I noticed you hadn't been down to breakfast the last couple of mornings. So I thought I'd bring you a bite to eat, here in your rooms, where you might have a spot of privacy."

Vincent was astounded by this uncharacteristic display of maternal concern. "Very kind of you, Mama," he said. "Afraid I haven't had much appetite lately. Other things on my mind, don't you know."

"I daresay," said the dowager, setting down the tray upon a table. Seating herself in front of it, she added, "It's not exactly comfortable having a parcel of company about the house all the time. I wouldn't wonder if you was tired of it. I know I am, and I sleep at the dower house, not here."

In a reserved manner, Vincent agreed that constant company could grow tiresome after a while. "It depends on the company, of course," he added with an inward thought of Constance as he seated himself at the table across from his mother.

"Aye, so it does," agreed the dowager. As she removed the cover from a platter of bacon and eggs, she added casually, "Those Lockes were nice people. I was sorry to see them leave so soon, for I took a great fancy to both of them. Mr. Locke was an amusing, lively sort of fellow, and his daughter a very nice gel. I wouldn't have supposed they bred girls like that in America. I'd always been given to understand it was a coarse, backwards sort of place."

Vincent gave his mother a sharp look. She returned it with seeming innocence as she continued. "I know Beatrice thinks a lot of Miss Locke, too. She's bent on getting her and her father to come stay with her in London after they've done their bit of sightseeing up north. Do you think there's any chance they might?"

"I shouldn't think so," said Vincent. He made a great show of breaking apart a roll as he added, "But of course I wouldn't know what the Lockeses' plans are. I'm not a correspondent of Miss Locke's like Trix is."

"No, I don't suppose you are," said the dowager. "It would be a very odd thing if you were. Unless you were engaged to her, of course."

These words made Vincent choke on his roll. "Engaged to her!" he exclaimed.

"Aye, engaged to her," repeated the dowager. She looked sharply at Vincent. "You mean to say you're not?"

"No!" said Vincent. The word came out with more force than he intended. After a moment he went on in a more collected tone. "I don't know why you should suppose there was anything like an engagement between me and Miss Locke. I am sure I've never said a word about such a thing."

"No, but I'm not blind though I *am* getting on in years," retorted the dowager. "I could see you was mightily taken with the gel. And it looked to me as though she was taken with you, too."

Vincent opened his mouth to speak, then closed it again. "I think a deal of Miss Locke," he said after a moment's pause. "And I'd like to think she thinks well of me, too. But that's all there is to it, Mama. She's engaged to a gentleman back in the States."

"Is she?" said the dowager. "Perhaps it's just as well. It's always a risky business, marrying a foreigner. And of course Miss Locke's not really in your class, for all she is a very nice, well-bred girl."

Vincent slammed the remainder of the roll down on the table. "Not in my class!" he exclaimed. "By God! If she's not in my class, it's only because she's a deal too good for me. I'd marry her in a minute if she'd have me."

The dowager gave him a keen look. "Is that so? But surely you don't mean to say she *won't* have you?"

"No, she won't," said Vincent bitterly. "I told you, Mama. She's already engaged to some Yankee fellow back home."

"But being engaged isn't the same as being married," pointed out the dowager. "If you're as crazy about her as you say, I'd have thought you'd have made more of a push to engage her feelings."

Vincent regarded his mother with openmouthed amazement. The dowager calmly took a piece of toast from the rack and began buttering it, seemingly heedless of his incredulous regard. "This from you, Mama!" he exclaimed.

The dowager gave him a quizzical look. "You'll catch flies if you leave your mouth hanging open like that," she observed. "Did you really suppose I'd forbid the banns between you and Miss Locke?"

"I'd have supposed that a deal more likely than that you'd advise me to make up to her!"

"But I'm *not* advising you to make up to her," said the dowager. "Frankly, I'd rather you married an English lady of your own class. But if you're in love with Miss Locke, then you needn't stop on that account. It's a poor sort of lover who needs his mother's approval to go a-wooing." Rising from her chair, she faced Vincent across the table. "An American daughter-in-law isn't a thing I'd have asked for, and I'd as lief not have one, all things being equal. But if you can convince Miss Locke to marry you, I daresay Larkholm will be none the worse for it, and neither will I. Now I'll leave you to eat your breakfast in peace."

After the dowager had left the room, however, it was a fact that Vincent ate very little breakfast. He sat crumbling the rest of his roll between his fingers, thinking over what his mother had said.

Her words had amounted to a tacit approval of his marrying Constance. It was a concession he never would have looked for. But of course it was meaningless unless he were able to persuade Constance to marry him, and that event seemed as unlikely as ever. Still, his mother seemed to think he had shown a poor spirit in letting her engagement stand as a barrier to his wooing. Had she been right? Vincent began to think perhaps she had been. His happiness and Constance's, too, hung in the balance. It would be cowardly to let her go out of his life without making every attempt to secure her.

*She isn't married yet,* he reminded himself. *That's the chief thing. As long as she isn't married, I've got a chance.*

Pushing aside the rest of his breakfast, he began to make plans. He decided he would see Constance and, if possible, convince her to delay her marriage to her American fiancé. She would be more likely to assent to such a request than a straightforward proposal to break her engagement and marry him outright, he reckoned. The delay would give him time—a few months perhaps—and in a few months much could happen. Vincent did not know exactly what he expected to happen, but for the first time in days he felt a stirring of hope. He pushed away his breakfast tray and went in search of his sister.

Lady Beatrice was very ready to help him when she understood what he wished to know, but the intelligence she gave him was of an alarming sort. "I just received a letter from Constance today," she said. "She and her father are in Portsmouth."

"Portsmouth!" said Vincent. "What would they be doing there? I had understood they were going to France after making their tour of the Lake country."

"They are not going to France," said Lady Beatrice. "It seems Constance is feeling poorly, and they have decided to return to America. It's a great shame, but—good heavens, Vincent, what is the matter?"

She got no answer, however. Her brother had already bolted from the room and could presently be heard demanding his valet to pack his bags at once and send to the stables for his light chaise and fastest horses.

Fortunately, Lady Beatrice was an intelligent woman, quite capable of putting two and two together. When Vincent appeared a short time later to bid her a breathless farewell, she merely kissed him, wished him well, and requested him to give her most affectionate regards to Miss Locke.

# Twenty-one

It turned out that his sister's regards were not all Vincent was destined to carry to Constance. Just as he was leaving the house, the butler came hurrying toward him at something more than his usual dignified pace. "I beg your pardon, m'lord," he said. "But this just came in the post for the young American lady, Miss Locke." He displayed a letter on a silver salver. "Lady Beatrice has been forwarding her mail, but when I took it to her just now, she mentioned you might be seeing Miss Locke in the next few days. And so I thought perhaps you might wish to take the young lady her mail directly rather than have Lady Beatrice send it on."

Vincent stared at the letter. It bore an America postmark and was addressed to Constance in a bold masculine hand. A wave of jealousy went through him. There was no doubt in his mind but that the letter must be from Constance's fiancé. His impulse was to consign it to the nearest fire, but reason prevailed, and he tucked it instead into one of his coat pockets. "Thank you, Harrison. I'll see Miss Locke gets her letter," he said shortly, and strode out of the house.

His spirits, temporarily elevated by the preparations for his journey, were depressed again by this incident. He began to feel there was no point in trying to see Constance. Probably he would arrive too late to see her at all. The letter saying she and her father were in Portsmouth had only reached Lady Beatrice today, and chances were they had already sailed. Vincent spent the first stage of his journey trying to calculate how long Constance's letter had taken to reach Larkholm. Such calculations were of course futile, for he had no idea what ship she and her father were sailing on or when it sailed, but he had to do something to occupy his mind. Left to itself, it was too prone to dwell on the horrible possibility that he would arrive in Portsmouth only to find Constance already gone.

As luck would have it, Constance was still in Portsmouth, though fretting at every day she remained there. She had urged her father into making inquiries at the transatlantic shipping office as soon as they had arrived in town, and had found the next ship sailing to America was a vessel named the *Fidelis*. Constance, desperate for affirmation that she was doing the right thing, thought this too clear a portent to ignore. Their passages had accordingly been booked on the *Fidelis*, but the morning she was due to sail a heavy storm had blown in, accompanied by strong offshore winds that prevented the ship from leaving her dock. By the following day the storm had passed, but the contrary winds remained, and Constance's father, making inquiries at her urging, was informed that no ship could leave the harbor as long as they did remain.

Constance bore these delays with as much resignation as she could muster. So thoroughly was she convinced that her first and foremost duty lay in leaving England, however, that she was inclined to think some diabolical force must be behind the winds that were keeping her there.

She had overborne every other obstacle in her way—although to speak truth, these had not been very many. Mr. Locke, who should have been the chief obstacle, had proved no obstacle at all. During their visit to the Lake District, he had frequently commented on his daughter's lack of spirits, and when he had questioned her concerning this lack, she had been forced to admit that the prospect of returning home seemed at present more attractive than the most sparkling Parisian society, the most spectacular view of the Alps, or the most magnificent Roman ruins.

On hearing this, Mr. Locke had assured her that he had no objection to returning home immediately. Yet though this was a victory for Constance, it did not bring her any joy. She knew how much her father had anticipated seeing the Continent, and the knowledge that she had deprived him of such a long-looked-for pleasure was yet another addition to the burden of guilt and misery she was already bearing.

She had done what she could to lighten that burden, seeking refuge in prayer as was her wont in times of difficulty. But on this occasion, there seemed no help to be got from divine sources. It was not that Constance expected a voice from heaven to address her while she was on her knees, saying she had done right in respect to Vincent. Still, always before she had risen from her spiritual communings with some sense of being refreshed. Reflecting on this phenomenon, Constance decided it must have something to do with the kiss she had exchanged with Vincent on the night of the fete. Although she had tried hard to regret that kiss, there was a part of her that not only did not regret it but wished to do it again.

Altogether, Constance felt it was no wonder if the Almighty turned His face from her. Yet when she was trying to do the right thing, it seemed to her that He might at least assist her in sending a favorable wind to put her out of temptation's way. Thus she felt doubly dismayed on the following day, when not only did the wind continue to blow but one of the inn servants brought word that temptation had descended full force upon her in the person of Vincent himself.

"Lord Yates?" repeated Constance stupidly. "But he cannot be *here*. He has a house party in Kent."

"That's as may be, miss," said the servant. "But it's

certain sure he's here now." And he stood aside to reveal Vincent himself, booted and great-coated and
wearing a diffident smile

Constance opened her mouth, then closed it again.
"'Evening, Miss Locke," said Vincent, bowing with his
customary grace. "I beg your pardon for calling on you
like this, but it's most important that I speak with you—
with you and your father," he amended with a sidelong
look at the servant

Mutely Constance opened the door for him. She was
unequal to speech at that moment, and Vincent
seemed to be unequal to it, too. Once inside the sitting
room, they stood and looked at each other for some
moments. At last Vincent spoke. "Don't mean to stand
here staring like a looby," he said. "But I thought I'd
never see you again."

"I didn't think I'd see you again, either," said Constance, drawing a deep breath. "Oh, Vincent, you
shouldn't have come."

"Maybe not," said Vincent. "But I couldn't let you go
without making another push to see you." As an after-
thought, he added, "Oh, and I've a letter for you. From
America." Reaching into his coat pocket, he handed
her the letter.

If Constance had been her usual observant self, she
might have noticed that he was watching her narrowly.
As it was, however, she was so flustered that she did not
notice at all. Neither did she notice the letter itself, but
merely accepted it with a word of thanks and laid it on a
nearby table. "You shouldn't have come," she repeated.

Vincent did not respond to this. He merely said,
"Constance, you can't marry that other fellow. What I
mean to say is, if you feel for me half what I feel for you,
it wouldn't be right at all."

Constance turned away. "Vincent, we have discussed
all this before," she said. "You know how I feel about it."

"No, I know how you *think* you ought to feel about

it," he returned. "But as for what you feel, I think it's pretty much what I do."

Constance made a helpless gesture. "You are only trying to confuse the issue," she said.

"And I think rather it's you who's confusing it. Which of us is right, I wonder?"

Constance made another helpless gesture. "Vincent, please," she said. "I tell you I have made up my mind."

Vincent was silent a moment, then spoke. "Seems to me I've always heard it's a lady's privilege to change her mind," he said. "Probably I've got no business to say so, but in this case I think you'd be wrong if you didn't, Constance."

Constance put up her chin. "How could I be wrong?" she demanded. "I am only acting in accordance with my principles."

"Well, if that's true, then all I can say is that you've changed your principles since I met you. That first evening, there at my sister's, I seem to recall you had a deal to say against the idea of marrying for convenience."

Constance shifted restlessly from one foot to the other. "Yes," she said. "But I don't know what that has to do with the present situation."

"It has everything to do with it, far as I can see. If you love me, yet go ahead and marry that fellow in America, I'd like to know what else that would be but a marriage of convenience?"

"It isn't at all the same!" said Constance. "If I marry Will, it wouldn't be for gain, or social position, or any selfish reason."

Vincent gave her an affectionate look. "No, it'd be just the opposite," he said. "You'd be marrying him because you didn't *want* to marry for gain or social position or any other selfish reason. But you'd still be marrying without love, and in the end, Connie, I think you'd regret it."

Constance was silent. Vincent went on, his voice softening. "Don't mean to tease you," he said. "I know you've your doubts about how well suited we are, and I can't deny they're in some wise legitimate. But if you've doubts on any score, I think you owe it to yourself to wait and not marry anybody until you're sure you're doing the right thing."

Still Constance was silent. Reason told her there was sense in what he said, but her spirit chafed at the thought of further delay. Having made up her mind that marrying Will was the right thing to do, she wanted to have the matter settled. Once it was settled, she might not be happy, but she would be at peace—a peace free of soul-searching and moral dilemma. The famous quote from *MacBeth*, which she and her father had seen recently at a performance at Drury Lane, pretty well summed up her feeling: "If it were done, t'were well it were done quickly."

Constance could wholly sympathize with MacBeth's sentiment. Yet when she thought about it, she realized this in itself might be a sign that something was wrong. The words she had quoted applied to an act that was wrong by any standards and ought not to have been done at all.

Once again Constance was thrown into doubt. "I don't know," she said, putting her hands over her eyes. "I don't know—I don't know—I don't know."

To see her suffering such agony of indecision was agony for Vincent, too. If there had been anything he could do to help, he would have gladly done it, but he could not reach a resolution for her, or make her happy with it once reached. "I'd better go," he said. "Forgive me, Constance." He turned away, then turned back. "It's true you're returning to America?"

Constance nodded. "Yes," she said desolately. "It's true."

Vincent's face was stricken, but went on in a matter-of-fact voice. "When does your ship sail?" he asked.

Constance gave a weak laugh. "By rights it already ought to have sailed," she said. "It was due to sail two days ago, but there was a storm, and the winds are still adverse, they say."

Vincent regarded her a moment in silence. "There's something in prayer after all, then," he said. "I was praying I'd catch you before you sailed."

Constance looked at him wide-eyed. For her part, she had been thinking the wind of infernal origin and the delay an undoubted evil. Yet now Vincent was admitting to having prayed for just such a delay. This news gave Constance an odd feeling. Almost it was enough to shake her in her certainty that she was doing the Almighty's will by quitting England. She was not, after all, such an egotist as to suppose God must favor her prayers above everyone else's.

On the other hand, the delay might be merely another temptation to test her resolve. Constance shook her head in bewilderment. She felt she needed time to sort all these contradictory ideas out. "I suppose we will sail within a day or two," she said uncertainly. "The winds must surely subside before much longer."

Vincent cleared his throat. "Would you mind if I came to see you off?" he asked. "As long as I'm in Portsmouth anyway, y'know. I'd like to come down to the docks and—and say good-bye."

Constance made a feeble protest about not liking him to go to so much trouble. Vincent gave her a pained look. "My dear girl! You must know that for the pleasure of seeing you I'd go to any trouble there was," he said. "Why, I'd go all the way to America with you if I thought it'd do anything but give you a disgust of my company." And with these words he turned and left the room, pulling the door shut behind him.

Constance stared after him, then began to laugh uncontrollably. Tears mingled with her laughter, so that she could not say whether her feelings were most harrowed or entertained. "Oh, Vincent," she said. "As if I could ever be disgusted with your company!" She could not help thinking of how delightful the long ocean voyage would be with him for company. But of course such an event was impossible. Constance put the idea firmly from her mind, but she was less successful when she tried to put from her mind the doubts that Vincent's words had inspired in her. Again and again she went over the same ground, arguing that it was wrong to be attracted him in the first place; wrong to let that attraction tempt her to break her engagement with Will; wrong to be tempted by a path so hedged about by worldly ease and pleasure when her duty clearly lay along the upward and rocky way.

But no sooner had she argued herself back onto the path of duty then she would recall how Vincent had told her that in marrying Will she would be making what was essentially a marriage of convenience. This was an abhorrent idea to Constance. Likewise abhorrent was his charge that pride was keeping her from following her heart. She had reason to know it was true, but she told herself that pride alone would not have prevented her from breaking her engagement if she had been otherwise sure it was the right thing to do.

"If only I were sure!" said Constance aloud. "There's the rub, of course." She was not sure about anything as matters now stood. Moodily she thought of all the hours she had spent on her knees during the past few weeks, praying that she might be guided to do the right thing. If only the Almighty had sent her a sign to indicate his will for her! It was true that adverse winds had kept her and her father from sailing, but if that was a sign, it was too equivocal for Constance's taste. She wanted a clear-cut, unmistakable sign that would tell her exactly where her duty lay.

And it was at that moment her eyes lit on the letter Vincent had brought her.

Slowly, advancing with almost superstitious fear, Constance picked up the letter. A glance showed her it came from Will. It had been fully a month since she had received a letter from him, a month in which she

had been struggling all the while with demons of doubt
and duty and indecision.

Constance picked up the letter, broke the seal, and
began to read.


Vincent, as he went outside to his carriage, was conscious of a sense of dissatisfaction. He had said to
Constance all he had come to say, but still he had the
sense that he had left something undone. Perhaps he
ought to have argued longer, to have wrung from her
an agreement not to marry her American fiancé for at
least a year. Perhaps he should have abandoned words
altogether and simply kissed her. Only he feared that
in following this course, he would be more likely to
look like a fool than a romantic hero.

*Not cut out to be a romantic hero, by Jove,* Vincent told
himself ruefully. *Been a fool all my life more or less. Except
when I fell in love with her, of course.*

Still, the sense of unfinished business remained with
him all the way out to his carriage. The footmen opened
the door for him, and Vincent started to ascend the
steps. Then he paused. He could not shake the sense
that he had left a duty undone—some duty connected
with Constance. He glanced up at the hotel facade, toward the window belonging to Constance's apartments.
At that moment Constance herself appeared at the window. She was waving to him frantically—waving with a
hand in which she was grasping something white.

Vincent's heart gave a leap half of fear and half of excitement. He could not guess why Constance wanted
him, but that she wanted him at all was a boon he would
not question. "Back in a minute," he told the surprised
footmen. "Forgot something, by Jove." Stepping down
from the carriage, he hurried back into the hotel.

At the door to the Lockeses' rooms, he waved aside
the servant who would have announced him and
rapped on the door himself. As before, the door was

opened by Constance. She had clearly been crying, but before Vincent could question her about this or even express his concern for it, she flung herself into his arms and kissed him.

Vincent was surprised by this turn of events, but not so much so as to fail to take advantage of it. "Constance," he said, kissing her back.

Constance tilted a tear-wet face up to him. "Vincent, I am such a *fool*," she said.

"That you are not," said Vincent warmly. "Couldn't be a fool if you tried." He thought a minute and then added scrupulously, "Except maybe when you fell in love with me."

Constance laughed in a slightly hysterical manner. "No, I am now persuaded that was my greatest stroke of genius. But I have done my best to ruin it just the same. Fool that I am! It doesn't seem you could want me after the way I have behaved."

Although her words thus far had been for the most part unintelligible to Vincent, he could understand this last statement and immediately undertook to refute it. When he would have kissed Constance again, however, she shook her head and drew away. "No, Vincent, you must not—not until you know what has happened. Oh, Vincent, the most mortifying thing! That letter you brought me—did you know what it contained when you gave it to me?"

"No," said Vincent cautiously. "At least . . . I supposed it might be from your fiancé in America."

"Well, it was. But he is not my fiancé any longer. Oh, Vincent, I have been jilted!"

"Jilted?" repeated Vincent stupidly.

Constance gave him a wry smile. "You may well be surprised! As I said before, it is the most mortifying thing. Will has fallen in love with Miss Mercer back in Boston, and he wants to break our engagement and marry her."

There were many comments Vincent might have

made at this point, but what he actually said was, "Who's Miss Mercer?"

"She's the daughter of a merchant there in Boston—a very wealthy merchant. And she is a most odious girl, or so I used to think. But now I am disposed to find her charming. She has saved me—saved both of us—saved *all* of us—a world of trouble. Only it's so humiliating, Vincent! When I think of how hard I tried to behave rightly by Will, even to the extent of cutting short poor Father's trip so I could get away from you. And all this time Will was falling in love with Miss Mercer!"

"Well, but it's the best thing that could've happened, ain't it?" said Vincent reasonably. "Relieves you of responsibility, what?"

"Yes, but it also makes me feel such a fool. After all my high-flown words about honor and duty! And then to be jilted at last." Constance made a noise that was halfway between a laugh and a sob.

"Best thing that could've happened," repeated Vincent firmly. "Now you can marry me. If you want to, that is," he added with sudden diffidence.

"Of *course* I want to," said Constance. "Only I don't see how you could still want me as a wife. I have made such a mess of this business. My pride—my conceit—I can see it all so clearly now. It was that as much as anything else that made me determined to stand by my engagement with Will. And now see what has come of it! Pride goes before a fall, they say, and there's no doubt I have stumbled badly on this occasion!"

Such a statement Vincent could not allow. He pointed out that the situation had been concluded in the best possible way for all parties involved, with everyone getting more or less what he or she wanted and no heartache on any side. "Mind you, I expect your ex-fiancé'll come to regret that he chose Miss Mercer over you," he added with a shake of his head. "But that'll be his lookout, not mine. I don't think I need scruple to profit by his mistake."

"No, indeed," said Constance with a weak laugh. "There have been too many scruples about this business already."

Vincent said warmly that he loved her scruples as much as any other part of her and reinforced his words by kissing her roundly. "I mean to see you don't ever regret marrying me, Constance," he said. "I know my situation in life ain't what you'd have chosen, but I'm willing to do anything to see you happy. Together we'll find a way to make it all work out—yes, even if it means giving up my title and moving to America."

Constance gave a shaky laugh. "Nonsense! Why are you to make all the sacrifices? If I marry you, then it means I am willing to take you as you are, even if it means being a countess." She gave another shaky laugh. "Oh, dear, that doesn't seem at all possible!"

"You'll be a wonderful countess," said Vincent, kissing her fondly. "Best countess there ever was, by Jove. You'll set an example to all the others, I shouldn't wonder. And I wouldn't be surprised if you didn't end by reforming the British aristocracy from the inside out."

Constance regarded him with an expression of wonderment that slowly changed to a radiant smile. "I never thought of that," she said. "It's true one can do more about changing a thing when one is a part of it rather than merely an outsider. We shall have to see." She looked seriously at Vincent. "Indeed, I am disposed to think that by marrying you I am doing exactly what I am meant to do. It's very strange how it all came about. Your bringing that letter when you did—and the winds that kept Father and me from sailing. Here I have been cursing them these two days, and all the while they were doing me a favor!"

Vincent agreed that the ways of the Almighty were mysterious. "Not that I'd presume to criticize Him," he added with a hasty upward glance. "He's done well by me this jaunt, and I mean to do as well as I can by Him in return. But—well, He knows my limitations. And you might as well know 'em too, Connie." He looked at her anxiously. "I intend to do my duty from here on out as well as I understand it, but I give you fair warning that I'm not the most quick-witted fellow around."

Constance laughed and said she supposed he would understand quite as much as he needed to. "You cannot deceive me, Vincent," she told him. "I have attended six lectures on ancient history with you, and I know perfectly well that you are as quick to grasp the essentials of a situation as anyone I've ever met. And in any case, you have common sense, which is a more uncommon thing than genius, I think—and certainly a more comfortable thing! I will never have to tell you to put on an overcoat when it rains, or to keep you from tipping the cabman a guinea instead of a shilling," she added with a sparkling smile.

Her estimations of Vincent's intellect were justified by his immediately grasping the import of this speech. "Aye, that's so. I daresay one genius in the family's enough," he said, smiling back at her. "We'll hope so, anyway." More soberly he added, "I hope your father won't object too much to our marrying, Constance. I can't help feeling badly that I'll be taking you away from him."

Constance said cheerfully that her father had never expected her to stay and keep house for him forever. "He has been expecting me to marry any time these two years, Vincent! We had already arranged that a maiden aunt of mine would come and stay with him after I am gone, and there is no reason those plans need change, though my bridegroom does! I am sure Father will be very happy when he hears the news, for he likes you a great deal, I know. Besides," she added with a rueful smile, "he is good enough to think anything I do must be right. Poor Father, he little knows how near I came to making a blunder of this business. But it has all come right in the end."

Vincent agreed that it had, although he told Constance he felt sure it would have come right in any case. "Even if you *had* gone back to America, I think we'd have come together eventually. It couldn't be otherwise, with both of us feeling the way we do. You'd never have gone through with marrying that other fellow, no matter how much you tried to tell yourself it was your duty."

"I hope not," said Constance. "I *think* not. At any rate, I have been most providentially saved from doing so!" She smiled at Vincent. "And I am very grateful to Providence on that account. Indeed, everything has turned out for the best. Do you know what makes me happiest about the way things have turned out?"

"No, what?" inquired Vincent with interest.

"That I need not feel guilty about having kissed you in the mausoleum! Will's letter was written weeks ago, long before the fete took place. It might be stretching a point, but I don't think it's unreasonable to count my freedom from the date it was written rather than the day I received it. It meant a great deal to me, that kiss, and now I need not be ashamed of it."

Vincent, too, was glad and said so. "I can tell you, it's made a deal of difference in the way I look at the family mausoleum," he added with a sideways smile. "It'll make a deal more seeing, as I can now, that it's the first place I ever kissed my wife!"

"Your wife," repeated Constance in wondering accents. "It still doesn't seem possible, does it? Vincent, I mean to stand by you regardless, but I hope your family will not be *too* dreadfully upset when they hear you are marrying me."

Vincent was able to reassure her on this score. "My mother's already given her blessing to the match. In fact it was she who told me I shouldn't give up just because you was engaged to another fellow. As for Trix, she'll be delighted, I know. So will the girls. They think a lot of you, those girls. Very discerning children, 'pon my word."

"They are charming girls, your nieces," said Constance. She gave a sudden laugh. "Won't they be pleased to know their lucky pieces worked after all!

Lady Julia insisted I wear her coral necklace at the fete, for which she claimed all sorts of miraculous powers, and Lady Diana gave me in addition a lucky sixpence to put in my reticule. At the time I didn't consider they brought me any great luck, but now I know otherwise."

"They'll consider themselves the lucky ones, when they learn you're to become their new aunt," prophesied Vincent. "Speaking of which, I hope it won't be long before that event takes place. Mean to say, I'll wait as long as you think necessary, but if it were up to me I'd marry you tomorrow, what?"

Constance smiled. "I'd marry you tomorrow, too, all things being equal," she said. "But I believe it might be better if we let at least a month or two go by before any engagement is announced."

Vincent was resigned to this delay and said so. "But what about in the meantime?" he asked. "You aren't still planning to return to America, are you?"

Coinstance shook her head. "No, for there is no longer any reason to do so. I shall doubtless want to return to America someday, for a visit, but for now my lot lies in England." She looked soberly at Vincent. "Still, there is one duty I must discharge before I settle here. And that concerns Father. I cannot feel right about having made him cut short his European tour. Since we are not returning to Boston after all, I would like to go on and visit the Continent with him as we had originally planned. Poor Father, he was so looking forward to seeing France and Switzerland and Italy, and it seems only right I should make him happy before I take my own happiness."

Vincent was much relieved to hear her duty was no more than this, and he warmly commended Constance for her filial scruples. At the same time, however, he could not help feeling rather wistful at the idea of being separated from her for what might be as long as several months. "So you mean to visit the Continent, do you?" he said, trying not to sound as unhappy as he felt.

"That means we can't expect to be married before October, I suppose."

"Probably not," said Constance. "But, Vincent—I was thinking that if you liked, perhaps you might accompany us to the Continent." She gave him a diffident smile. "Father would be delighted to have your company, I know. And of course it goes without saying that I would! And after we have spent so much time together, our friends and relatives will be much less surprised than they might be otherwise, when we announce our engagement."

Vincent regarded her with fixed attention. "By Jove," he said, "that's a good notion, Constance. A really *clever* notion, by Jove. I'm engaged to the cleverest girl in the world—aye, and the most beautiful." He reached out to stroke Constance's face with a reverent hand.

"Vincent, you are too kind," she said. She looked at him, her expression half smiling and half worried. "Indeed, I can't help thinking you must be deceived, to heap so many encomiums upon me. When I think of all the really beautiful girls you might have married! It seems as though you must wake up someday and realize you'd made a mistake in marrying me."

"Never," said Vincent with assurance. "You needn't ever worry about that, Connie. Once I make up my mind to a thing, I'm the steadiest fellow going. You can ask anybody who knows me."

There was that in his tone that convinced Constance, and she made no further protest when he drew her into his arms again. "I believe you really do know your own mind," she said. "But I am sure people will doubt whether a Yankee girl and an English lord could ever be happy together."

"Well, it'll be up to us to convince 'em we are," said Vincent. And he proceeded to kiss Constance in a manner that must have struck anyone watching as very convincing indeed.

## ABOUT THE AUTHOR

Joy Reed lives with her family in Michigan. Her newest Regency romance, MR. JEFFRIES AND THE JILT, will be published in August 2003. Joy loves hearing from readers and you may write to her c/o Zebra Books. Please include a self-addressed stamped envelope if you wish a reply.